THE CHOSEN HEIR

A DARK ROMANIAN MAFIA ROMANCE

MONIQUE MOREAU

MEET MONIQUE!

Join Monique's Newsletter (and receive goodies and release information)
https://bit.ly/SteamyReadNewsletter

Join Monique's FB reader's group, she'd love to hear from you
Possessive Alpha Reads

Like her Facebook Page
https://bit.ly/MoniqueMoreaufb

Follow her on TikTok
@moniquemoreauthor

Follow her on Instagram
https://bit.ly/MoniqueMoreauIG

Follow her on Book Bub
http://bit.ly/MoniqueBookBub

Learn all about Monique's books
MoniqueMoreau.com

AUTHOR'S NOTE

A quick note about the Romanian mafia, or *mafie*. After doing quite a bit of research on the subject, I can honestly say that there isn't a plethora of information. I've let my imagination run wild and taken liberties by inventing rules and societal norms I have not found any proof of in the real world.

I've also given certain Romanian words special meaning within this unique world. I've introduced the Lupu clan, the main Romanian *mafie* family, whose center of power is in "Little Bucharest," a name I've coined for the small Romanian community in Sunnyside, Queens, New York City.

The surname Lupu does in fact mean "the wolf" in Romanian, but I created the Lupu tat, a wolf baring its teeth, that is required of all members of the Lupu *mafie* clan.

And with that, I'll leave you to enjoy Alex and Nina's story!

Monique

P.S. If you'd like to read Tasa's story, it's in the last book of my MC Romance series, *Whistle's War*. While technically a biker book, it's more of a hybrid biker-mafia book.

1

"F ucking hell," I gritted out as I read the text over my grandmother's shoulder. Tasa was safe and she begged us not to look for her. *Really, Tasa?* As if I'd leave my baby sister to hang out to dry, regardless of whether she'd run away from home or not. Oh, and had she conveniently forgotten about her fiancé, Cristo? And what part of the term "dangerous enemies" had not penetrated her thick skull, despite my relentless repetition of that threat?

Bunică gave a nonchalant shrug of her skinny shoulders and a grin that showed off her gold tooth. That woman could get her teeth fixed a thousand times over, but she wasn't one to put on airs. As she always said, "I was born a peasant girl, and I'll die a peasant girl."

Peasant girl, my ass. She was as sharp as they came, and while she loved to ham it up with her country ways, she'd graduated from Romania's finest medical school. No lie, she could dig out a bullet and sew up the wound in under half an hour. It had come in handy on more than one occasion, when the doctor on our payroll didn't arrive quickly enough.

"What is she thinking?" I spat out. "She's roaming the country doing God knows what. No protection, no bodyguard, no—"

"Oh, hush, you act as if Tasa's an invalid instead of a smart young woman who can take on the world with one hand tied behind her back. She'll be fine. And you best leave her alone," she warned, poking at my chest with her bony finger.

I stared down at her, incredulous. Leave my sister to roam the country unprotected? *Is she insane?*

"Christ, *Bunică*, she's a female. Alone."

My eyes rolled up to the kitchen ceiling, seeking patience, as I took a seat on one of the stools scattered around the island in the kitchen of our family home. This was where *Bunică* practically lived so this was where family members came to talk to her. Was I the only rational one in this conversation? It wasn't like she didn't know who we were. It's not like she wasn't acutely aware that our enemies would start crawling out of the woodwork to kidnap Tasa.

"A *lone* female," I reiterated, emphasizing the word "lone" in hopes of getting through to my grandmother. "Of the *Lupu* clan." My gaze passed over the midnight-blue double oven range my father had imported directly from Italy when he busted out the back wall and extended the kitchen to please his mother and wife. The chrome from the state-of-the-art appliances gleamed under the bronze farmhouse lights.

We are the Lupus, the Romanian upstarts who quickly rose to the top of the New York City mafias. The speed of our rise was a point of embarrassment for the Bratva, the

Russian mafia, and the main reason why they're so intent on destroying us. As for the Italians, they were a shadow of what they were before the takedowns and trials of the '90s. Which had left a vacuum for my father to fill when he arrived in New York, solidifying our foothold in Sunnyside, Queens. Better known now as "Little Bucharest."

Returning my attention to *Bunică*, I reminded her, "Enemies? Remember them? Why do I need to mention this? It's not like you don't know what I'm talking about. She's in real danger."

She let out a cackle as she whipped out a bottle of *palincă*, a traditional Romanian spirit from the region she came from. Plunking down two small glasses, she poured two shots and pushed one over the kitchen island to me. The other, she threw back like a pro.

"What's obvious to everyone but you and your mother is that Tasa is her own woman. She's smart, and she's not going to get caught by some two-bit *mafie* idiot. She'll be fine."

I narrowed my eyes at her. She was too relaxed by far, considering her youngest grandchild had just run off to god-knows-where.

"What do you know?" I demanded.

Fluttering her wrinkled hand weakly in front of her chest, she lied without a shred of remorse, "Who? Little old me? Why, nothing!"

"You're as deceitful as the day is long," I snapped, my patience finally fraying.

"Back off," she warned, her innocent features turning dark. *Ah, there's the real* Bunică. "I don't happen to know anything, but if I did, you bet your last dollar I wouldn't tell you. I won't help you drag her back here and keep her prisoner until she marries that worthless *tâmpit*, Cristo. *Uck.* He's barely a man. And he has a little two-bit hussy of a side piece. Each of you must marry in the *familie*, but why him? *Bah!*"

"You're unbelievable, you know that, right? Come on, out with it," I insisted, flicking the fingers of my open hand at her.

"Like I said, my lips are sealed." She made a gesture as if locking her lips together and flinging away an imaginary key.

My jaw clenched. Women. The bane of my existence. And those two stuck together like super glue. It was hopeless on my part to try to sever the unbreakable.

"Fine, then," I replied, releasing a long, exhausted breath. "You're not the only person I can press for information."

Her hand nabbed the sleeve of my jacket, crushing the fine wool between her bony fingers. "Leave that poor girl alone. You know she's in love with you. Don't you dare take advantage of her."

My grandmother was talking about Tasa's little best friend, the beautiful, supple Nina, of course.

Nina.

Damn, that girl. Smelled like jasmine and a hard fuck waiting to happen. Just the thought of her brought crackling heat to my skin and a stiffness to my cock. That woman was my Achilles' heel, if ever there was one. Sweet as could be, with large brown eyes and a chest I could face-plant in and suck on for days on end. Annnd...

And she's also like a sister to you, asshole.

Not.

There wasn't a shred of brotherly feelings toward that little minx. Unless one included the taboo kind.

Laying my forearms heavily on the smooth wood of the kitchen island, I warned, "*Bunică*, it's Tasa we're talking about here. My little *sister*. For some insane reason, you don't think she's in jeopardy, but I happen to know exactly what our enemies are capable of. I know exactly what they do during a torture session. Once it's out that she's gone, finding her and using her to get to us will be at the top of their list. This is like a nuclear arms race, during the Cold War." I tapped the watch around my wrist. "Time is ticking, and I can assure you that this won't finish well. Least of all for Tasa. Who's going to want to marry her if she's tarnished? Think about that and come talk to me when you've regained your common sense."

"*Băiețel*, don't speak to your *Bunică* like that. I wiped your bottom when you couldn't even feed yourself. Any man should be grateful for the chance to marry my little girl."

I snorted out an exasperated sigh. I hated it when she called me *little boy*. Deciding it was in my best interest to pretend I didn't hear her last comment, I bent down low and dropped a kiss on the crown of her head. "Do you think I enjoy this? Do you think I enjoy having to lay down the law and act like an enforcer with the people I love?"

"You *do* enjoy it," she shot back. "You always think you're right. In that way, you take after your father. Regardless of what everyone in this family thinks, he wasn't a saint, you know. He was human, and he made his fair share of mistakes."

Yeah, right. She always said that, but it was never quite believable. The man was a brilliant businessman and strategist. He loved his family and was the paradigm of how to behave in our twisted world. He was honorable to his core. If I could live up to half of the man he'd been, I'd die content. Which brought me back to the issue at hand: Tasa's marriage.

"I've been negotiating with Nelu on this marriage contract between Tasa and Cristo for *years*. It's more than a simple wedding, as you well know. What's going to happen when he finds out his future daughter-in-law ran away? It will be perceived as a stain on his honor. It could legitimately lead to war when we've only just begun our truce. Not only is business booming, but Tata would be disappointed in me. I gave him my oath that I would do everything in my power to make this happen. There's too much on the line," I finished with a frown.

The responsibility of taking care of my family fell heavily on my shoulders, but on days like today, the weight was crushing. Although *Bunică* was whip smart, the truth was she couldn't relate. She'd always been taken care of. First by my grandfather, then my father, and now me. She could afford to focus solely on the personal, not the big picture. No, that fell on me.

"Pfft. And so you had to sell Tasa to do this? Of all people, you chose to sacrifice your little sister?" Reproval shimmered in her eyes at me.

"*Tata* would've commended me for it. *He* would've thought it was a brilliant move. With the Popescus, Tasa will be taken care of. She'll be protected. And it would solidify a peace that's eluded our families for decades."

Bunică stared at me like she was about to spit on the ground. "Don't make it seem like you're doing this for Tasa, Alex. It's beneath you to lie."

"I *am* doing it for her," I ground out, fists balling at my sides. Christ, this old woman was never satisfied. She was spoiling the girl with notions of love. Our life was based on duty and, for women, that included the duty to marry a man chosen by her family. As the boss or *șef* of this family, I might be given a leeway regarding this rule. But for a princess of marriageable age like Tasa, it was unthinkable.

"She's the baby of the family. The Popescus, curse their name, are worthless mongrels. Animals. Unlike the Lupu clan, they didn't gain power until the fall of Communism. That's a blink of an eye in the span of history, and you sold your precious sister to those heathens?"

I snorted. "They're powerful enough now; I can tell you that much. We can look down on the Popescu clan all we want, but only a fool would underestimate their potential to do damage. They're *vicious*. Ruthless. You know this as well as anyone." It was also common knowledge that their tempers were like hair triggers. One wrong move and *kapow*. I made a dismissive wave. "In any case, it's done. My hands are tied. There's nothing I can do but retrieve her and make sure her marriage goes off without a hitch."

She stalked up to me. Barely five feet tall, she went toe to toe with me and spat out, "Then, you will get no help from me. I will do everything in my power to thwart you. The marriage be damned."

"You're impossible," I heaved out, throwing up my hands. "You know the situation."

When Tata was bleeding out in the ambulance roaring through the quiet streets, his dying wish had been for me to take care of the family. I'd already failed on that promise, with Tasa stranded somewhere out there, alone and vulnerable. Possibly hurt. My back teeth ground together at that last possibility.

The second oath had been to reconcile our family with the lowbred Popescus. I didn't disagree with *Bunică* that every one of them was a bottom-feeder. No education, no class, no nothing. Violence was their greatest attribute. The

two families had been at each other's throats for genera-
tions, clawing their way to the top by throat-punching the
other. We may be at the pinnacle, but they came in at a close
second.

Nelu, their şef, and Tata were always vying to be the top
dog. Tata often said that it was too late for their generation,
that there was too much bad blood. But at his death bed, he
declared, "There needs to be a marriage. It's the only way."
Those last words were the proverbial nails in my coffin.

"Go back to your fancy apartment in Columbus Circle,
Alex. I don't want you under my roof until you come to your
senses."

Goddamn, this woman was impossible. She refused to
acknowledge the possibility of a looming war. Instead, she
was banishing me to the penthouse floors of the two towers
of the Time Warner Center building in Manhattan, where
my brothers and I lived.

Tasa had moved in with Nina a few avenues over, in a
nice high-rise building overlooking the Hudson. Of course,
Tasa, always with the rebellious streak, couldn't share an
apartment with her twin, Nicu. Oh no, our building was too
snooty and fancy for her. And Tasa was as opinionated as
the day was long. Thank Christ, she had her little best
friend living with her.

My back teeth ground down harder, my fists flexing by
my sides, but there was nothing I could say when Bunică got
into one of her fits. Turning on my heel, I marched out of
the kitchen, grabbed my coat from the hallway closet, and
stalked out of the house. What in the ever-loving fuck?

Tasa gone.

Contract in ruins.

Potential war on the horizon.

Everything I'd worked for gone.

Gone.

I was an abject failure. No, I refused to let that stand. I didn't care what it took to make this right. I'd fulfill Tata's oath. I'd drag Tasa back by her hair to marry the Popescu if need be. I'd make my father proud if it fucking killed me.

2

"She's driving me fucking crazy, Nina. I swear I'm going to kill myself if she doesn't get off my fucking jock," Yo-Yo uttered into the phone during our video chat as he did another curl with the weight in his hand. My little brother had been getting jacked, lately. I supposed I should've been happy that he'd found a way to blow off steam. More than anyone, I understood how much he needed release. I had hoped my little rebellion at the cusp of leaving home would've smoothed the way for him by the time he reached his late teens, but no such luck. Mother was as wound up as ever. Even more so because he was a boy. There were no excuses for a boy. A boy had to succeed.

Walking through the living room of the Upper West Side apartment I shared with my best friend, Tasa, I gazed out at the overwrought, gold-leaf furniture as I crossed barefoot over the Persian carpets on my way to the kitchen.

Propping my phone against the shiny toaster, I grabbed a teakettle, filled it with cold water, and slammed it on the stovetop. I cringed at the clanging sound of metal hitting metal. Mother was losing her mind. I didn't know what it was about adolescence that seemed to tip her over into pure, unadulterated insanity. The shouting. The recriminations. The fear she projected on us. The older we got, the worse she spiraled. In the end, she'd create an explosion of massive proportions. At least that's how it had been with me, and the same thing seemed to be playing out with Yo-Yo.

Once the water was heating, I flipped open the cupboard and grabbed the French press and stainless-steel container of ground coffee. If Tasa were here, instead of out gallivanting somewhere, she'd be preparing a nice cup of Turkish coffee, and I wouldn't have to resort to pre-ground coffee and the French press. Glancing up at the clock, I noted that it was past nine a.m. Again, I wondered where my best friend had spent the night. Her family's home, next door to mine in Queens? Highly unlikely. With her former lover, that vocal instructor from school? Doubtful. *Where can she be?*

"You know Mother. She has to have a meltdown the instant we turn eighteen because it marks her impending loss of control. That, on top of a general fear of the future, and *ka-boom*." I flicked my hands open to emphasize the bomb analogy.

My mother always liked to remind us how her family went to great lengths to get their only child, a girl no less, smuggled into the United States. Now she was a regional manager at the company she worked for. But that horrific trip across the world? It'd left her terrified of the unpredictable. And nothing seemed as scary as a child on the cusp of adulthood who didn't have a career mapped out to retirement.

"You know how it is with her and careers. Not just any

career either. It's not like I can be honest with her and say that I want to get married and have a gaggle of kids," I complained to my brother.

A sigh escaped from my lips. Tasa and I often commiserated that fate had played a cruel joke on us, dropping us in the womb of the wrong mother. Her mother only wanted to see her married to a nice Romanian boy, with kids tugging at her skirt. My mother was appalled by the idea. Our home had been a battleground for years, before Dad finally convinced her to let me go to Juilliard to pursue singing. That didn't stop her from working me half to death with vocal lessons and specialty summer camps. Her intention had been for me to go to Yale, not Juilliard.

Every once in a while, she still shuddered at the prospect of my future. But at least I'd chosen an honorable career. One that had to do with culture and history. Unlike Yo-Yo, I wasn't bitter. I had long been resigned to my mother's pressure. Although, Yo-Yo's current struggles reminded me of my upcoming graduation, and what that meant. It was only a matter of time before her attention turned toward me.

"Yeah, but at least you got into Juilliard. You don't mind playing the game and pretending to be a good, obedient daughter." His unspoken words were that, unlike me, Yo-Yo didn't have the tolerance for subterfuge or any kind of bullshit.

"It's only for another few months," I said, trying to put it in perspective for him. "It's not like I care to pursue a competitive singing career after I graduate in the spring. Then I'll be right back on her radar."

I had no idea what I was going to do. If anything, I'd work with kids, but Mother would go ballistic if I suggested becoming a music teacher for children. A college professor would be acceptable, but that was definitely not a good fit for me. My shoulders bunched up as I ruminated about my future and my mother.

"Anyway," my brother said, switching the conversation, "I'm sneaking out tomorrow night to go to a hip-hop show at a loft party in Bushwick."

"Just don't get caught," I counseled, because, really, what could I say? I'd snuck out on more than one occasion to meet up with Tasa as a teen. Not that we did anything particularly exciting. Mostly, we took the subway to The Village in Manhattan and tried to get into bars with bad fake IDs. We never could trick those bouncers and would end up hanging out in Washington Square Park until we got tired and dragged our butts home.

"Do you want me to try talking to Mother again?" I suggested. I'd do anything for my little brother, even hopelessly attempt to convince my mother to back off.

"Like that's gonna make any difference," he grumbled. "Sure, go ahead. Why don't you come over tonight for dinner? Try talking her down from the ledge."

I grimaced.

"Is an entire meal necessary?" I quipped.

"See? And you're out of the house. Imagine how I feel," he fired back.

"Has Dad been helpful?"

"As much as he can be. He's not exactly hyped about my plans, but at least he sees me as a separate human being with my own set of dreams."

"Yeah," I replied on a sigh. If it took our mother ages to accept Juilliard, the idea of a career as a hip-hop artist was close to unfathomable. The fact that he was insanely talented, had a cover-model kind of way about him, and had the sweetest temperament in the world were inconsequential. None of those things mattered to her. She might have approved if he were a cellist, like the musician he was named after. Luckily, Yo-Yo doubled as a dope stage name.

"Okay. Anything for you. If I can't talk her down, at the very least, I can act as a buffer."

"Damn straight. You know I miss you, right?" Yo-Yo said, giving me a lopsided grin.

"Yeah, yeah, as long as you don't give me that nonsense about me being your favorite sister when we both know I'm your *only* sister."

That got a guffaw out of him. I breathed in relief. Anything to make that boy smile.

I hung up with him and checked my social media for signs of Tasa. There was a text from an unknown number. Usually, I erased them without checking, but something told me to read it.

TASA: I'm okay. I had to escape. Couldn't go through with Cristo. Don't try to find me. Texted Bunică. Love u.

"Oh, Tasa," I groaned out, smacking my thigh.

Honestly, it wouldn't be that bad to get married if Cristo wasn't such an idiot. Starting a new life and a family seemed like a good thing. God knows, it was what I wanted for myself—with the right guy. She would've been free of the pretense of pursuing a career she didn't care for in the opera, which her family had decided was the only viable option to a suitable marriage. Real opera freaks, that family. Tasa hid it from me, but I knew she'd changed her major to avant-garde modern dance, which was frowned upon by her people, compared to the sophistication of opera.

But to run away? *Really, Tasa?* Such a drastic move.

Then again, I was a wimp.

Thing was, her family had enemies. Bad enemies.

Thank God the girl had the sense to text her grand-mother; otherwise, they'd assume she'd been abducted, and all hell would break loose across Queens. Possibly across all five boroughs of New York City. When Tasa's father was gunned down on Queens Boulevard, war broke out that lasted over a year. I was only twelve at the time, but I overheard the nightly news my parents watched. Names rattled off by the anchors ending in the "*ou*" and "*itch*" sounds. Romanian and Russian names. Didn't take much to realize the war was between two different mafias.

Finding out that my best friend had absconded to God knows where, I was worried but I wasn't *that* worried. My girl was nothing if not clever. Knowing her, she'd planned this break for months, if not longer. It hurt to realize that she'd had to plot behind my back, but I understood why she'd struck out on her own. I couldn't leave Yo-Yo. Was I saddened by that? Yes, of course I was. But we both knew I couldn't keep a secret to save my life, and her family was constantly around. I mean, her twin, Nicu came over on a weekly basis.

A flurry of anger flapped in my chest. Alex had led her down this path with his ultimatum. I always tried to look on the bright side when we talked about her looming marriage, but deep down, I was disappointed by his persistence. Her brothers treated her like a princess, so I assumed he'd eventually relent. He was so bossy. While it was a turn-on for me, it would push someone like Tasa to the brink.

Hip propped against the counter, I tapped my fingernails on the delicate porcelain cup with gold filigree as I contemplated what this meant.

With the problems Yo-Yo faced at home, I might as well move back for the rest of the semester. The whole point of this apartment had been to move out of Queens and live with my best friend. The deal was that her family would pay for the apartment and her mother would be given free rein to decorate it. Ugh. It was almost a deal breaker; that's how much we hated her mother's taste, but we caved since we both wanted to live away from home.

I may love the woman to death, but her decorating skills? Awful. It would've been a perfect fit for a drafty old nineteenth-century castle. Down to the precious cup I was holding to drink a simple cup of coffee out of. One day, when I had my own home, I'd decorate it the way I wanted and drink from cups I'd picked out myself.

I was taking another long sip of my first cup of coffee when another text came in. Picking up my phone, I checked it and my cell phone almost tumbled out of my hand. My first summons from Alex.

Alex. Alex. *Alex.*

Oh God.

Worrying my bottom lip, I got my first taste of what Tasa went through each time she was summoned by her oldest brother. The butterflies taking flight in my tummy were maniacal. Besides being the imposing head of the Lupu family, Alex was my kryptonite. Whenever he turned his piercing emerald-green eyes on me, I melted into a pathetic puddle. The man dripped with sex appeal.

Seriously, it was obscene.

Besides being hot as sin, he was huge, towering over me whenever I found myself standing beside him. It was as if I had a huge warrior beside me, treating me like a precious, coveted thing he'd protect with his life. Yes, I realized that my imagination got the best of me. Whenever I daydreamed about starting a family, he was the primary star of my fantasies.

Tasa had prodded me to go for him, but the risks were too great. First, she and Alex sometimes acted like each other's nemesis. Tasa needed me by her side. She was my support system, and I was hers. No man was getting between that. Also, I had no idea if he wanted me. The humiliation would've crushed me if he saw me merely as his little sister's best friend. No, I couldn't take that chance.

Anyway, like Tasa, the man was obliged to marry one of his own. He was a demanding man. Not only did he stick to the rules, but he also imposed them on others. I could fantasize about him all I wanted, but that was where it ended. My fate was to pine after him from a distance.

Staring at the text with a time (11:30 a.m.), place (his office), and a warning ("Be there."), I understood why Tasa meticulously kept every detail of her escape plan from me. She knew I'd be summoned and that, once in his presence, I was defenseless. Even thinking about him had my stomach in knots and my panties soaked in anticipation. Damn that man.

Not that he'd do a thing to hurt me, physically or otherwise. There was no chance of that, despite my fantasies of being tied to his bedpost. No need to resort to coercion when he had other means at his disposal. Manipulation being number one. Not that I blamed him. I'd be the same way if anything happened to Yo-Yo.

My best chance of fending off his inquisition was to go on the offensive. I'd give him a piece of my mind because none of this would have happened if he'd been more understanding of Tasa. As a perfectionist, he'd pushed too far, and look where it had gotten us? A shudder coursed through me. Executing this plan while beating back my lust was going to be one hell of a challenge.

3

At a quarter to eleven, I stepped outside our building on 71st Street and craned my neck, looking for my ride. A black Mercedes, with Tasa's former chauffeur-slash-bodyguard at the wheel, rolled to the curb by the entrance. Nikki stepped out of the driver's seat and opened the back passenger door for me with a nod. I settled inside, the plush leather seat smooth under my fingertips, and tried engaging him in conversation. He was stubbornly silent. His stoic face might as well have been carved out of marble for all I could get out of him. I had no idea how Tasa ever got him to talk, much less how she'd convinced him to allow her up in the front passenger seat. Apparently, he was smitten with her. No surprise there.

Long before her father's very public assassination, I had already learned that Tasa didn't come from an ordinary family. The word mafia had been whispered about her from the time we were in elementary school. By the time I understood the significance of what her family did, it was too late. She was already my bestie and my crush on her brother had long been well established in my soul.

The drive across the city to Sunnyside, Queens was nerve-racking, but Nikki finally stopped the car in front of the Dacia Café. Owned by the Lupu family, it was situated next door to Tasa's house, which was next door from my house. Thank God, it was the middle of the day and my mother was at work. As a regional manager of a country-wide floor installation company, I'd bet my last dollar that she was on some conference call with a subsidiary out West.

As awkward as it was to wait in the back seat for Nikki to hold the door for me, I knew better than to do it myself. I watched impatiently as he stepped out of the car, circled around the trunk, and opened the door. I paused at the entrance to the café for him to prop the door open for me before I passed through. Again, I waited for him to usher me across the ground floor bustling with patrons, to a set of stairs near the back that led up to Alex's office.

Knocking gently, he waited until a deep-bass tone vibrated through the thick wooden door, ordering us to enter. Nikki swung the door open, prodded me forward with a little shove, and firmly shut it behind me. It swooshed closed with a soft click, and there I was, alone in the same room as Alex. Pressing up against the padded leather upholstery of the door, the indentation of the squabs molded against my back.

Lifting my eyes to him, I swallowed over my suddenly parched throat. My courage shriveled into nothing. My intention to scold him about Tasa died a quick death. Sheesh, I'd be lucky if I managed to speak normally.

Lord, he's as gorgeous as always.

Alex sat behind a majestic antique wooden desk at the other end of the lengthy room. His taste leaned toward the past, but without the gaudiness that so attracted his mother. My eyes darted around the room, from medieval wall hangings to little classical paintings, with delicate lamps casting light over them.

I crept over the expensive, plush rug and almost stumbled as I passed a frame hanging from the wall. I blinked. *Is that a L-Leonardo drawing?* Sure looked like one, but I didn't have the guts to stop and inspect it closely. Beneath the drawing was a credenza with a variety of liquor bottles and cut crystal. A little farther off was a small table with a chessboard and two chairs. Intricately carved pieces of ivory and black wood were spread across the board as if the players had stopped midgame. Everything was somewhat familiar. The leather, silk, and luxury were reminiscent of Tasa's familial home, but the office was markedly simple and masculine. God, I could imagine a room like this in my home, when I finally settled down.

Surely Alex heard the door open and shut, but he continued to work on his laptop uninterrupted. Reaching his desk, I stood with my hands clasped in front of me and waited. After a few moments, he pushed back the large bloodred oxford leather armchair he was sitting in. Uncoiling his body like a lazy panther, arrogantly confident, he rose to his feet.

My gaze followed his rise until he towered over me.

I'd known this man practically my entire life. I'd seen him at Tasa's home, the café, and even at the apartment I shared with her. This was one of the rare times we were alone. My blood pumped hard, and my heart thumped double time in my chest.

I swallowed the flashback of the one time I'd seen him half dressed, as he thrust into...*never mind*. Hesitantly, I took a step closer. The fingers of one of my hands curled over the back of the chair facing his desk and clawed the thick leather.

His glittering eyes watched me intently, scrutinizing me as if I were a small rabbit. Feeling distinctly vulnerable, I bit down on my bottom lip. Granted, I was always nervous around him. Always wanted him to see me as more than Tasa's friend.

In the past, I'd lost my faculties of speech once or twice, but to be the center of his complete focus was a whole other level of unnerving. Silence reigned, and I didn't have the nerve to break it.

As always, he exuded an otherworldly beauty that shunted the breath out of my lungs. It wasn't simply that he towered over me, that his broad shoulders blocked out the light coming from the windows behind him, that the bulges of his defined biceps stretched the sleeves of his jacket. He'd always worked out. As a youth, he was into competitive fencing. Even now, two crossed fencing swords hung on the wall behind him, above his head.

His sable hair was impeccably combed and coiffed, although I knew that it curled up on the sides when he sweat, one rogue lock falling over his forehead. A broad forehead that looked as if it was cut from a single block of granite. But it was his eyes that took my breath away. Deep green, with lighter shards that danced, teasing me. Those glittering emerald eyes were flinty and soft at the same time. He was the most beautiful male specimen I'd laid eyes on.

Worse still was the underlying aura rippling beneath the surface. I always felt it as a sexual, languid thing, like some spell had been cast over me while he licked his chops, circling me like I was his next meal. The hairs on my nape pricked up in fear, excitement, and...stupor. It made no sense. No sense at all. But there it was. That was the effect this man had on me.

Fidgeting ever so slightly from foot to foot, I couldn't

take the silence anymore and blurted out, "What's going on, Alex? Where's Tasa?"

He continued to watch me in that intense, predatory way of his. His jaw tightened, adding to the jut of its razor-edged sharpness. *Sheesh, I could cut a hole in the drywall with that thing.*

"You tell me, Nina," he drawled back, the gravel in his voice like roughened fingertips rasping over my heated skin. His voice resembled the best cognac.

To keep the silence at bay, I whooshed out in a rush, "I got a text from Tasa. She's run away but says she's safe. She sent the same text to your grandmother."

My eyes swept down to the rug and stayed there, evading his intense gaze. In that moment, I forgave Tasa completely for not telling me a thing. I'd do anything he wanted without a second thought. If he told me to drop to my knees and open my mouth to receive his cock, I'd do it. Squeezing my eyes shut, I fought to block out the image of his huge cock. Because I had seen it. I knew.

Great, now I was getting wet. Discreetly rubbing my thighs together, I reprimanded myself. *Not now, Nina. NOT NOW.*

But forcing myself to stop thinking about his junk didn't alter the truth. Without skipping a beat, I'd gladly fall to my knees and beg him. I was putty in his hands. *Putty.*

Snapping my eyes open, I licked my lips at the thought of his cock tucked away inside that pristine suit. A suit I'd love to muss up by making him come all over it. His eyes darkened, like a line of evergreens on the side of a winter mountain. Falling into them, I saw nothing but green. I could drown in that color.

"Sit," he ordered, gesturing impatiently as he glided elegantly around the desk and approached me.

I jumped to do as he asked. Uncurling my death grip on the chair, I scurried around and dropped into the nearest seat. He reached my side and crouched beside my chair. My mouth went bone dry. Swallowing to get any saliva down my parched throat, I stared down into his face. I was riveted, my pulse pounding in my eardrums at his nearness.

He was so close I caught the faint sandalwood of his cologne. *Dear God.* A little gasp escaped. I cursed myself under my breath. His hand landed on the curve of my knee and gripped it gently. Going from parched to salivating, my throat muscles worked audibly to swallow the pool of saliva in the well of my mouth.

His eyes followed the movement of my throat, and then dropped to the arm of the chair. I felt the loss of his gaze. It was as cold as the howling wind coming off a frozen tundra.

His eyelashes cast a shadow over his cheeks in the low light of his office, and I couldn't help but think again of how deep my infatuation ran. Since I could remember, I'd felt something for him. Before I knew lust, it was the awe one felt for a distant but coveted being. I'd always ached to have his attention on me, and whenever he acknowledged me, I would float on cloud nine for days afterward.

"Sweetness," he murmured in a low tone, the endearment wreaking havoc on my sanity. "You need to tell me everything."

I swallowed again. "I-I don't know...anything, really. She didn't tell me anything before she left. I didn't know she was gone until this morning. I texted her, thinking maybe she slept over in Queens, although that didn't make sense, because...because she was mad at you and your mother..." I trailed off when his eyes lifted and held mine, freezing my brain.

Nodding his head, his strong fingers around my knee

flexed to encourage me to continue. Shifting under his touch, I was thrilled, yet discomforted. Wetness gathered between my thighs, and I threw out a prayer of thanks that he had no idea the effect he had on me. The mortification would be more than I could bear.

"She didn't answer," I went on. "That's when I started to worry. I went on social media, but there were no new posts. You know she always posts *something*. I mean, at least once a day. While I was poking around on my cell, I got a text from an unknown number. I don't normally check them because they're spam, but..." I gave a light shrug of my shoulder. "Call it instinct. I thought that...well, you know..." My heart pounded so loudly I could hear it in my eardrums.

His eyes drilled into my face like a hawk, piercing me with his hunter's vision. "No, I don't know. Tell me what you thought."

My eyes trailed away from his concentrated gaze. Our conversations rarely got this heavy and never reached this level of truth-telling.

Are we really doing this? Are we going to speak about who you are? What the Lupu family is?

"Nina," he called me back to him. My eyes snapped to his.

I guess we are.

Grasping the armrests for strength, I took a big breath and announced, "I thought she might've been kidnapped."

His gaze burned my face. The warmth of his hot focus raised flags of red to my cheeks. Seriously, if looks could burn, I'd be scorched earth at this moment. A tidy pile of ashes is all that would be left of me.

"I see," he murmured. "And you don't think she has been?"

"No, honestly, I don't. From the tone of the text, it was

absolutely her. I'm not an expert, but there's no reason for someone to kidnap her and then go out of their way to contact *me* to convince *me* that she's safe. I'm nobody. Kidnappers would contact *you*, not send me a text to relieve me of my worry. Only Tasa would do that."

His lip twitched. "Yes, I believe you're right. I'd be the first to be contacted, as the *head* of the *family*." The emphasis on those two particular words was significant.

"Exactly." I nodded in agreement. "As the head of the family."

"I see very little reason to be anything but perfectly honest with you, then," he observed dryly. "How long have you known?"

"A long time." Then I hurried to add, "I've been around your family, like, forever, and it doesn't take much to put two and two together."

He chuckled. God, the sound of his rumbling laugh rolled through me like the languid smoke of incense. So. Sexy. I doubted the man could do anything that wasn't sexy. He was the embodiment of everything sinful, luxurious, and indulgent.

"We're currently working under the assumption that she hasn't been kidnapped, because of the text my grandmother received. It seems that Tasa feared a war might ensue if we thought she'd been taken. Which leaves me to deduce she has concocted this little rebellion on her own."

His thumb swiped back and forth over my knee, mesmerizing me with its languid rhythm. The heat of his touch melted me, and I had to tighten my grip on the armrests to keep myself upright.

His eyes sharpened; shards of crisp moss gleamed with focused intent. "Am I to assume you knew nothing of this, Nina? Hmm? You're her best friend, are you not? You go to the same school. You live with her. You practically finish each other's thoughts."

"I didn't know," I rushed to say. "You have no reason to believe me, but I really didn't."

He cupped the side of my face and leaned in, close enough for me to pick out the different shades of green in his irises. Unwittingly, I moved closer. The sandalwood fragrance assaulted me, pulling me in and dragging me under. *Does he feel anything toward me, or is he using my attraction to him to get information about Tasa?*

We moved toward each other, closer and closer. Alex took a sharp inhale and twisted his head away at the last moment. An expression of pain crossed his beautifully sinful face. His eyes shuttered tightly for a second and then he was back, his mossy green eyes on me. "I believe you. We both know I can extract every secret from you. If I so chose. Tasa knew as well, and she spared you from that fate," he said softly.

My breath stuttered in my chest. His words were true, of course, but that didn't take away from their impact. We had never spoken of the attraction I had for him. Not in a joke. Not in a whisper. Nothing. *Had I been that obvious over the years?* God knows, I'd never had the guts to hit on him. Never had the bravery to even flirt with him. Still, mortification crept up my throat in a red flush.

His hand lifted and slid down the side of my face, along my chin, and halted to cup my throat. His strong fingers wrapped around the front, just below my chin, and tilted it up.

"Tasa made certain not to tell you anything. She's shrewd enough to know I'd tear down anyone to find her. I'd make you talk, and talk you would."

His fingers slipped down the column of my throat, over

my collarbone, and landed on the top button of my silk top, nestled between the curves of my breasts. Tinkering with the mother-of-pearl button, he popped it open and traced his finger into the dip of my chemise. My lower jaw dropped open. *Oh my God, oh my God, oh my God.* What the hell was going on? My breathing sped up a mile an hour.

His thumb swiped down the slope of one breast, and I jerked in my seat. A breath of surprise escaped me. My brows drew together in a frown as I stuttered, "Alex...w-what are you doing?"

He drew closer. So close I could feel the puffs of his breaths against my lips. "Christ, these perfectly ripe tits. Feels better than I imagined, and I've imagined them for a long time, Nina. Always loved those moments when I'd catch you watching me with that hunger in your eyes. That *greed.* Are you greedy for me, Nina?" he inquired in a silky voice that drifted over my skin like a lazy caress.

I sucked in a breath. That touch and those words shot hot jolts of electricity straight to my clit. *Yes, God, yes, Alex, I'm greedy for you. More than you can possibly know.*

But I wouldn't cop to any of it. Even though he admitted to desiring me, even though he currently had his hand on my breast, I refused to admit to my obsession. I had some pride, after all.

With bravado that I didn't feel, I tossed out, "More to the point, Alex, is whether you're greedy for *me.*"

"Yes," he growled. "Don't tell me you don't know. How many times have I watched you from the window in my office at home. Since you were sixteen, Nina. Since you've grown these luscious tits. How many times have I passed you in the hall and was seconds away from shoving you against the wall and taking *what I wanted.*"

My mouth gaped open.

Ahhh...no. No, I had no idea. My butt shifted around in the seat of my chair like it was on fire. My panties had practically melted and peeled off my skin only to be doused by the wetness of my pussy.

His eyes were at half-mast.

"Apparently not," he drawled.

I wet my parched lips. Once. Twice. His eyes smoldered on them. Nervous, I bit down hard on my bottom lip. Then my body chose that moment to rebel. With a mind of its own, my back arched to give him greater access, silently begging him to reach my nipple. He made a noise at the back of his throat. Finally, *finally* he smoothed his thumb over it. Taking it between his fingers, he pinched hard, as if to punish me for my obliviousness.

Twisting in my seat, I threw caution to the wind, wrapped my fingers around his nape, and pressed my lips to his.

Moaning, he parted his lips, and I thrust my tongue inside. His remarkable taste exploded in my mouth, better than I ever imagined. It was something akin to bourbon mixed with the smoke of a bonfire. Abruptly, I was whisked off the chair and onto his lap. He took over. The soft glide of his tongue moving against mine was divine. Growing dizzy with pleasure, I heard pathetic mewling sounds. Barely registering that they were mine, I absorbed the lashes of his talented tongue. Without warning, he tore his mouth from mine.

Panting harshly in the quiet of the room, he swore, "Fuck, that was never supposed to happen."

Bereft but desperate for more, I stammered out, "What? Don't stop."

He licked the side of my throat, getting a whimper out of me before pulling back for good.

"Fuck, sweetness. At the rate we're going, I'll have you spread out beneath me. And once I feast on that sweet pussy, it won't be long before I'm breaching your tight clutch. Then, all hell will break loose."

Clasping the ends of his collar, I tugged him closer as I yelped, "Why?"

"You're Tasa's best friend," he snarled, frustration igniting the emerald flames in his eyes. "She'll be back, even if I have to drag her home by her fingernails. We don't get along well enough as it is, and it will only get worse. You'll be dragged into our drama, becoming one more thing we struggle over. She needs you by her side more than I do, Nina. You've always been there for her, and she'll need you more than ever."

He was right, of course. I knew that. Hell, I agreed with him, but at that moment...I couldn't let go. Instead, my hold on him tightened. Crumpling his collar between my fingers, I begged, "No, please."

His eyes snared mine and held. "You know I'm right."

"But she left me," I cried out. Struggling to get ahold of my sudden anger and long-standing sexual frustration, I crushed the starched cotton between my fists. After taking a deep breath, I tried in a more even tone, "She left for good, Alex. If she worked this hard to get away, do you really believe you can keep her against her will?"

"I have to try. I have no choice but to find her and bring her back," he ground out, wrapping his hands around my waist and placing me back on the seat of the chair as if I weighed nothing. "It's my duty, and duty is my *raison d'être*."

Hearing the steel in his tone, I collapsed back against the chair, pressing in so hard that it dug into my spine. He was as attracted to me as I was to him. Shocking, but also true. The man desired me. Perhaps not as much as I wanted him but close enough. Heck, anything in the same ballpark worked for me. Over the years, I'd convinced myself that he barely noticed me. Alex, the oldest sibling and head of the Lupu family, wanted little ole me. *Me.* If he hadn't given me the kiss of my life, if he hadn't said those wicked, dirty things, I'd never have believed it.

It was admirable of him to sacrifice his own desire for his sister's comfort, but Alex either didn't know her very well or he was living in denial. Tasa wasn't coming back. And if she was gone for good, as I strongly suspected, then he was mine.

If duty was his reason for living, then I'd become part of that precious duty of his. For once, my virginity would come in handy.

Releasing his crinkled collar, I patted it gently and said, "Alright then, Alex. Go find her. Good luck because you'll need it."

"Nina," he pleaded for my understanding. "She's in danger. Serious fucking danger. The kind of danger that could have her tortured. Is that what you want?"

"Of course not! I'd never want Tasa to be anything but happy. You haven't asked for my opinion on this, but if you find her—"

"*When* I find her," he interjected.

"When you find her, I suggest you listen to her carefully. She obviously planned this for a long time. There's a reason she left, and you can't ignore it anymore. Not unless you want a repeat or to make her miserable for the rest of her life."

He shot to his feet, hands on his hips, and glowered down on me. I shrank back into the chair until he released a sigh. Shaking his head, he relaxed his stance and reached out slowly, as if afraid of startling me. His knuckles tenderly grazed down the side of my face. "Are you truly scared of me?"

"You seem so...angry. I don't like it," I muttered, my eyes bouncing around the room to avoid the pain and offense in his. My insides shuddered, and I gripped the arms of the chair for support again.

"I'd never hurt you," he swore.

"I know," I mumbled. Darting a glance his way, I uttered, "I don't like to see you so wound up. Upset. It's hard to watch."

He threw his hands up a little. "I'm stressed out as fuck. My little sister is gone. Anyone could have grabbed her by now. Cristo's father is going to lose it when I tell him. Not that I give fuck all about him compared to Tasa's well-being, but it's a tricky situation. One that needs to be handled delicately. If he finds out on his own before I get a handle on the situation, he'll take it as a direct insult to his son and his honor."

"Shhh," I replied, the sound coming out unexpectedly. The urge to calm him drove me hard. I'd do anything to bring his emotions down a notch or two. I gently took his hand and tugged until he took the seat beside me. His head dropped back against the chair, and he let out a low, exhausted breath.

"Relax, Alex. This won't help you find her or deal with the fallout of her running away."

A twinge of pride took residence in my chest as he took in a deep inhalation while I continued to caress his hand.

"There's something that can take the edge off," he said, tilting his head forward, eyes boring down on me.

I wasn't sure exactly what he was referring to, but I knew how I'd like to take the edge off for him. Be of service to him. If I could, if we had that kind of relationship, I'd slip my hand into his pants and touch, pet, and stroke to my heart's content. Better yet, I'd go on an adventure of discovery with my lips, tongue, and mouth. I'd taste every inch of him and bring him to completion until he flooded my mouth, until my throat was raw from the way I imagine he would take it. One thing I'd always admired was how he was his own man, utterly comfortable in his own skin, at ease with his physicality.

I licked my dry lips, dying to taste more of him.

"Don't do that. You don't know what a fucking cock-tease move that is, but trust me, Nina, you do not want to be teasing my cock right this minute. I'm at the limit of my control, as it is."

I turned fully toward him. "Tell me what I can do to help you, Alex. I'll do anything to soothe you, to make it better."

"Kiss it better, you mean?" he teased, with a twinkle in his eye.

I flushed from the roots of my hair. God, he could read me like an open book. But I hurried to deny it, "That's not what I meant. I just want to help. If you're serious about Tasa being in trouble, then I'll do anything to help you find her. Anything to help relieve your anxiety and bring her back safely."

Slowly, I stood up and went behind the chair he was sitting in. Tenderly, I laid my hands on his shoulders and pressed my fingers into his tense muscles. Holy hell, they were like steel underneath my touch. I dug a little deeper, eliciting a low groan from him. It was an unholy, gravelly sound. I wanted more of it, so I kneaded deeper into his shoulder muscles. It was like working with granite, but eventually, his shoulders dropped, and he relaxed deeper into his seat.

Whenever I caught sight of him, whether visiting Tasa's

family home, the café, or at our apartment, Alex was always busy. Busy moving, busy talking on the phone, busy throwing out orders. Excusing himself as he took a call into a hallway while the rest of the family gathered for Sunday brunch or one of their many parties. He was always working. Even when I'd occasionally see him sitting still, his mind was clearly elsewhere, preoccupied with business.

Here, with me, I wished for him to unwind. My fingers seemed to be doing something for him, because his head dropped back against the back of the chair. The tension in his muscles seemed to ease under my attention, and I worked deeper into the tissue around his taut tendons. His sharp-angled jaw tilted upward. His eyelids drooped, leaving two shadowy arcs of dark lashes to fan out across his harsh cheekbones.

"I should have you come here every day to do this," he mused in a low, velvety voice. "Your fingers are magic."

"I'm glad," I murmured back. Inside, I was going, *squeee!* To be this close to him, to be able to touch him and make him feel good was incredible. Helping this strong man garner the energy to go on, I was doing something meaningful. It was a heady experience. I could practically hear Mother laughing at me, but I shoved the disapproval away and allowed myself to enjoy my moment.

"Even your voice relaxes me," he conceded, and that little flare of pride burned brighter in my chest. I had the power to change the mood of this dynamic, challenging man.

"You flatter me," I replied.

His hand caught mine. I stuttered to a stop. He squeezed it tightly. "I don't say anything I don't mean. I don't do anything I don't want to do. Or stop doing something I want to do. You know that already, don't you?"

"That I do," I rasped out between dry lips, attesting to the truth of his statement.

Alex was referring to Tasa's high school graduation party. It had been a wild affair, with a mix of kids from high school, the neighborhood, extended family, and business associates. Needing a break from the overwhelming energy of the crowd downstairs, I hunted for a quiet place. Winding through the hallways of the top floor, which was shared by Tasa and her twin, Nicu, I wandered past a bathroom when I heard sounds.

Grunting sounds.

I should've kept walking, but instead, I stepped closer. There was another grunt, accompanied by a moan. Creeping closer, I peeked through a crack of the open door of the bathroom. What I saw had me step away for a brief second. Unable to help myself, I promptly returned to my spot and peered around the wooden frame. My eyes slid down to the woman on her knees, moaning around the largest and only live cock I'd ever seen. For an eighteen-year-old, I was inexperienced and the first cock I ever laid eyes on was Alex's. It was a side view, but I could see it well enough. Perhaps I should've been scared. I was anything but.

I stared, riveted as his buttocks clenched each time he thrust into her mouth. *Good. God.* The bad internet porn I'd watched had nothing on this.

I think my hand went to my mouth as that girl, a senior just like me, moaned greedily around his dick.

Lucky wench.

"Play with your tits," he ordered. Unbuttoning her shirt, she pulled out breasts way smaller than my own. Alex hadn't lied when he said earlier that by sixteen, I was well in the throes of being well-endowed. It didn't seem to stop there either.

"That's right. Like that. Good, baby," he praised her. His dirty, filthy words bounced off the walls of the small bathroom and echoed in my heart.

My own hands followed his command, voluntarily moving to my own breasts and massaging them.

"Stop," he growled.

She did.

So did I.

I pressed my lips together to suppress the moan about to escape. My thighs were glued together and started rubbing quickly against each other to relieve the pressure.

His hand landed on her head. He wrapped her long blonde hair around his fist and took control.

"Suck it good, baby. Take it down that throat." He made a particularly rough thrust. "Now swallow," he demanded as he held her down, choking her. "Breathe through your nose," he instructed. Snorting through her nose, tears leaked from her eyes, but they burned bright for him. For this lesson on how to deep throat him. How to pleasure him.

Damn her. I wasn't a jealous person by nature, but at that moment, envy charged through me like a stampede of wild horses. Here, this lucky bitch had him in the palm of her hands. All that control with just her mouth and tongue. What I would've done to be in her position.

My chest rose and fell, faster and faster. One hand slipped down the taffeta of my dress and pressed between my thighs. Between the erotic image in front of me, the illicitness of my voyeurism, and the jealousy rushing through me, I was soaked.

Alex pulled out, stepped back and shifted her slightly. She shuffled on her knees to follow his lead and then he was back inside her mouth. This time, however, something must have alerted him to my presence.

His head snapped up; his eyes caught mine in the mirror. *Shit, shit, shit.* I wanted to fall back and hide, but his glittering green eyes impaled mine as his cock impaled the girl's mouth beneath him.

"You want this?" he asked. Whether he was asking me or her or both of us, I had no idea.

The girl moaned around the crown of his shaft.

"Do. You. Want. This?" he ground out. "I'll give it to you just the way you want it, sweetness," he murmured directly to me through the mirror.

Entranced, I froze. He was clearly speaking to me while his cock was in another girl's mouth. I was his little sister's best friend, and this man already featured in every one of my fantasies, at least a few times a week. For years. My mouth opened as if to speak, but nothing came out.

His eyes dropped to my fingers. "Yes you do, you dirty girl."

Caught.

I was so caught.

A flurry of shakes overtook my body as I stood there, finger moving frantically between my thighs. Eyes on my fingers, his lower jaw dropped open as he continued his steady thrusts, not breaking his rhythm. Not going faster, not going slower. In. Total. Control. Control of her. Control of me. Meanwhile, my body went into some kind of shock. Shudders racked my body. I was on the cusp of the greatest orgasm I'd ever had. It was baring down on me fast, but I didn't dare let go.

With more self-restraint than I knew possible, I yanked my fingers away, whirled around, and flew down the hall. The words "dirty girl" taunted me as I fled the scene, running as if I'd witnessed a murder instead of the filthiest sexual act to date.

That was the moment Alex was referring to when he stated he didn't do anything he didn't want to do or stop doing something he wanted to do. Perhaps, whatever this was between us had started that night, when he taunted me with my own raging lust while thrusting into another girl's mouth. It had been the hottest moment of my life and was a recurring fantasy from that day on. Only, my fantasies featured him taking *my* throat.

A silence descended upon us as I worked his muscles until they were supple in my hands. When my fingers slipped off his shoulders, his eyes snapped open. He opened his mouth, about to say something, when his cell phone rang. With a heavy sigh, he grabbed the phone, checked caller ID and answered, "What?"

He listened for a moment before replying, "Hold on. I'll be back."

Muting his phone, he murmured in a tone oozing with regret, "I have to take this, Nina. Don't for a moment think we're done here. I expect your full cooperation on this. If you hear anything, if you're in touch with her in any way, you contact me immediately. Now go. Nikki's waiting downstairs to drive you back to the apartment."

With that, he dismissed me. He stood, turning his back as he walked to the window and resumed his conversation. Reeling, I glared at his broad back. God, it was so easy for him to switch lanes, while I stood here, burning with unrequited lust. I bit back a sob of frustration and turned on my heel. Quietly crossing the long room, I darted one last desperate glance at the outline of his broad shoulders before slipping out of his office.

Next time, he wouldn't get away from me so easily.

4

I took a sip of whiskey as I brooded in my booth in the VIP section of my club, The Lounge. It was where I conducted business in the evenings, where I socialized with other men like me, and where I picked up women when I needed to scratch an itch. One perk of opening this club in my neighborhood was its proximity to the college campus of Fordham University. Downstairs was usually full of college students.

My eyes lazily glossed over my empire, pausing at each cluster of customers lounging on black and red velvet chaise lounges and low couches that surrounded low cocktail tables. Trying to maintain an air of classiness, a series of large black crystal chandeliers hung from the ceiling. I scanned the row of scantily dressed women sitting at the bar, advertising their availability to men like me. *Blonde, brunette,* my eyes squinted, *purple, and blonde again.* This was where women looking for a hookup or more sat. For me, it never went beyond a hookup. I had too much on my mind to spend more than a night with the same woman.

My business meeting had concluded, but the slew of

women hadn't yet noticed the vacated spot beside me. When they did, a little catfight might ensue before a couple of them made their way to my booth. There were rules to hooking up with me. For one, I never gave out my number, and if by some unfortunate misstep, they did get access to it and dared send me a text, I made sure they regretted the violation. If I happened to have the same woman more than once over the years, it was just that. Happenstance. I was a busy man; I might have repeats, but never on purpose.

Almost a week had passed since I saw Nina, but thoughts of her never drifted far from my mind. Goddamn, it had been a mistake to touch her. A few touches, a few kisses, and I was going half mad with lust. That woman was something else. Her full, warm tits had filled the palms of my hands just right. Her beautifully stiff nipple rolling between my fingers was a teenager's wet dream. And the way she tasted? Like jasmine, vanilla, and fucking. Hard as a steel pipe, I'd let her hands rove over me. What a pity it was such a brief taste.

It was almost too much to stop, but I'd forced myself before it went too far. There was no denying it was a struggle, but I had little choice in the matter. With three egotistical brothers, Tasa was the lone girl in the family. Nina was more than a best friend; she was like a sister. Tasa had been my father's favorite, and Nina was possibly the most solid relationship Tasa had since his death. I couldn't tear their friendship apart and deprive my sister when she'd need it most, once I dragged her back home.

Nina was almost too much to take in. I'd noticed her since she was in her late teens. Long dark hair cascading down in waves like a waterfall. Large doe eyes the color of tempered chocolate. She was as sweet and delicious as the chocolate *Bunică* used to make for cakes when we were children. She tasted like home.

I'd known the girl most of my life, so I knew how loyal she was to her family. To Tasa. And there was the rub. I'd wanted her for a long fucking time, but I'd never touched her, even after she caught me fucking that girl in the mouth all those years ago. One time alone with her, and my infamous control collapsed. I wanted to dive into her like one dove into the refreshing waves of the ocean on a hot summer day. She was an oasis for my soul, that woman. Soothing and yet stimulating in all the right ways.

But Tasa was coming back, whether she liked it or not. Knowing my sister, she'd need all the emotional support she could get. After Tata's death, Nina helped Tasa through her grief, and she'd be there for her again. I couldn't pull the rug out from under Tasa by snatching away her closest confidante. The way she'd see it, I shut down her joyride and then poached her friend. I could practically hear her sarcastic tone demanding, "Of all the women in the world, you just couldn't help yourself, could you? You just had to take Nina!"

I adjusted the gold cuff links on my sleeves and took hold of the glass of whiskey. My grip tightened around the glass when, speak of the devil, Nina stepped past the velvet rope my bouncer graciously lifted for her. *What the hell is she doing here?* Christ, she was crafted by the gods for the sole purpose of tempting me.

She was wearing a red dress that left little to the imagination, especially around her tits, and my teeth audibly clanged together. When she turned slightly, I saw her slinky red dress was backless. Back*less*. Leaving her beautiful porcelain skin gleaming under the brighter lights by the entrance. The possessive brute inside me wanted to rip off my tailored jacket and throw it over her shoulders to hide what was mine.

Mine.

Fuck, that word should not pass through my head when it came to her.

Even her lips were painted red. She rarely wore makeup, so it was noticeable from my seat, halfway across the room. Knowing those red lips were near, my cock stirred. Hell, they were made to wrap around my cock and leave a ring of red around the base.

I broke my death stare on her because what the hell was she doing, waltzing into *my* club dressed like that? Was she trying to attract other men? Abruptly, I noticed a man's hand settle possessively right above the curve of her luscious ass. My teeth ground down so hard I was surprised my jaw didn't snap from the pressure. I was sure to crack the whiskey glass I was holding. *What in the actual fuck?*

My youngest brother, Nicu, leaned toward me and said, "Two o'clock."

"Yeah, I see."

"You see, and you're not happy," he observed.

"Thank you, Mr. Fucking Obvious," I gritted out. Nicu was the smartest of us when it came to instincts and street-sense. I was certain he'd long caught on to the fact I had a slight obsession with the little girl next door. The strange man's hand above her ass reminded me that she was no longer so little.

Since she was sixteen and grew a pair of tits on her that rivaled a porn star, I'd kept my distance. Even though she was jailbait, I couldn't help spying on her from the office window in my family's home, which looked directly into her bedroom. I caught her undressing once or twice, and quickly threw the curtains closed before I did something regrettable, like jack off to the sight of my little sister's best friend.

Those pouty lips weren't helping my cause, either. Her bottom lip was fuller than her bow-shaped upper lip, teasing and taunting me by its very existence. Speaking of which, her bright-red lips were curling up on the sides, throwing a brilliant smile to the fucker who ushered her to the far end of the room. She took a seat on a low sofa in one of the alcoves and he quickly followed.

Unable to take my eyes off them, I rubbed the stubble along my jawline and swiped at my mouth. I once entertained the idea that I lusted after her because she was off-limits. After all, Tasa would've cut my balls off for touching her friend. She was a vicious little thing and loyal to the core —one of the many reasons I adored my little sister, even if she made it her mission in life to make mine a living hell.

The other thing about Nina was that she was almost as shielded as Tasa. They spent so much time together that I knew as much about her as I did about Tasa. Despite Tasa's little affair with her vocal instructor at The Juilliard School, I knew she was still a virgin. I didn't even have to threaten her lover. He unequivocally confirmed to me, the day Nicu and I paid him a little visit at the beginning of their affair, that she had no intention of losing her virginity to him. My brother and I made it clear to him that we'd slit his throat if that changed in any way, shape, or form. I had hoped a lover would help her let off steam, but her running off clearly proved it hadn't done enough.

Tasa was good by design, but Nina was good by nature. She was the epitome of everything sweet and soft. It was one of the reasons I got so hard around her. Although I didn't think she was a virgin, just the idea of sinking into that tight flesh, the possibility of tearing through the thin but irrevocable barrier, had my teeth on edge. The way she'd looked at me in my office, bashfully peeking out from under her dark eyelashes, got me spurting a little in my pants. Her innocence was devious; it got under my skin like nothing else.

I had been able to stay far away from her, but the first time Tasa was out of the picture I cracked within hours. Yet, I managed to regroup in time and force myself off her.

Then, she had the audacity to walk into my damn club.

Fuck.

My eyes narrowed to slits as I watched Nina and the tall man. He might've been wearing a suit, but I knew, better than anyone, that was no guarantee of decency. Unbuttoning his jacket, he had the nerve to place his arm over the back of the couch. I squinted as his fingers lightly played with a few strands that had come undone from her upswept hair. The muscles of my stomach clenched and twisted. While she might not be inexperienced, she'd never had a boyfriend. Unlike Tasa, she didn't have the duty to remain a virgin hanging over her head.

But what if her pussy was unused? By the way he was pawing at her, given half a chance, he'd rip into that soft, yielding flesh like a fucking animal. The thought tore at my gut. This was why I spent as little time with her as possible. Because I knew what I was. A possessive motherfucker.

Fists balled at my sides, I forced myself to remain still as the tall man loomed over her bombshell of a body and whispered into her ear. Even from this distance, I saw the telltale blush crawl up her throat. A waitress stopped to deposit drinks at their table. Swinging her glossy dark hair over one shoulder, Nina scooped hers up like an inflatable life ring and guzzled half of it down.

"She's nervous," Nicu noted.

"You think?"

"She's going to get drunk if she keeps that up. You know what a lightweight she is," he added, as if I didn't know that about her. Even Nicu, who felt for her only as a brother, shifted in his seat. He was as possessive as I was, and he didn't like what he was seeing. Beautiful, innocent Nina alone in a club and drinking fast due to nerves.

I should go there and smack her behind for bringing a fake ID into my club because she's not twenty-one yet.

"What am I supposed to do about it? I'm not her keeper."

"Do what you've always wanted to do," he counseled. I rolled my eyes. Nicu and his perceptive comments. I'd guided him into this twisted life as soon as I could morally do so. Like me, he'd killed his first quarry at the age of fifteen.

Ripping my eyes away from Nina, I turned to my brother. "What the fuck are you suggesting, *frate*?" I returned, my tone dripping with sarcasm.

"Yes, I am your brother, and as your brother, you can't hide from me. Christ, Alex, you've been panting after that woman for years. Get her before someone else does, because, believe me, you won't like it if they do."

"The fuck do you mean *before someone else does*?"

Nicu arched an eyebrow, throwing me a blasé stare. We had a little stare down, as only brothers could.

"I'd break her," I argued.

"I highly doubt it," he drawled.

"You know how my tastes run," I reminded Nicu. And myself.

"I'm sure she knows. Everyone knows." He paused a beat. "It's not exactly a secret, and she knows more than most. If she doesn't, I'm sure you'll break her in gently.

Nina's stronger than she looks, and she wants you. She's got a little subbie in that lush body dying to come out and play. It's part of the reason you've had a hard-on for her since she sprouted that rack."

"You know, the real problem is that she's Tasa's best friend."

"Please, motherfucker. Tasa's gone and forging her own life. She's left the city, and she's not coming back. You've got free rein, brother."

The tall man's fingers glided up Nina's bare arm to her shoulder and squeezed. My blood went from a low simmer to a boil in a second flat.

"Don't say that. I'll find Tasa and bring her back safely," I swore to him.

Ignoring my oath, he asked, "How do you know she didn't come here on purpose anyway? Not only does she know who owns this place, but she knows this is our spot. Are you trying to tell me that since she walked in here, her eyes haven't strayed over here once? Doubt it. And if she is avoiding us, then it's for the sole purpose of making you jealous."

"She's too innocent to make a play like that...plus Tasa needs her ten times more than I do."

"Alex, this little stunt is right out of our dear little sister's playbook."

The man captured Nina's chin and crushed his mouth on hers.

"Fuck!" I cursed harshly.

5

I was out of my seat and stalking toward her before I realized what I was doing, but then I was too far gone. By the time I reached her, her mouth was being devoured by this other man. Completely oblivious to my presence, it took every ounce of my self-control not to rip the bastard off her.

I let out a growl. Hearing it, she started and attempted to pull away, but the man's grip on her nape kept her in place. I heard a soft whimper, and my fist was seconds away from obliterating this motherfucker.

"Nina," I ground out, loud and harsh.

Nina shoved at the man's chest, dislodging his mouth from hers. Her head snapped in my direction, eyes flaring wide in shock and fear.

At this point, fear was good. She should be fucking afraid.

"A word," I snapped.

"What the hell—"

Nina grasped the man's arm and stopped him midsentence. "This is the brother of my best friend, Tasa. You remember Tasa?" she asked hurriedly, nodding her head as if that would help him understand the severity of his situation.

He frowned at her. "From school?"

I ground my jaws together, my patience wearing thin. "Nina. Now."

"Hey!" the man called out, but Nina was already on her feet and skirting around the low couch to get to me. Good girl. The growling, snarling beast pacing in an endless circle in the cage of my chest tossed its head in impatience.

Wrapping her fingers around my arm, she implored the guy, "Gregory, order another drink. I'll just be a moment."

Although her touch, combined with her immediate submission, cooled off the worst of my rage, I could've ripped the face right off *Gregory*.

Tugging at my arm, she tried to move me, but I stayed right where I stood because I was nowhere fucking done staring down at this cocksucker. If he had any sense, any sense at all, he'd be gone by the time I brought her back. *If* I brought her back. A big if.

"Alex, please don't make a scene," she urged, her bulging eyes edged in white. "I'm coming with you."

My head swung toward her. "Me make a scene? After getting your face sucked off in the middle of my club. You're kidding me, right?"

"Please," she begged in a low, husky tone that caught hold of my attention. Or, more to the point, the attention of my dick. Not only had I never seen her with a man before, but tonight, I was forced to watch the bastard swallow her whole. Whipping around, turning my back to the other man, I allowed her to drag me away by the lapels of my jacket. She pulled me to the far end of the lounge and down a hallway going toward the restrooms. When we turned the corner into a darker hallway, I abruptly took control and backed her against the wall.

With her caged in my arms, we stared at each other for a long beat. Our chests were heaving, although probably for different reasons. I scrutinized her face, looking to see if she was drunk, aroused, or both. What I saw was anticipation mixed with fear, and I couldn't deny that it pleased me greatly. My gaze dropped to the full bright red lips that had taunted me from afar. Smudges of lipstick circled her mouth and fury abruptly caught hold of my throat once again.

My jaw ticked away as I catalogued every trace left by that bastard.

"What the fuck are you doing, Nina?" I demanded in a dangerously intimate tone.

"I-I'm on a date," she stammered out, averting her eyes.

"This is how you let a date treat you?" I scoffed, corralling her closer until her panting chest brushed against the open sides of my suit. "In my establishment?" I pressed closer. "Under my very nose?" I dipped my head and let my nose graze the side of her throat, scenting her. The sweet fragrance of jasmine and vanilla hit my bloodstream, bringing my lust to a boil. Turning me ravenous for another taste.

"I-I don't know," she stumbled over her words.

"You don't know?" I inquired in an innocent tone laced with warning. "You come into my establishment, dressed in a sexy red number like this, looking like a fragile rose. Then you stick a thorn in my side by letting a strange man maul you in front of me, and all you have to say for yourself is that you don't know? You want to poke the bear, Nina? Because I'm more than willing to let it loose on you. If *any*one touches you, especially in here, that man will be *me*. You come in here, flaunt yourself, and throw another man in my face? It's like waving red in front of a raging bull. You wanted a reaction, little girl? Have no fear. A reaction is what you'll get."

I pulled back to watch the effect my words had on her. Her mouth opened to speak, snapped closed, and opened again.

Nothing came out.

Pushing open the door of the employee restroom beside me, I flipped on the light switch and hustled her inside. Seeing her blinking up at me like a deer in headlights drove my hunter instinct *hard*. Her momentary weakness summoned the rampaging predator clamoring to be let loose on her.

"Wipe your mouth," I commanded severely.

She raised trembling fingers to her mouth and wiped it with the back of her hand.

"You're going to forget you ever kissed that fucker," I promised her. "And I'm the one who's going to make you forget."

Tangling my fingers into her silky tresses, I yanked her head back against the cold white tiles. "We're going to play a little game, you and me. The rules of this game are simple. I ask a question, and you answer me honestly. Understand?"

She nodded as much as she could with my claiming grip on her hair.

"Did you or did you not come, knowing I'd be here?"

She blinked a few times.

Twisting her dark locks in my fingers, I tugged a little harder. "Answer me."

"I came, knowing you were here," she confessed, her voice hoarse.

I grazed my lips over hers. So smooth. So soft.

"Good girl," I praised. "That's it, Nina. Never lie to me."

A small whimper escaped her parted, moist lips, shooting straight to my balls.

Gaze boring into her, I insisted, "Did you think to make me jealous?"

"Ye-s," she cried out, the word cracking in the end.

I leaned in and licked up the length of her jawline.

"Such a good girl," I commended her. Placing another gentle kiss on the corner of her lips, I asked softly, "Do you know what happens to good girls?"

I leaned a little bit away to look her in the eye because I wanted to make sure she understood what was at stake here. The beast was out, and it wasn't leaving without its pound of flesh. Her eyes were glued to mine, searching my face. This was me at my most raw. I was usually driven by goals, by demands and expectations, but tonight...my demons were in the driver's seat. My objective was simple. Take her and make her mine. She'd asked for it, strolling into my territory accompanied by another man. That wasn't simply an insult but a gauntlet thrown. One I was gnashing at the bit to pick up.

"Do you?" I repeated.

A notch formed between her brows. "N-not really."

"Let me make it clear to you, then. Good girls get fucked," I replied bluntly.

I paused, waiting for her reaction. There was a sharp intake of breath, but her eyes blew out. They dilated like she'd taken a hit of coke, leaving but a thin circle of dark brown around her wide pupils.

I rasped out a bark of a laugh. "You expected that didn't you, Nina? Coming into my territory, acting like a naughty little girl. You know what kind of bad man I am, deep down inside. I locked that shit up around you until you showed up in my club and gave another man what's mine. Well, you're going to pay for making a move like that."

My fingers tightened around her locks and tilted her head back farther to capture her mouth with mine. She opened instantly. My heart soared at her immediate surrender. Slanting my mouth over hers, my tongue went deep to plunder her hot, wet mouth, tasting of robust brandy. Jerking at the spaghetti straps of her red dress, the low-cut sweetheart neckline dipped lower and exposed her luscious tits.

"Fuck," I rasped. "You're not even wearing a bra. You're in so much fucking trouble, you filthy little thing." I cupped one of her large breasts and held it for a moment, cradling its divine weight in the palm of my hand. How many times had I jacked off to fantasies of them? They were bigger and riper than when I stood, rigid in the shadows of my office, spying on my little sister's best friend.

"Holy hell," I moaned before ducking my head and sucking one large nipple into my mouth. I mauled that breast like a mad berserker, rampaging her silky skin with my tongue and teeth. It tasted just like her scent, that beguiling mixture of jasmine, vanilla, and dark sensuality.

Nina's fingers slid up the sides of my face and twisted in my hair as I transferred my attention to her other nipple. Scraping the rough bristles of my jaw against her delicate skin caused her to gasp out loud.

Sucking on as much skin as I could reach, I made sure to leave red love marks. Her chest was already rising and falling with her accelerated breath, but I was only getting started.

"You deserve to be wined and dined. To be treated like a princess," I murmured into the delicious pillowy flesh of her breast. Then I stepped away and whirled her around to face the sink. Planting her hands firmly on either side of it, I grabbed the slinky material of her dress and yanked it over her hips.

"That's what you deserve, sweetness," I whispered into the crook of her neck as I gripped her hips and ground her fine ass into my groin. "To be fucked like a princess in a bed of silk sheets."

Unzipping my slacks, I pulled out my engorged cock. "But I'm a dark prince."

Pushing her panties down, I finished, "And I don't fuck nice. We're going bare, Nina." Through clenched teeth, I said, "I'm clean, but I need to know whether you're protected from pregnancy."

She nodded.

A nod wasn't good enough. I didn't get women pregnant, period. That only happened within the confines of a marriage. As badly as I wanted to plunge inside her tight heat and feel her skin to skin, I'd stop and put on a rubber.

"The words, Nina," I growled.

"Yes, yes, I'm on the pill, and I'm clean, too."

With that admission, I thrust inside. Wrapped around my shaft, her cunt throbbed hot. Her fingers clutched at the porcelain as her mouth dropped open on a harsh exhale. I'd only gotten the crown and maybe an inch inside of her when her slick flesh clenched down on my cock, keeping me out.

She was slippery wet alright, but she was tight. Real tight.

"Spread your legs," I commanded roughly.

She obeyed, and I pressed in deeper, but her inner walls cinched tighter in lockdown. Fuck, that felt good, but her pussy was tighter than I'd ever had to handle before. Sliding one hand to her front, I found and caressed that little beaded pearl while my other hand palmed her thick breast roughly.

I shifted on my feet. The movement caused my hips to punch forward on their own accord and then I felt it. A little tension. A...wall? I heaved out a breath. I wasn't imagining it; that thin membrane was undeniable. I ceased all movement. I was fucking a virgin. I was pressing into untried territory.

Oh, this girl was *so* mine, it wasn't funny.

Mother*fuck*— but before I could finish my thought, Nina curled her fingers around my hips and slammed herself back, impaling herself on my cock and ripping through her hymen.

Shocked, I demanded, "Look up, Nina. Look at me."

Her eyes met mine in the mirror, glistening with unshed tears. I caressed her hair, soothing her until her body relaxed bit by bit. Holding tight, I remained still to allow her to adjust to the penetration of my cock. Without breaking eye contact, I placed open-mouthed kisses along her shoulder and up her throat as I praised her for being so strong, so brave and sexy. And especially for being mine. Damn, she was always special, but knowing I was the first man to breach her had sealed her fate.

Once her muscles loosened sufficiently, I began to rock slowly until her eyes glazed over. Lower jaw hanging open, saliva gathered at the corner of her mouth and almost slid over the curve of her bottom lip. Suddenly, she leaned back and went limp against my chest, her gorgeous rack thrust out. I wanted to bellow and pound my fucking chest like the savage I was.

I had done this. I had speared her tight cunt with my cock and reduced her to a wanton creature.

"You like my cock inside you?" I murmured.

She nodded once.

"I want to hear the words, Nina. Convince me this is what you want."

"Yes, Alex, I've waited for you. Please, I've always wanted you. Please take me," she begged. Tilting her hips up, she pressed back to take another inch of my hard cock. My nostrils flared. By her swift intake of breath, it was too much too fast, but I admired her courage.

"Christ, you're *tight*," I gritted out, shaking my head to chase away the buzz overcoming me. Grasping her hips, I pulled away a little to get a prime view. Oh, and did I get it. I saw the lips of her pussy spread almost obscenely over my shaft. The shaft pulsing in and out of her slow, but relentless. Each time, I pushed in half an inch deeper and paused to give her a moment. My thick cock wasn't easy to take in general, much less for an unbroken cunt like hers.

"This is what I've dreamed of, even before I caught you in the bathroom. This is what I've always wanted," she breathed out.

"What is that?" I rocked in deeper.

Her breath stuttered in and out. She bit down on her bottom lip, but I heard the tiny whimper of surprise she tried to suppress. Little did she know I wanted everything from her.

Her pain and her pleasure.

Her whimpers and her cries of ecstasy.

"Your cock. Inside me," she clarified.

Pleasure ricocheted through my body, pulling my balls tight. My thighs trembled from the strength it took to hold back when all my body wanted to do was thrust and fuck and claim this woman. She wiggled her butt a little, eliciting a deep, pained groan from me. I blew out a long breath.

My fingers, which had stilled as I wrangled to regain

control, came back to life, and I resumed massaging her swollen clit. They slid down to trace the outline of her lower lips stretched taut around my girth, dripping juice and blood and pre-come. Getting my fingers slick, I returned to teasing her clit.

Ever so slowly, she whirled her hips into a few tight figure eights and declared, "I'm ready."

I'm rarely left speechless, but she'd caught me unaware. At that moment, it dawned on me that I'd been played by a not-so-innocent little virgin. Thoroughly and completely played. She'd showed up at my club, taunted me to lose control, and got me to fuck her virginity out of her.

An involuntary laugh puffed out. "I'll never fucking underestimate you again, Nina."

"I told you I've waited for years. Tasa's gone." Her voice dipped in sadness. "The only upside is being taken by you."

Then, courageous girl that she was, she pulled off my cock and shoved back into me again. Fuck, this woman and her cunt were incredible.

"Do it again. Let me see," I demanded, desperate to watch as she speared herself on my cock, spreading her pussy lips over my rigid flesh. Following my command, she dragged off my massive cock and impaled herself again.

Tightening her grip on the porcelain sink, she arched her back so I could get a good view of my cock, slick with juices and smears of blood. *Blood.* My breath was trapped in my lungs. Blood was sacred to a *mafie* king like me. Blood was the foundation for the deepest of bonds. In the moral universe in which I lived and breathed and would one day die, it was the building block of bonds. Bonds that defied death because they passed to the next generation.

The one time in my fucking life when I slipped and look what happened! Whether either of us wanted it, she was bound to me and I was bound to her. She was not only mine, she belonged to my family. But she wasn't *mafie*, a voice in my head whispered. *Doesn't matter.* This woman was mine. She was under my protection.

The pressure around my skull intensified as the smears of glistening blood disappeared when she pushed herself back onto my cock again. Watching my slippery cock swallowed by the stretched lips of her pussy snapped the last threads of my restraint. Taking hold of her hips, I rammed myself fully inside. Lust, conquest, and fear gripped me by the throat.

Virgin.

Played.

Blood.

Bond.

The last one crashed through my brain in an endless loop. Blind and mindless, I rutted into her like an animal in the throes of madness, driven by the urge to brand that tight cunt. If it wasn't for her delicate flesh shuddering around my cock, I would've thought I'd hurt her, but *thank fuck*, she was right there with me, shouting out in pleasure with each of my thrusts.

"You want your virgin pussy taken? You wanna get fucked hard? Oh, it's happening, little girl. I'm the man who conquered this pussy. Look at those perfect pink lips stretched wide around my cock. *I'm* the one who busted through this tight cunt. *My* cock is baptized in the blood of your sweet cherry. Come for me, Nina. I need you to come," I begged, my voice cracking as I gave her ass a hard smack.

Rearing back, I took full control of that tight, wet hole. *And it was fucking heaven.* Her pussy was a gold mine of pleasure. She threw her head back until the crown banged against my chest as I pounded into her like my life depended on it. The come I had stored up for this girl came thundering out at the same time as my roar. My soul fractured in a million pieces as an onslaught of sensations throttled me.

Through the oncoming blindness of my orgasm, I saw her eyes turn glassy with pleasure as her body shook from the intensity of her climax. Hot come kept churning up my cock and spilling into her. I couldn't stop thrusting as her pussy bore down on me, clutching and choking and milking me for all she was worth. Her body instinctually sucked every drop out of me as if this would be her one and only time.

Over my dead fucking body.

6

Holy. *Shit.* I knew that walking into the club, using Alex's name to get access to the VIP lounge, and letting Gregory stick his disgusting, sloppy tongue in my mouth might be worth the trouble I was courting, but I'd never *ever* thought it'd turn out this well. Color me stupid, but sex was *incredible.* Way better than what the average woman suggested. It was Alex. Besides a few moments when it'd hurt like hell, this was *insane.* The pressure of his cock when he pressed into me, the burn of the stretch, and then the climax at the end? Put the orgasms I'd had by my own hand to shame. To. Shame.

I knew there was a savage beneath that suit, covered over with only a thin veneer of civilization. The beast is what called to me the most. The kindness and protectiveness he'd shown me through my childhood was nothing compared to the time I spied him beating the hell out of a man around the corner from his house or pounding into my classmate's mouth. Those two moments—okay, especially the last one —were when I realized that I didn't only want him, I needed him. Strong. Demanding. *Brutal.* It called to everything inside me that was soft, that wanted to yield to his rough commands.

I'd planned it right, banking on the chance that once he was inside me, he wouldn't stop even after discovering I was a virgin. It had paid off. He had the kind of ruthlessness I craved. Alex had called me a princess, but there were zero regrets for losing my virginity in a nightclub bathroom. Princess, *pssht*. It was cute of him to think so. My only response was, thank God it hadn't stopped him from fucking me like I wasn't one.

Now, it was done.

I cast a look over my shoulder and found him tucking his beautiful cock away and zipping up his pants. Grabbing a few paper towels from the dispenser, I scrunched my nose and asked, "Don't you want to clean up?"

He shot me a wicked grin. "Not a chance in hell. You know how I am about blood."

"Um...I do?" I knew Romanians like him considered blood to be symbolic and that virginity tied a man and woman together in the *mafie*. While I'd plotted, I wasn't sure the blood bond applied to me. I was just a regular American girl.

He nodded. "You do. I want your bloodshed on me, Nina. I earned it. It stays on until we get home, and you can clean it off me at leisure," he promised darkly.

Yeah, I definitely didn't know anything about not cleaning up afterward, but for some inexplicable reason, my chest burst with pride. God, was I as bloodthirsty as he was? I matched his cocky grin with one of my own. We'd clearly both gotten off on tearing through my hymen. *That's okay, we'll be sick together.*

But that didn't mean this wasn't a one-off. My smile slipped. He'd talked about me cleaning him up at *home*, but that wasn't enough clarity for me. I mean, Alex was a gorgeous, powerful man who could fuck like a stallion. He could have any woman he wanted.

In a hesitant voice, I prodded, "What happens now, Alex?"

His eyes sharpened as he smoothly pried the paper towels from my death grip and twisted the faucet open. Drenching them underneath a stream of scalding-hot water, he squeezed them and crouched down. Ever so gently, he cleaned me with soft swipes, folding the paper towel to expose a clean side before going in again, until he'd decided that I was clean enough.

"What happens now is that I'm going to drill into that sweet pussy until it's stretched out to the size of my cock. But before that, it means you're going to get rid of that fucker you came with." His eyes flicked up and locked on mine. "You belong to me now. I'll give you the kindness of doing it yourself. Otherwise, believe me, I'll gladly take care of him." His eyes glittered like hard gems. "My way."

A shot of delight thrummed through me. The raw possessiveness behind his words was music to my ears.

"Oh," I replied, my grin coming back tenfold. *Happy, happy, joy, joy.*

He snagged my panties from the floor and tucked them into his pocket. "My trophy," he explained smugly. "Now be a good girl and get rid of that bastard before I do, Nina."

I smoothed down the front of my dress. "Give me five minutes."

"*Five*," he ground out, pinching my chin and tilting my head up. "Trust me, Nina, you don't want to test me on this."

Noticing the muscle in his jaw doing jumping jacks, I nodded my head vigorously.

I turned to go, but he held on tight and ordered, "Wash your mouth."

"My mouth?"

"Yes, your fucking mouth. I want to kiss you."

"You already kissed me," I reminded him.

"That wasn't a kiss. I want all remnants of that man gone," he snapped harshly.

"I can assure you, Alex, I don't have the slightest memory of him."

"Damn it," he muttered before taking hold of my nape and bringing me in for a fierce, claiming kiss that had me melting against him. He gorged on my mouth like I was a feast and it was his last meal. My lips were tingly and puffy by the time he finally took a step away and released me.

"Now go. I want you at my table in exactly five minutes," he pronounced as he took out his cell phone and pressed on his timer.

Holding the door open for me, I flew out and rushed to Gregory.

※※※

By the time I sent poor Gregory off on his way and made it to Alex's table, the scowl on his face told me that my five minutes were up. Thankfully, he must've seen how hard I'd worked to get Gregory out of his club and chose to take pity on me. Somewhat. His eyes stalked me, promising retribution, as I slunk over to his table.

Taking a deep breath, I slipped into the seat he patted beside him. Nicu gave me a nod of acknowledgement and greeted me with a little smirk, "Hey, Nina. Fancy meeting you here."

Heat crawled up my throat, and my eyes sped away from him. Mortified, I tried to remind myself that he didn't necessarily know what happened in the bathroom, unless I outed myself by my own stupidity. Trying to summon up a modicum of maturity, I cleared my throat and replied, "Hey, Nicu. How's your night going?"

Alex's arm came and wrapped around my shoulders. Nicu's eyes paused on it. "Not as well as yours, I imagine."

I groaned, and Alex gave his little brother a hard stare. The kind of stare I wouldn't want to be on the receiving end of.

"Sorry, Nina. Didn't mean to be crude," he conceded.

"Better," retorted Alex as he brought me into the warm comfort of his embrace and nuzzled me.

The way he burrowed into my hair felt divine. Taking a possessive hold of my throat, he brought my mouth to his and gave me an all-consuming kiss until I moaned. By the time he broke it off, my head was swimming. I had never felt coveted like this before, and that, along with the lust thrumming beneath my skin, settled the nerves rioting in my belly from the newness of my situation. While I'd known Alex and Nicu almost my entire life, I'd only been around them in the context of their family. I'd never been alone with either of them, much less with both at the same time, and rarely in public. Then there was the fact that I'd just barely finished losing my virginity to Alex in the employee bathroom of his club.

I couldn't help but think of what Tasa's reaction would be regarding Alex and me. Hopefully, she was being genuine the times she'd pushed me to admit how I felt about him, insisting that she wouldn't mind if we were together. I always downplayed my borderline obsession with him around her. First, because my loyalty lay with her, but also because I had little hope that anything would come of it. As much as I missed Tasa, her running away had instigated a wild beginning to a new chapter in my life.

This was a rewriting of the rules of engagement, and I had no idea how to handle it. But Alex's decadent scent and the warmth of his body heat provided an anchor for the elation rivaling my nerves and anxiety.

It almost felt surreal, but when I shifted in my seat, the slight soreness between my legs was a delicious reality check. That, and the unfamiliar weight of Alex's arm around my shoulder. With new courage, I edged closer to him.

A large man, swaying on his feet, loomed over the booth where we were sitting. Instinctively, I shrank back, and Alex wrapped me deeper into the protection of his broad chest. Hmm...after years of daydreaming about this, it was beguiling to be nestled in the cove of his embrace.

"Alex," the man slurred, giving him a salute with a hint of mockery. The whiff of alcohol coming off him was staggering. He could've disinfected a toilet bowl with the amount he'd consumed.

With a wobble of his head, he turned to Tasa's twin and said, "Nicu."

Gazing up, I blinked as the light from above illuminated the stranger's face. Cristo. Tasa's soon-to-be husband. He was a large guy, not unattractive if you liked the football-player-kind of physique. I'd always thought he had a good head of wavy brown hair and nice brown eyes, but wasted was not a good look on him. His normally well-coiffed hair stuck out every which way, his eyes were glassy, and his lower jaw was slack, a bit of drool collecting at one corner of his mouth. A jolt of anger ran through me. Sure, people had the right to party and drink, but he wasn't worthy of Tasa. In that moment, I was grateful she'd escaped him. She should never have to marry this guy.

"Cristo," Alex replied with a tone that could freeze a man's blood. It was clear Alex saw him for what he was. But then *how* could he have given Tasa over to this man? Some of my indignation toward Cristo was siphoned off and directed toward Alex. *What was he thinking?*

Cristo squinted down at me, and I ducked my head to avoid his scrutiny. We'd met several times over the last year as the marriage negotiations progressed at a steady clip. He and his parents had been invited to every public social event hosted by Tasa's family, but he'd always been on his best behavior.

"Nina? That you?" he slurred.

I gave him a hesitant wave. *Awkward.* I didn't dare glace at Alex, but I felt the tension in his muscles. Did Cristo or his father know Tasa was missing? Is that why he was drunk? He didn't seem particularly torn up by the idea that his bride-to-be had run away.

"Where's Tasa?" he inquired, his blurry eyes roaming around.

Well, that answered my question.

His head swiped left and right as if he expected her to appear at any moment.

Nicu's jaw clenched, and I could almost hear the grinding of his back teeth, a bad habit he had. Tasa's twin didn't do "uncomfortable." To anyone who didn't know his expressions, he simply looked stone-faced. Stone-faced blank was his resting bitch face, after all.

"She's busy at school," Alex lied, his arm tightening around my shoulder in warning. He didn't have to worry. I had no intention of saying a word. But listening to them discuss Tasa brought on a fresh wave of yearning for my best friend. It was because of these two men that she was gone. "As you well know, it's her last semester, and she's working on some big senior project."

Good one, Alex. Since Cristo had never gone to college and seemed to care little about Tasa's life, he'd eat that up. My irritation at Cristo flared brighter. She deserved better than a guy who was so disinterested in her life that it was easy to pull one over on him.

"Never understood why you insisted on everyone in your family going to college. Waste of time, in my opinion. But then again, you are the *Lupul*," he sneered.

The *Lupul*? I recalled Tasa explaining it to me...that it was a form of respect for Alex, as head of the Lupu clan.

"We go to college because we're not ignorant heathens like the typical *mafie* crowd. We go to college because we have to face the Bratva, and every one of those bastards holds a PhD in chemical engineering or financial management. *That* is why we educate ourselves," spat out Nicu. "And you should know better than to criticize the head of the clan your father so desperately wants join, in holy matrimony no less."

Nicu had never thought Cristo was good enough for his sister, and while I knew he chafed against Alex's insistence that he go to college, he'd show a united front to his sister's fiancé. Like with my mother, education meant a great deal to Tasa's family, especially since Alex had had to drop out of Columbia University after his father died.

"She must be busy 'cause I haven't seen her on Insta," Cristo remarked, dodging the steaming pile of shit he'd just stepped in. "She usually posts every day."

"Yeah, well, she's working day and night, slaving away on a big opera at the Met. They're allowing only a few seniors to intern, and you know how *Carmen* is her favorite opera."

It was *La Traviata*, actually. But since *Carmen* was the big hit on the winter program, Alex had no choice but to go with that one. "Oh, yeah, yeah, sure it is. That's gotta be a big deal for her. Huh, I figured she'd be all over that shit, posting everywhere." Cristo's reply was more proof he didn't know his fiancée, making me seethe inside.

"They're not allowed to take pics, what with Angela Gheorghiu singing. You know what a diva she is."

"Gheorghiu, you say? She's the most famous Romanian opera singer in existence."

"Yes, exactly, and no one loves her more than Tasa. So despite her addiction to social media, she refrains from posting out of deference to her idol."

I buried my face into his chest to hide, stifling a giggle that bubbled up. Sheesh, he was laying it on a bit thick.

"I'll have to tell my father," Cristo went on to say.

"You do that," Alex replied tersely, his patience clearly at its end. Alex didn't do lies, but covering for Tasa's betrayal was a necessity.

"What are you doing here, Cristo?" I cut in to move the conversation off the subject of my best friend.

He gestured with the hand holding a glass. Alcohol sloshed out and splattered across his button-up shirt. "With friends. Over there."

I leaned over and caught sight of his group. My body stiffened, outrage exploding inside. I recognized Cristo's current girlfriend from the photos Tasa had shown me as she laughed at the absurdity of her situation. That alone should've tipped me off that my bestie had no intention of marrying him. Tasa had a jealous streak a mile wide. Raised as a princess, she'd never share her man, of all things.

Like me, she was a romantic at heart. Tasa had had every chance of losing her virginity with her one lover, but she walked away with her hymen intact. She didn't need to tell me why. I knew. Like me, she wanted to lose her virginity to a man she felt something for. In that, we were in total agreement.

Alex noticed my reaction, and his gaze followed to where I was staring. He must've spotted Cristo's girl because his eyes narrowed dangerously and his face froze in place like a death mask. Generally the disciplined type, there was no missing the fiery temper beneath that thinly veiled facade of calm. Nicu wasn't handling it any better. Fuming with rage, he looked like he was seconds away from tearing Cristo apart, limb by limb. Nothing triggered him more than a perceived insult to his baby sister.

Cristo was a true idiot to dare frequent Alex's place with his woman in tow. He probably assumed Alex didn't know or figured he could get away with it by hiding her in a large group of people. If he'd had his wits about him, he would've realized what a bad idea it had been.

Then again, Alex was also at fault. Seeing stupid Cristo, drunk and with his woman, fueled a new flare of courage. Maybe it was fueled by the fact that I had just lost my virginity to a man of my choosing when Tasa would've been forced to give hers up to this moron. Whatever it was, it had triggered a rare burst of temper inside me.

"Great seeing you again, Cristo. I'll make sure to let Tasa know you checked in on her. Have a wonderful evening," I said overly brightly as I leaned over Alex and shoved at Cristo's large body to move on. God, I couldn't wait to get rid of him.

Either he got my message or he finally noticed the death glares he was getting because he quickly replied, "Oh, okay.

Yeah, good to see you. Alex. Nicu," and hightailed it out of there.

"Fucking asshole," Nicu snarled. "I'm going to dismember that motherfucker. There won't be a body for Tasa to find on her wedding day."

"There won't be a wedding day," I rushed out in relief. There'd been no sign of Tasa whatsoever in the past week, from my end at least.

Casting a glance at Alex, I inquired worryingly, "Have you found anything?"

He shook his head brusquely. "Nothing. She withdrew from school and had the tuition reimbursed. Emptied her bank account and vanished into thin air. Nothing to tip me off as to where she's gone."

Turning to face him fully, I took a big breath and said, "Alex, I'm begging you. Please, you can't let her marry him. He's an idiot. Besides the fact he has a girlfriend that he's clearly smitten with—"

"You know this?" His eyebrows jutted downward in two severe lines. "Tasa knows this?"

"Of course, she knows. You live in a small world. Did you think she'd blindly walk into something like her marriage without finding out what kind of person he was? That's so not Tasa."

"Apparently," he drawled.

"Come on," I huffed out, frustration and anger bubbling over. "Of course, she knew she had to marry an appropriate husband, but that doesn't mean she liked it. That doesn't mean it was fair to force her to marry *that*." I flung out my hand in Cristo's direction. Pressing my lips together, I barely held my tongue from running on.

"Nina," he said sharply, "in our world, we have responsibilities. We may not like them, but we have to fulfill a certain set of expectations."

"Alex, *you* had responsibilities thrust upon you when your father was killed. Having lived with such a heavy burden, why would you put that on your baby sister? You should've protected her. You could've left her to follow her own path, instead. Especially, knowing how independent and stubborn she is. She's not one of these silly, airheaded *mafie* princesses," I grumbled.

The corners of his mouth tightened when I used the Romanian word for the mafia. I rolled my eyes. "I've practically lived in your home. Did you think I picked up nothing over the past eighteen years?"

"Damn," murmured Nicu.

"This is none of your business, Nina," Alex replied sternly.

"But it is," I insisted. "Tasa is my best friend." I clenched my fists, my nervous tension rioting inside me. "She's gone, and I haven't returned to our apartment, because I can't stand being there without her."

Taking a deep breath, I forged on before I lost my nerve. He had to see what he was doing to her. "Other than vacations, I've spent almost every day with Tasa. We've lived next door to each other since we were *two years old*. We're practically sisters. You pushed her to this and look where it's ended. If she's willing to abandon her entire family and me to escape this marriage, then she has no intention of coming back. That much, I can guarantee you."

"Nina, you don't understand everything that's on the line with this marriage, but I can tell you we rose to the top because every member of my family and clan has done what was required of them, whether they liked it or not," he replied bluntly. "That is the only way we survive."

While I was sure he wasn't wrong, I tackled the anxiety gaining ground on me, because I had to make him understand. This was about Tasa and, like with Yo-Yo, I'd do anything for her.

Bracing myself, I pushed on in a soft but insistent tone, "I know you believe what you're saying, but this could've been avoided. You were too hard on her. She's not like you." I motioned to Nicu. "Or him. And now she's gone for good." I sniffed and swiped away a few errant tears. Dammit, I didn't want to cry.

My cheeks flaming from embarrassment, I stood up and snatched my clutch off the table.

I rarely lost my temper. It was an even rarer event for me to pick a fight. Confrontation was definitely not my thing, but as much as I might adore Alex, he was in the wrong. He'd handled Tasa badly for years, and it had led to this catastrophe.

"Maybe it's because you're both men that you don't miss her as much. Maybe it's because she's been out of the house for the past three and a half years and you're not used to seeing her every day. But *I'm* used to it, and *I* miss her."

I glanced over at Nicu, who stared at me with eyebrows arched up, eyes wide with shock, and mouth slightly agape. I snagged the flesh of my bottom lip and gnawed on it. Besides Tasa, I didn't know anyone who challenged Alex.

Glaring up at me, he snapped, "Where the hell do you think you're going?"

Clutch pressed tightly to my chest, I blinked down at him. "I-I'm leaving. I sh-should probably leave," I stammered.

"Sit your ass down," he commanded in a dark tone.

My butt instantly hit the cushion of the banquette.

"If you have something to say, then by all means, say it,

Nina, but watch your tone. I don't tolerate temper tantrums from my family, and I sure as hell won't tolerate it from my woman."

My woman?

My eyebrows shot up.

"I'll take a switch to that tight ass in a heartbeat, sweetness," he declared. Leaning in close, he continued in the curve of my ear, "And I'll enjoy every damn second of it. Test me on this." He paused a beat, challenge flashing in his eyes. "I dare you."

Why did he seem so serious when he spoke those words? *Um...because he is.* The glint in his eyes advertised that...yup, he was dead serious. A thrill skated down my spine while goose bumps coursed up my arms. I shouldn't have been aroused by his threat of getting punished, but I was. Moisture gathered at the junction of my thighs, and I wasn't even wearing panties to protect me from embarrassing myself if I left a wet spot on my dress.

Dear God, help me.

His hand shot out and caught a lock of my hair. Twining it around two of his fingers, he tugged me closer and closer until I was once again plastered to his side. Taking hold of my clutch, he gently pried it out of my clenched fist and returned it to the table.

"Now. What will you have to drink, baby girl?"

"A martini?" I croaked out, still somewhat stunned by what had just happened. I'd gotten the guts to stand up to Alex and made it to the other side, with an arousing threat of punishment thrown into the mix.

His lips thinned into a straight line. "You're not twenty-one yet."

I tossed my head, my movement cut short by his hold on

my hair. "In two weeks from now," I whispered, sinking into two pools of emerald that masqueraded as his eyes.

"Then in two weeks from now, you'll get that precious martini you so desire," he affirmed.

"I want it dry," I demanded with a pout.

One side of his mouth hitched up in a sexy little smile that turned my insides into liquid. A dimple popped out on his left cheek, and I swear I almost dissolved into a puddle, right then and there.

"Dry. Got it. Until then, what will you have?"

"A Coke?"

"You sound unsure," he answered in a low, sensual voice that had me practically panting. *Is it hot in here suddenly, or is it me?*

"Yes, I'm sure," I rasped out, my voice scratchy.

He snapped his fingers in the air. A moment later, a cocktail waitress materialized as if she'd been waiting in the wings, listening for his signal.

"A Coke," he ordered, eyes still on me.

"Yes, Mr. Lupu," she replied in a silky voice that had my head jerking to the side to throw her a narrow-eyed glare. Her tone made me want to scratch her eyes. I sat back with a little huff, somewhat shocked by my reaction. What the heck was happening to me? First, I'd started an argument with Alex as if I were some bold, brave woman, who I most certainly was not. Then I had a jealous pique over a strange woman hitting on Alex, when that was par for the course. He was gorgeous, rich, and powerful. Who was I to expect anything less from a red-blooded woman?

"Thank you," he replied with a dismissive wave of his hand.

It was clear that Alex had noticed my sudden ire, because his little smirk transformed into a huge grin. "I'm learning new things tonight about my little bird, Nicu," he said while staring straight at me. "She gets upset on behalf of others. She gets riled up when another woman tries to catch my attention."

"I do not," I hissed out vehemently, lying through my teeth because, yeah, he was spot on. Even though I'd known them most of my life, I suddenly felt exposed and too *seen*. Tasa was the blooming rose, while I preferred being the... trellis in the background?

While we had spent time together, Alex and I were strangers in many ways. He mentioned he'd noticed me for years, but there were huge differences between us. He was a busy man who might've lusted after me during breaks from his demanding life, but I was a lonely, shy girl with way too much time on my hands. My sense of who this man was, having stalked him for years, was far more refined than what he thought he knew of me. Oh, sure, there were parts of his life I knew little about, but I had a strong grip on who he was, on his character. I did not, for an instant, think it was reciprocated.

As if sensing my discomfort, Alex assured me, "You'll get used to it. You'll have to. I'm a demanding man with high expectations of everyone around me. Now, that includes you. Your loyalty and your passion will serve you well. Believe me, in the dog-eat-dog world I'm about to introduce you to, you'll need both in spades."

7

I tucked Nina's lithe body against me and leaned back to relax. I wasn't lying when I said I liked her spirit. She'd surprised me tonight, and I was learning that there was much more to this woman than her soft, sweet persona. While that was the core of who she was, she also had a wiliness and courage that showed in the little plan she'd carried out to get me to fuck her raw. Then there was the hissing kitten she'd transformed into when defending my sister and fighting for her cause. Good. Nina would need a spine to be with me.

I took a sip from the new whiskey the cocktail waitress slid in front of me, and my gaze returned to that fucking little shit, Cristo. I'd always hated that son of a bitch, and Nina had been spot on when she'd stated that he didn't deserve my sister. Truth was, he'd never measure up to Tasa.

If her disappearance had accomplished one thing, it was to make me realize she'd be miserable married to that asswipe. Peace or no peace. I had misconstrued Tasa's little rebellions, thinking they were just that, simple teenage rebellion. I had assumed she knew the drill and was willing to go through with the marriage.

She was expressing her dismay, and instead of catching on, I'd pushed her over the edge. I loathed being wrong, and I disliked making mistakes even more. Mistakes were dangerous. They could easily lead to pain and death. Being wrong left a burn of fury in my chest. Fuck, I couldn't afford the mistake I made. Especially with my little sister. She was an innocent.

I studied the group of young Popescus and hangers-on partying brashly at the far end of the upper floor. Rowdy and loud. Tacky. Christ, that family had always lacked in class. Even if I found Tasa...I swallowed the fear clawing up my throat...*when* I found her and brought her back home safely, I wouldn't force her to marry that prick.

Speaking of pricks, I had to somehow salvage the situation with Nelu, the Popescu boss. I certainly couldn't lie again. Falsehoods were beneath me, and I'd almost choked on my own spit when I spewed that shit in front of Nicu and Nina. Hell, Tata would've never lied. Under any circumstances. His moral integrity was ironclad.

It'd been six years since his death, and after a long, drawn-out, exasperating negotiation, Nelu and I had finally agreed to a marriage. A marriage that was tied to the business deal of the decade. Nelu had access to a new product coming out of Afghanistan: the native ephedra plant. Turns out it was a game changer in the worldwide production of crystal meth. Nelu the Dirty, as he was known in the region, had struck deals with warlords and had unlimited access.

He may have had the product but I controlled the illicit trade routes out of Afghanistan into Europe and the rest of the world. I could put a stranglehold on all the best channels. Once the tit for tat between the Lupu and Popescu clans was eradicated, we'd work together for the profit of both.

The linchpin to all this?

The marriage between Tasa and Cristo.

But that had gone to hell. Of course, I'd always been uncomfortable with giving Tasa away, but I'd convinced myself that each of us had to sacrifice for the greater good of the clan. While our relationship was strained at times, I lived under the illusion that she'd understood and accepted her lot.

No more.

Hearing the pain I'd inflicted on my sister, seeing Nina blame me for Tasa's defection, was a double punch to the gut. Making Nina cry...well, *fuck*. I was close to smashing my fist into a wall.

I did that. I made this sweet, gentle girl cry. I'd forced my sister to run for her life. Ultimately, I failed her. And by failing her, I not only failed in my duty but I also betrayed the last oath I gave my dying father. Which left me with only one viable option. I had to make this right.

My hand slid over Nina's dark, silky tresses as she took a sip through the straw in her Coke. Those lips, so delicate and full, still had traces of her outrageously red lipstick even after I ravished her mouth. They innocently wrapped around the straw, tempting me to distraction.

I'd already torn through this poor girl's hymen, ripped through her wet cunt, and yet I was nowhere near done with her. Sure, her pussy had rippled around my cock. Sure, she'd come so hard the first time I wrenched open her unused flesh. But it had only whetted my appetite for more of her delectable pussy. There was no denying that I was an unrepentant savage.

Slapping my palm on the table, I turned to Nicu and said, "Time to go home."

My brothers and I occupied the penthouse floors of the Time Warner Center building off Columbus Circle, on the Upper West Side. There were two towers, consisting of two penthouse apartments in each tower. Tatum, my closest friend and *consilier*, lived in one tower with me while the other was shared between Luca and Nicu. Although, more often than not, Luca ran off to his home in the country.

Nina didn't raise her head but, instead, leaned into my touch in a manner that had my breath stuttering in my chest.

Eyes downcast, avoiding me, she fiddled with her straw as she reminded me, "I moved back home. To Queens. Do you mind having me brought back to Sunnyside?"

I huffed out a mirthless laugh. She thought I was going to discard her so easily? Christ, she had no idea who I was.

"You're staying with me," I stated unequivocally.

Her eyes shot to mine.

My grasp on her locks tightened. "You're not going anywhere. My enemies have not magically disappeared since our time in the bathroom, and Cristo saw you here, at my table. *With me*," I emphasized.

"But you and Cristo's family are okay now that the marriage contract has been set in place," she argued.

Nicu barked out a sharp laugh. "Marriage or no marriage, we will never be friends. They can turn on us in a heartbeat. Especially once they learn about Tasa, which can happen at any time. Things are tense until we find Tasa and resolve this shit show with Nelu, Cristo's father."

Nina rolled her eyes. "I know who Nelu is, Nicu," she chided him softly.

He turned a devilish smile on her. "I shouldn't have doubted you would. My bad."

"You're under my protection, Nina." I tugged her head back until her gaze was fully back on mine. "You stay with me."

Her eyes, large and bright, melted on me as she murmured her assent, "Okay."

"Good girl," I crooned in a low voice for her ears only, and she shifted in her seat. It pleased me to see her reaction to something as simple as the change in my tone. She was so attuned to me already. Nicu had mentioned her nature was compatible with mine, and this was proof she was indeed my good girl.

Rising, I assisted Nina to her feet. With a goodbye nod to my brother, I firmly planted my hand on her lower back and guided her out of my club to a waiting car.

"Isn't Nicu coming as well?" she queried, peering out the window of the car.

Stegan, my driver, chuckled from the front seat. He knew what we all knew. Nicu went hunting at night, whether the prey was a woman or an enemy whose throat he'd slit. His nickname wasn't the Vampire for nothing. He was the most brutal of us, with a craving for spilled blood. But these were the kinds of details Nina should never be aware of.

She may know more about our life and family than I had anticipated, but that didn't mean she'd be privy to the gory details. We did our best to shield our women, but who the hell knew what she might inadvertently find out. She was an innocent, and I couldn't expose her to the ugliness of my world. I wouldn't be able to stand it if her soft eyes turned on me in disgust.

Whether we had a blood bond or not, Nina would always be mine to protect. When it came to outsiders, blood bonds weren't clear-cut like with a *mafie* girl. There was some wiggle room around marriage, but an honor-bound man like me didn't walk away from a woman after taking her virginity. That's why *mafie*-made men avoided virgins.

But that was done and over with. Regardless of the requirement that I marry my own kind, regardless of the blood bond I'd triggered by popping her cherry, deep in my fucking soul, I knew Nina belonged to me. My gut seized at the mere notion of letting her go.

"He can find his own way home. It's enough that we work together and practically live together. We don't have to travel together as well," I responded, although I liked that she worried about him. Truth was, no one handled a threat better than my youngest brother.

Closing the privacy screen between Stegan and us, I turned to touch her again. Before I could say a word, her lips met mine. Her clutch toppled into the footwell as she pressed her gorgeous tits against my chest. Fuck, I wanted to delve deep and never come up for air. Her lips were soft and gentle, her tongue tentative, but I forced myself to break off our kiss. There was an issue that needed to be addressed before we went any further.

"Nina..." I started.

She batted her eyelashes at me, her big brown doe eyes clearing although her little hands fisted into the lapels of my coat and tugged me closer.

"What?" she asked in a hoarse voice, squirming in need. In need of me. Every cell in my body screamed at me to take her, mark her, and teach her what it was like to be mine— teach her that every inch of her perfect, lush body was mine alone and that I was the only man who'd satisfy the itch between her legs.

But I didn't rise to the pinnacle of the Romanian *mafie* by getting distracted, even by someone as luscious as Nina. I jerked at the collar of my fitted button-down shirt. Who was I kidding? When it came to my self-restraint, this girl was my weakness, as evidenced by my major slipup earlier. But that tension had been in the making for years. When we finally came together, the energy was explosive. Hell, it was beyond even my tight control.

"There's one issue we need to get straight before we move forward with whatever this is between us," I continued.

Releasing me, she nodded her head eagerly, her eyes centered on me with renewed focus. Something I regretted but knew was necessary. Folding her hands primly in her lap, she gazed up at me with her full attention, lips slightly parted, the bottom one taunting me to lay the tip of my cock ever-so-gently on top of it as I command her to open up and suck. What a precious little wifey she'd make. If only she were Romanian and of my world, she'd be a perfect fit.

I was already in over my head. Shedding her virgin blood had called to something deep in my soul. That made her mine to protect forever, but to make her mine in every way was...problematic, to say the least. As the head of my family, I had some leeway, but everyone expected me to marry *mafie*.

One more taste and—*focus.*

Squinting my eyes marginally to indicate I was serious, I made my tone hard as I warned her, "You can't run away from me, Nina. That's a no-no."

"Run away?" she queried, her brows drawing together.

"Earlier tonight," I reminded her, "when you got upset about Tasa. I explained I won't tolerate any disrespect or flaring tempers like the one you exhibited. That is particularly true in front of other people. Nicu is my brother and knows you, so I allowed it to slide, but you cannot under-mine my authority in public. People trust me with their lives, and my power must seem absolute."

I flicked my hand to dismiss that issue once my position was stated. She was a smart girl. She'd understand. Grasping a hold of her upper arms, I dragged her closer and continued, "But what truly pissed me off was when you were about to stomp off. To *run*. That's unacceptable. Tasa already ran away from me, and the fallout of that may turn out to be a disaster. I will not abide you running from me. If you're upset, hold it in until we're alone. Then you can go at me as fast and hard as you like. Be assured, I can take anything you throw my way."

Nina blinked up at me. Was that shock I read in her eyes? If so, then fine by me. If this woman was going to be by my side, this was her first lesson. Let's see how she handled it.

Hauling her up to me until our lips almost touched, I resumed, "We can scream it out. We can fuck it out. What-ever you want. But one thing I cannot, *will not* take, is you running. I'm going to fuck you hard enough as it is, sweet-ness. Believe me when I tell you, you do not want me running you to the ground to fuck you. Make no mistake about it, Nina; I will do both should you pull a stunt like that again."

Crashing my lips to hers, I gave her a hard kiss before putting her away from me, on the other side of the car. "You've been forewarned."

Inching toward me, her eyes luminous in the half-light of the car, she whispered, "Tell me, Alex, how hard would that make you fuck me *exactly*?"

Her soft, lilting tone had my cock going rigid. It'd perked up at her kiss, but the inquisitive, barely restrained excite-

ment in her words, especially when *fuck* fell from her innocent lips, had my cock stiff and raring to go. She had no idea
how close I was to the edge, or she wouldn't taunt me with
her big eyes, glistening with arousal, pushing out her pouty
bottom lip and speaking to me in that breathless voice.

My eyes bulged slightly. Fucking hell, this woman would
be the death of me. Was fucking her roughly the only part of
my diatribe that had penetrated her skull? Was that the part
that held the most value for her? Because there was no
doubt she was highly aroused.

"How hard do you want it, Nina? Tell me," I
commanded, my voice more beast than human as I loomed
over her.

Flushed with desire, she picked at the edge of her coat
and murmured, "Maybe I'll run on purpose just so you can
catch me."

Oh, that insinuation frayed the limit of my control.

"Is that right?" My voice was pure gravel.

"Hmm..."

Goddamn, that humming sound fired right at my dick,
tightening my balls high against my body.

"You want me to hunt you?" I enunciated. "Run you to
the ground and drag you by these silky locks?" I took one of
her tresses and circled it around my finger before dragging
her close. My lips whispered over hers, "You want to fight
me? Try it, baby girl, so I can take it from you, take it against
your will. I'll tie you up. Hands. Legs. Then I'll thrust my
tongue into that sweet pussy. Haven't had a chance to taste
this yet."

I gently cupped between her thighs, and she squirmed
right away, taking advantage of my touch. "But I will. And
when I do, I'll make you an addict. You won't come with any
man but me. But I won't let you come, will I? Not for a long

time, because if you run from me, I'll have to tame the wild in you. Teach you a hard lesson on how to be my good girl. Running can get you killed," I growled between clenched teeth as her fingers clawed my shirt, scraping at the skin beneath, "and that will *never* happen. Not on my fucking watch."

Her harsh breaths and little moans echoed through the small space of the back of the car. I felt the tiny puffs of air from her pants against my own lips. She gazed up at me, her throat and cheeks flushed red, her chest billowing up and down in excitement. I'd hit on one of my little girl's dirty fantasies. Biting her pouty lip, she begged me with her eyes.

Now.

Now, it was time to take her lips.

And I did.

I crushed them, forcing her to open to me, and she did, willingly. *Eagerly.* As I consumed her, I only hoped and prayed I didn't fuck this up.

8

The sleek black car stopped in front of my building and idled until I ended our kiss. Nina made a distressed sound as I pulled away, her fingers clutching at me desperately. Her lips were red and bruised from my attack on her mouth. Goddamn, but seeing her disheveled, where my fingers had gripped and twisted her hair, with her puffy lips and the flush racing up the delicate column of her throat made me want to throw her down on the seat and finish what we'd started.

Instead, I reeled it back and, ordering Stegan to stay, helped Nina out of the car. I looped an arm around her waist when she wobbled on her heels, until I was sure she was steady. With a few last directions to Stegan, I bid him a good night and guided Nina into the lobby of my building.

When the Time Warner Center was nothing more than a rumor, my father had put in a bid with the developers for the penthouse floor. As the plans developed, it'd turned into each floor of both towers. After my father died, Tatum and I had renovated the apartments in one tower, holding on to the two in the other tower for when Nicu and Luca grew up.

Nodding to the doorman, I reminded myself to put Nina on the list of guests who had access to the penthouse floor. I never locked my door since only my brothers and Tatum had special access. We were constantly in and out of one another's places at all times of the day and night, so pesky things like locks got in our way.

Once I got Nina inside my apartment, I stripped my coat off and flung it on the chair beside the door. Unlike my family home in Sunnyside, which had been decorated to my mother's antiquated taste, this place was all mine, and I liked my space minimal.

Nina's gasp beside me told me my modern taste was a surprise to her. Casting her a side-glance, I teased, "Did you think I'd allow my mother to decorate my home like she did the apartment you share with Tasa?"

"I had assumed..." she replied as she slowly unbuttoned her coat. I went behind her and took hold of it, giving a prayer of thanks that the black coat had hidden her in public. It seemed I was a possessive mofo when it came to this woman because the thought of her sauntering around in that dress would've had me going ballistic.

For the first time since moving into the penthouse, I turned the lock of the door behind me. Tatum had a key, but this was an unprecedented move on my part. I smirked as I imagined how he'd react when he turned the knob and found it locked. Arrogant bastard.

There was no way I'd have him walking in on me and Nina. More to the point, there was no way he was getting an eyeful of my woman. *My woman.* Christ, but I wanted that statement to be true. In my heart, she was already mine. There were more blocks on my path to that trophy than I was willing to dwell on at the moment.

Right now, with Nina in my home, I wanted to savor her.

Stepping away from me, she crossed the marble-and-onyx foyer, her fingertips gliding over the wood-and-bronze bannister of the three steps descending into the spacious living room, which was decorated in gray and white, with accents of lapis lazuli. She traversed the space, inspecting the minimal modern furniture and pausing for a moment in front of a Rothko painting before continuing toward the two walls of three-paneled floor-to-ceiling windows overlooking the city on one side and Central Park on the other.

"This is an amazing view," she breathed out in awe. Having followed her, I took a step closer until her ass was nestled against my front.

Nuzzling into her jasmine-fragranced hair, I said, "Yes, it is," although I was speaking of the woman before me, not the city sprawled below us. "Would you like something to drink?"

Shaking her head, she traced an invisible line on the windowpane. Glancing over her shoulder, a little frown notched between her fine-winged brows as she politely inquired, "How rich are you, Alex?"

Oh, she had no idea.

All she'd seen of me besides my club tonight was the brownstone where I was born, where my mother and *Bunică* continued to live, and the café next door. Those properties were but a small drop in the pool of Lupu wealth.

"Very rich," I stated simply. "Although, my father bought this condo as an investment when the building was first conceptualized; it's worth far more now. I have great wealth, Nina. With it, comes great responsibility and great enemies. That's why it was so foolish for Tasa to run away. Just as it would be foolish for you to do the same."

"I will never," she promised fervently.

"You say that now, but you may not be able to handle my

lifestyle. If it were a simple question of lifestyle or money, there'd be room to negotiate, but my wealth is intricately wrapped up in the honor and safety of the Lupu clan. They are interlocked and can never be unbound. And now, having given me your virginity, you *should* be as bound to me as I am bound to the Lupus."

Her head tipped up, staring at me with her big bright eyes, and she asked, "And am I bound to you? What will you do with me, Alex?"

I broke my stare on her and gazed across the expanse of darkness, over the multitude of sparkling lights below.

"I'm not sure," I replied honestly.

"I want to be with you. I don't want to scare you, but it's only been you, Alex. Only ever you."

Scare me? Firstly, I didn't scare. Ever. More importantly, her admission was bliss. Her honesty. Her loyalty. The bravery she showed in her confession. They humbled me. But none of that guaranteed she would be mine.

My eyes returned to her. I grazed the delicate skin of her cheek with my knuckles. "You're exquisite, Nina. In every way. Never doubt how precious you are to me. But I can make no promises. Some things are beyond my power. I have pressing issues that need to be resolved. Besides finding Tasa and securing her protection, there's Nelu to deal with. He's a formidable negotiator. He will have my balls in a choke hold over this. I don't know what I will have to sacrifice to appease him. Then there's the fact that I am the symbol of my clan and family. I am the *Lupul*. The expectations of whom I marry are clear-cut."

The corners of her mouth dipped, and her beautiful brown eyes grew infinitely sad. I wanted to rip at my chest and pound on the windowpanes until they shattered, but I would not hold the truth from her. There were many things

I could not tell her about my life. I wouldn't add to an already necessary evil.

"What expectations?" she inquired in a careful voice.

She already knew. After all, she'd seen what I put Tasa through. Still, she deserved a straightforward answer.

"I'm expected to marry like Tasa. You accused me of imposing too great a burden on her, but it's the same burden my brothers and I carry. I did not ask anything less of her. We're not average people who can simply marry for love. Even my own parents' marriage was an alliance. They *found* love, but my father married my mother because she's a direct descendant of the last king, King Michael I. That elevated my father's status in certain circles in Romania, Central and Eastern Europe, and the Russia Federation. It legitimized the Lupu family name to be aligned with royal blood."

I didn't have the heart to go into the question of whether my clan would accept her. My nuclear family wouldn't be a problem; they knew her and loved her. But the rest of them? As şef, I was given certain latitude, but I had no idea whether my clan would forgive such an infraction. It had never been tested before.

The corners of her mouth dipped down.

"I see..." Her eyelids dropped to hide from me, she sounded defeated, and that tore at my heart. Fucking hell, but I wanted her to be mine. My soul thundered that she already was. I'd taken her virginity, for Christ's sake. Even if it had been done in an exceptional lapse of sanity, it was physical proof of what I already knew to be true. Why did life have to be so difficult? As hard as being şef was at times, even Tasa's disappearance didn't tear me up like this. The walls pressed in on me. I felt trapped.

I took hold of her nape and snarled in her face, "No, you

do not see. Not the complete story. I am more than the *Lupul*. I am my own man as well. There are so many balls to juggle at once, decisions to be made, and consequences to be dealt with before I am free to decide. Some things have barely played themselves out. But I swear to you that until everything is resolved and the dust settles, you're with me."

She stiffened in my hold. I felt the taut tendons of her neck against my palm. Of course, she was upset. This wasn't what she'd expected. She thought I was a man with the same choices as any other man. While that may not be true, it didn't mean I'd let her go. Was it fucked up what I was asking of her? *Yes.* Was it too much? *Probably.* Did it dishonor her? God above, I prayed *no.* I had to believe that, because I couldn't let her go. I could *not.* Not after we'd just gotten together. Not after feeling her lips on mine. Not after taking her, when I'd fantasized about it for so many years. Christ, it was even better than my imagination, and that was saying a whole lot.

"My intention isn't to disrespect you. You're not a whore, so don't even think that—"

"It did cross my mind," she cut in.

My chest tightened. I squeezed my eyelids shut. Fuck, that was painful to hear. Snapping them open, my gaze burned into her. "Listen to me. That's not true. I'm not using you. How many years have we known each other, Nina? You're my sister's best friend. You're the closest a person has gotten to my family. There's no way I'd take any of this lightly."

"I waited for you," she confessed, her eyes bleeding dismay. "I remained a virgin because, deep down, whether I fully admitted it to myself or not, I wanted my first time to be with you."

"And it was a fucking honor, baby. It was a precious gift

you gave me and not one I take for granted." My hand caressed down the curve of her back and palmed her ass, bringing her flush against me so she could feel how aroused I was. I ground gently into her. "You have no idea what a good thing you did. I didn't deserve it. You bestowed your virgin blood on me without me having to work for it. A truly selfless present. There are forces at work holding me back right now, but I'll never take you for granted. It's the opposite. I intend to treasure every fucking moment we have together."

Not knowing if I could keep her, I'd cherish every inch she gave to me.

"Can we not try to get to know each other better? Spend time together. Let's see what this grows into because nothing will prosper if there isn't a foundation built between us. Would you give me the gift of your time to explore this powerful thing between us? Give me time to figure a way out of this clusterfuck Tasa left us with. It's a big ask, I know, but that's what I can honestly give you right now."

Nina fiddled with the top button of my shirt, her eyes glued to the movement of her fingers. It was a rare occasion when I was nervous, but I waited for her answer with bated breath. The pressure around my chest intensified until it felt like a crushing vise that would snap my ribs. I'd never felt more impotent in my life. Even when Tata was murdered, I had revenge to focus on and a clan to take over. This...this was a mindless agony. I'd never wanted anything for myself as much as I wanted Nina.

"Okay," she acquiesced. "I've given over so much already. I can gift you my time." I released a breath. Her eyes flicked up to mine. "Can you say the same? I know you're a busy man."

"I am a busy man. That's why I don't fuck around with

women...until you. My duties are demanding, but every moment I'm not working, I'll be with you. That much, I can promise."

"For a powerful man, you don't seem to have that much power," she mused with a small sad smile.

"Tell me about it. My life is dedicated to a cause much greater than myself, but I am a man with needs. Those needs include you, and I'm willing to fight to have you in my life, baby girl."

Did I sound as confused and fucked up as I was? I was trying to speak my truth, but the truth was messy. I needed Nina and I needed time. Time to figure out how to pull it off and walk away from these crushing expectations, but I had to believe I could make this work.

Her shy eyes glanced away and then fixed on mine. "Will you take me to bed?"

"Hell yes," I swore. Bending at my knees, I scooped her into my arms and stalked into my bedroom. "This night is nowhere near finished."

9

A little gasp slipped out when Alex swept me off my feet, my fingers hanging on to the front of his shirt for purchase. He bounced me a little before settling me into his strong arms.

His back and forth was a little confusing. One moment, he was talking about duty, and the next moment, he was claiming to need me. I'd witnessed what he'd put Tasa through. Marriage was a big deal, and like with his parents', it was used for leverage. Despite my promise to give him time, our conversation left me with a sense of urgency. I was desperate to make the most of us because, who knew how this would end?

"Can we take a shower?" I suggested and clenched my eyes as flashes of heat shot up my face. There were still traces of dried blood on my inner thighs, I was sure.

Recognizing my concern, he teased softly, "There's nothing to be embarrassed about. I was there, you know. I was the reason for it."

Walking into a huge bedroom, which continued the minimalist design of the rest of his apartment, we entered a spacious bathroom, decorated primarily in black marble. The lights came on automatically as Alex gently put me on my feet. I expelled a little nervous sigh, feeling exposed under the brightness.

"Undress," he instructed.

Although I had lost my virginity just a mere two hours ago, I was suddenly anxious, and my gaze bounced around the bathroom, landing anywhere but on him. I took in the brilliance of the white sink and bathtub, which sat in stark contrast to the black marble of the floor and walls. The gleaming white porcelain highlighted the white veins in the black marble.

Taking my hands tenderly, he brought them to the top button of his shirt and proposed, "Why don't you start with undressing me."

Gulping, I nodded. I had more nerves and butterflies now than in the employee bathroom of his club. It had been easier when everything was a flurry of action under time pressure. Here, we were facing each other. In silence. No distractions, no time crunch, no possibility of getting caught. Our movements were slow, almost languid.

My fingers popped open the top button of his crisp dark shirt. Spreading it open, I realized for the first time that I hadn't yet seen his chest. I unhooked the second and third buttons, picking up the pace with growing anticipation. I wanted to see his tat. The same tat I'd seen a hundred times on Tasa.

A few more buttons, and his shirt gaped open. I wasn't distracted by the defined ridges of his abs or the trail of dark hair pointing south. No, my gaze shot to the image of the wolf baring its teeth. The distinctive Lupu tattoo. Every member had this tattoo, although Alex's and his siblings' tats were a slight variation in color from the others. Tasa told me that if one did not share Alex's blood, then one must shed blood, either through a blood oath or marriage, to get the honor of the wolf mark etched on their skin. My fingertips grazed longingly over the wolf's fierce expression. What I would give to have that inked on my own skin.

"It's the same," I uttered, cringing at stating the obvious.

"As Tasa's? Yes, it is," he replied.

It was beautiful, really. The wolf had the same emerald-colored eyes as its owner, bright against his olive skin. My fingertips grazed down the ridges and valleys of his abs and landed on his belt, feeling the pressure of his cock pressing behind the zipper. Raising his arms behind my back, he blindly undid his cuff links. They dropped to the floor with a *ping* and another *ping* and then he drew his shirt off his broad shoulders.

By this time, I'd finished opening his pants and shoved them down along with his boxer briefs. My eyes dropped, and I got a good look at his long, hard shaft.

Damn.

The flared tip was large and demanding. A thick vein snaked up his jutting cock. I couldn't help but lick my lips. He was larger than I expected; he was definitely going to stretch my throat, but I was more than ready for it.

"Don't do that unless you want my cock down your throat," he forewarned me, as if reading my mind.

Is that a threat? Oh, he had no idea how long I'd fantasized about this. I was about to fall to my knees when he took hold of my forearms to stop my descent.

"No one wants those plump lips around my cock more than I do, but I have your blood on me. I have no trouble lapping up the blood from that cherry I popped. That's exactly the kind of monster I am, but you're a different creature altogether. You're everything good, sweet, and yielding."

Bending his head down to me, he counseled, "You should run, knowing how little I fear. The taste of blood doesn't bother me. Not in the least."

Glancing down, I now noticed the smudges of dried blood on his groin and even a streak or two on his shaft. He was trying to scare me, but I was too far gone on this crazy ride for that. I already knew the savagery flowing through his veins. It only intensified my attraction to him.

"I'm not afraid of you."

"You should be," he insisted.

"Maybe, but I'm not," I reiterated. I'd already chosen this man. I wasn't going to back down over a little spilled blood.

Toeing off his shoes, he stepped out of his clothes and reached for the zipper on the side of my dress. Helping me out, he groaned when it slithered off me and hit the ground, leaving me completely bare. I hadn't worn a bra, and he'd taken my panties with him when we left the bathroom at the club. My sensitive skin crackled like sparks off a bonfire whisked away by a seaside breeze.

Stepping into the shower, he opened the faucets, testing the water until he was satisfied with the temperature.

He reached for me.

I slowly placed my hand in his.

His fingers folded over mine tightly and pulled me toward him until I was under the warm spray. Hot water rushed out of more than one showerhead. Glancing around, I was surprised to discover a glittering wall of white marble, including a seat made of the same large slab of rock.

Taking a bottle of gel from a small high shelf, he lathered his palms and slicked them down my sides. I shuddered at the contact of his hands on me. His large cock bobbed between us, taunting me, testing me. There was no way I had the patience to have him wash me down. His resolve might be that strong, but I was desperate to feel the silky skin of his cock between my lips.

Grabbing the bottle, I squirted gel into my hand as well, building up the lather before taking his cock and rubbing vigorously. I scrubbed the blood off his thighs, crouching down as I did it. The pounding of scalding water made his tat glisten, especially the green jewellike eyes of the wolf. His hair, plastered around the shape of his skull, curled at the ends like when he was younger.

Once I washed off what I needed cleaned, I tipped my head up and stuck out my tongue to tickle the tip of his shaft. Grunting, he grabbed hold of my nape and obliged my silent request by gliding his cock right where I wanted it. Moaning around his slippery skin, I took in a deep breath through my nostrils, scenting the musk beneath the fragrance of his pine soap.

"Fuck, Nina. Fuck," he cursed, his eyes drilling into me. He ground his teeth together. His tip was already slick with pre-come when I got my first real taste of him. *Man, oh man.* He tried to stifle his groan, but it came out nonetheless, a choked sound of desperation. Inside, I preened like a flattered prima donna after an encore. I was going to unravel his infamous control. Having already succeeded earlier, I was addicted to provoking his surrender.

Humming around his smooth hard flesh, I made sure it was loud, so that the pulsation reverberated up his shaft. Pulling my suction off his dick with a small popping sound, I then licked the crown. Around and around like a lollipop I went until he grunted out, "Cocktease," and shoved himself halfway inside.

I almost chuckled with glee.

That was when I sucked hard. I may have been a virgin, but I was no nun and knew my way around oral sex. Giving and receiving it. Kneeling below him with my cheeks hollowed out, I must've been a sight to behold. Both of his palms slapped the wall behind me as he drove down my throat.

I inched slowly backward until I was flush against the wall. Tilting my head up, I elongated my neck and opened my mouth wider still, silently challenging him to thrust harder and faster. Like I'd hope, it was too much of an offer for him to refuse, and he pushed in hard, brutal almost. My tongue was pinned down as his cock shoved in, choking me. Tears sprung from my eyes as I gagged. *That's what I'm talking about!* My teeth scraped over his shaft, but the pain only egged him on. He hissed and took my throat harder. I was getting slick between the legs, my inner muscles clenching in need.

"Is this what you want, sweetness? You want me to use you like the little throat slut you are? You don't like me when I'm nice, do you? Bad girlie."

I shook my head. Finally, he was getting it! Sure, losing my virginity was going to hurt so I'd wanted his gentleness then, but otherwise, I liked it rougher. I liked him to take control and lose control.

He drew out to the tip. Then his hips punched forward, thrusting deeper and faster.

"Take it," he urged. "You want it hard, yeah? Oh, I'm going to push you to the limit, girl." I didn't even realize my hand had moved until my fingers were rubbing my clit.

"Swallow," he commanded, a harsh, impatient sound, and I did so instantaneously. "That's right, let me into that tight throat."

Already breathing through my nose, I struggled to get enough oxygen. Relaxing my throat muscles, I adjusted to the intrusion. It didn't matter though, because I wanted Alex to hit my limits and shove past them. *Really shove, Alex, shove.* Taking my hair in his fist, he rocked his hips, hitting the back of my throat repeatedly. My clit sparked off when his cock twitched and swelled.

"Pinch your clit," he urged. I did as I was told an instant before his come first hit. It flooded my mouth and shot down my throat. White-hot bliss flashed hot through my body. Moaning and whining, my own climax ripped through me a second later, whisking me along like I was on a rickety Cyclone roller-coaster in Coney Island. I swallowed and swallowed as my body shuddered through a powerful climax. There was too much, coming too fast, and his seed dripped out the sides of my mouth. Clasping his ass, I drew my nails sharply down his buttocks. His big body shook above me, his cock jerking inside my mouth.

Once he emptied himself, Alex stumbled back a few steps. His eyes were rapt on me, wide with shock. I felt the shaking of the ground beneath me when his back smacked against the wall.

Pleased as could be, I sat on my haunches, and lapped at my lips like a cat after gorging on a bowl of cream. A warm flush of pride swept through me. I did that. Tasa's little friend had brought big, bad Alex to his knees. Put that dazed look on his face. He stared down at me with disbelief. I glowed, knowing I'd not only met his expectations, I'd exceeded them. It was something I planned to repeat, again and again. I wasn't a little virgin anymore.

Instead, I was the woman who'd handled him.

10

Tatum's dark eyes locked on my face. Arms crossed over his broad chest, he loomed near the head of my bed. My gaze shot right to Nina.

Yup, there she was, sprawled naked on her belly beside me with my arm securely wrapped around her waist. Not only did I wake up with her in my bed, but I hugged her protectively into my body. I shot Tatum a glare over my shoulder. Did the bastard take my hint and look away? Not fucking likely. Instead, a big ole snarky grin spread over his arrogant face.

Fucker.

The sheet barely covered the curve of Nina's ass. Her long back was on full display, and it made me want to tear the eyeballs out of his head. Grasping the edge of the sheet, I slid it up until she was completely covered. The movement caused her to wiggle her ass as she shifted on the mattress, which had the unfortunate side effect of making my stiff morning wood twitch in interest. Letting out a little sigh, she settled back into her dreams. Goddamn, I wanted to stay there and wake her up with my tongue on her clit. That was the way she should wake up every morning.

I waved Tatum off, silently ordering him to exit my bedroom. That garnered a nice glare from him, but I didn't miss the gleam of humor in his black eyes.

"You locked me out for her?" He swept his hand back, gesturing to Nina. "Seriously?"

Pressing my index finger to my lips, I gestured harshly toward the bedroom door again. I needed to get him out, out, *out*. Even after what we'd done last night, I already wanted back into that sweet cunt. Tatum could be the biggest cockblocker when he chose to be. Even without the possibility of sex, I just wanted him out. Out of my bedroom, where my woman was peacefully sleeping, and out of my apartment. Out of my space, period. Plus, I just knew I'd get an earful from him. The impending scolding was practically vibrating off him.

An intense desire to smash his face hurtled through me. With effort, I stuffed it down, reminding myself that it wasn't his fault. He was only doing what he'd always done. Amazing how a habit built over years suddenly needed to be disposed of ASAP. Nina was here to stay for now, and my apartment should be a safe space for her. For us.

Flashing me one final glare, he stomped out of the room as I slid out of bed. Grabbing a pair of sweats, I put them on and pattered out into the living room. Following the banging sounds to the kitchen, I leaned against the doorjamb as he pulled out the *ibric*, a small, long-handled pot used to make Turkish coffee. I preferred espresso, but Tatum was as old school Romanian as they came, and old school Romanians drank Turkish coffee exclusively.

Christ, I didn't want him in my kitchen, brewing up coffee. His mission was to torture me. His purpose in life was to sit on my shoulder like a devil's advocate and advise me, but the only thing I wanted was to be alone with Nina. Preferably, in bed. I could already see the mixture of disapproval and pity on his face. My shoulders bunched up to brace myself.

"What the fuck, Alex?" he started in without missing a beat.

And there it was. Normally, I wouldn't put up with that kind of questioning from anyone, not even my brothers. But Tatum was not only my oldest friend from childhood, but he was also my *consilier*. As my advisor, he had more leeway to speak frankly to me.

On more than one occasion, I'd prayed for Tasa to crush on my friend so I could marry her off to him. But when I mentioned it to Tatum, he only gave me a long-suffering sigh. Knowing me well, he first ticked off a list of reasons why I would desire such a union. Then he'd flat out denied me with a slew of counter arguments. He ended his diatribe by begging me to let it go because he knew how stubborn I could be when I got an idea in my head. I should've known by the way they squabbled that they were nothing more than siblings at heart, but I had to try. Hell, if I were a woman, I'd marry him in a heartbeat. He epitomized the qualities of calmness, rationality, and stability.

"The whole point of locking the door was for you *not* to see my woman half naked. Should've known you'd ignore a direct order, you ingrate," I griped.

He abandoned the *ibric* on the stove and threw his hands up in exasperation. "Your woman? Let me clarify here, you're speaking of Nina, right? Nina? Tasa's best friend who's twenty-fucking-years old?"

"For now, yes."

"Christ, Alex. I've never taken you for an idiot. You do

realize Nelu is going to insist *you* marry his precious daughter to make this fucking mess with Tasa right?"

"Don't blame Tasa," I cautioned him, choosing to ignore the greater problem he'd brought up. Of course, it had crossed my mind, but I already planned to avoid that at all costs, even before I hooked up with Nina. The thought of Cristo being linked to my family was hard enough to swallow. At least Tasa would've moved in with the Popescus. But to have one of them on my territory? In my home? No, that was too much.

"Yesterday, you were practically cursing her name," he fired back, shock lacing his tone.

"Tasa may have run away, but she didn't create this situation. I made the arrangements...without realizing the impact it might have on her."

"And now you realize it?" he remarked, amazed.

I stared past him, out the window. Nina's words from yesterday reverberated in my head and guilt dug its claws deeper into me. "Yes, I do."

"Well, at least you got something right. I'm assuming this has to do with Nina. No other way you could make such a quick about-face. I should thank her when she wakes up. If you had listened to me ages ago, this whole situation might've been avoided."

"Alright," I offered. "I fucked up. I get it, but don't act like you don't know why I wanted this. Tasa was getting wild, going to sex clubs." I waved toward the bedroom. "Dragging Nina along with her. Part of my reasoning for getting her married was that once she had a man and a regular sex life, she'd settle down. Cristo's girl brags about his cock, so at the very least, he knows how to use it properly. The marriage plan clearly backfired. Can we move the fuck on now?"

"Sure we can move the fuck on, but that doesn't change

the fact that Nelu is going to bleed you dry of everything he can get. He's going to want you to make it up to him by taking Tasa's place. Why should he settle for a sibling when he can have the big kahuna and put his pretty little daughter into your home as his spy?"

"That's not going to happen," I gritted out. "No man will force me to do anything I don't want to do."

"You're a *șef*, boss man. You aren't your own man," he oh-so helpfully pointed out. "You have a family. A clan. And an empire that crosses continents. Your job is to protect those three, regardless of what you want."

"Like hell, I'm not my own man," I ground out. Again, I felt the walls closing in on me. The burden of what was expected of me was pressing down on my shoulders like a ton of bricks. How far was I willing to go out on a limb?

Pretty damn far, I decided.

"What the hell's happened to you? Last night you were on your way to a business meeting at The Lounge, and this morning, I find Nina, of all people, in your bed. I can count on one hand the number of times you've brought a woman back here. And you were plastered each and every one of those times, but you don't look worse for wear to me." He looked me up and down critically. "Then you lock the door on me because you don't want me to see her naked. Fuck, Alex, we've shared multiple women. Multiple times. In the same bed."

I waved him away. "This is nothing like that. Nothing," I insisted.

If anything, it was the opposite of sowing my wild oats. Everything I felt for Nina was soaked in the scent of hearth and home. Family and children. *Fuck, what am I saying?* I'd barely spent time with the girl, but I couldn't help it. I knew her as part of my family, and those were the things she dragged out of my soul. As a man who followed my gut as much as my intellect, my instinct screamed that she was mine for the long haul.

"Of all the women in the city, you had to go for her. Tasa will carve out your balls with a butter knife and stuff them down your throat for breakfast."

"Nice image, Tatum. Real nice."

"I'm being real, not nice. And you are in definite need of a reality check," he retorted as he flipped on the tap and filled the *ibric* with water. Reaching for the canister of ground coffee, he measured out the grounds with brusque, impatient movements. He thrust the coffee canister away and grabbed the sugar bowl, from which he distractedly dumped in a few spoons of sugar. I grimaced. Fuck, I hated it when he made the coffee too sweet.

"Tasa's gone, so how exactly is she going to butt into my private life?"

"And you called her 'your woman for now,'" my friend observed as he vigorously stirred the ingredients in the *ibric*. "I don't know which is worse. That you've fucked Nina, that you called her your *woman,* or that you called her your woman *for now*. Are you losing your mind right now? Is that what's happening? Should I call doc like when there's a gunshot wound that needs stitching? 'Cause you're acting like your brain is bleeding out."

"Thanks for your vote of confidence," I grated out between clenched teeth.

Rolling his eyes, he gave me a hard stare before turning his focus back to the stove.

Stirring again, he tried pleading with me, "I get it. She's beautiful. She's sweet. She's pure." At that last point, he shot me a knowing glance. He was already thinking that I took her virginity. He didn't want to acknowledge it out loud because that would imply marriage, and he didn't want to go there. Unbeknownst to him, I'd embrace marriage. Not only was it high time, but I *wanted* to lock Nina down. I wanted to spend every day with her. I damn well needed her in my bed every night. And I was too possessive not to put a ring on her finger.

Unfortunately, this clusterfuck with Nelu had to play itself out. Frustration clawed at my chest yet again. It was becoming a common occurrence. What the hell was happening to me? Since when did I feel stifled by being șef?

Since Nina.

"I really get it," he went on, "but you need to think with your brain, not your dick."

"Have I ever thought with my dick?"

"No, but that doesn't mean there isn't a first time for everything," he rejoined with a snort. "You have Nina in your bed, and that's not something I *ever* expected to see. This is a sensitive time, Alex. We need to focus on settling this situation, which is shifting by the day. Hell, by the hour."

"I'm completely focused on my work, Tatum. It's Sunday, for Christ's sake. I can take a few hours off."

The only reason Tatum pulled his scowl off me was to pay attention to the foam building as the coffee brewed. Being a perfectionist, he couldn't miss that moment of opportunity. If he took his eyes off it, he'd be pissed for fucking up the coffee.

"I've been completely honest with her," I explained. "I told her what I could and could not do."

He glanced up for a second. "What is that exactly, Alex? Do you even know?"

"Not completely," I admitted. "One thing I do know is that I'm moving her in here for her protection, and I'm locking my front door because I don't want you barging in on us. I need to make certain she's safe, at least while we're searching for Tasa and resolving the marriage contract with Nelu. I can't get distracted by worrying about her. That *would* take away my focus, and if Nelu truly wants me as a son-in-law, I'll need my wits intact."

"It makes sense for her to stay here, but are you sure that'll make her any less of a distraction? Although," he pondered, "you will be getting off, so the upside is that it'll leave you more relaxed. You're always more focused after a good fuck."

I growled at him. "It's not only about sex, Tatum. She does something for me. Her calm presence soothes me, and I'm wound up as fuck with everything that's going on."

Taking the coffeepot off the stove top, he poured the foam out and returned it for another fifteen seconds to build up again. He gestured for me to get the cups for Turkish coffee. I placed them on the counter just as he pulled the *ibric* off the stove. Then he poured the coffee, grounds and all.

Bringing the cup to my lips, I sipped the bittersweet beverage.

"Too sweet," he grunted.

"Yup," I confirmed. I knew it would be, with the amount of sugar he'd inadvertently added.

"Shit," he said and whisked my cup out of my hand. "I'll make another."

Oh, hell no.

I grabbed it back. "Like hell, you will. You're not throwing it out." Tatum could be a control freak on his own time. I needed him out of my apartment before Nina woke up and found him here.

Taking another sip, I held back from pursing my lips at the sickly sweetness of his coffee and lied, "It's fine."

At that moment, soft footsteps padded behind me. I stifled a groan and checked over my shoulder as Nina quietly stepped into the kitchen. She was wearing nothing but one of my sweatshirts. Knowing she smelled like me made my stomach clench with need. While I internally writhed in frustration that Tatum was still here, I couldn't help smile at seeing her covered in something of mine. That, and the fact that she knew better than to wear that slinky red number in front of Tatum. If that had happened, I'd have no choice but to knock him out cold. Although...my sweatshirt only fell to midthigh, leaving her long, lean legs bare.

Shyly tucking a lock of hair behind her ear, she announced her presence with a soft, hesitant, "Hey."

I could only imagine how uncomfortable it had been for her to wake up in a strange bed without me there. Then she'd had to roam my apartment until she found me, only to be faced with Tatum. The walk of shame and all that.

Bringing her warm curves into my side, I cajoled, "Good morning, sweetness. Did you sleep well?"

Ducking her head, she averted her eyes and half hid in my chest. I wrapped my arm around her and ordered Tatum to say hello in Romanian, "*Salut-o.*"

"Hey, Nina, hope we didn't wake you with our loud arguing. We're loud and we argue. Might as well get used to it because that's how Alex and I communicate best."

"*Idiot,*" I rumbled out in Romanian.

He gave me a shit-eating grin, the fucker.

Pointing to his coffee cup, I lifted my chin toward the front door. "Why don't you go back to your own apartment? I'll meet up with you in a few hours."

Taking the third cup, he pressed it into Nina's hand and said, "Good to see you again, Nina."

He threw me a warning look, one he didn't bother to hide from Nina. My jaws clenched. She didn't need his judgment on top of the mess I made of things last night with my equivocal bullshit answers and excuses. She deserved better than that. Better than me, if I was to be perfectly honest with myself. That honest assessment didn't mean I'd let her go.

Once Tatum was finally out the door, I let out a sigh of relief and braced myself to deal with the nervousness pouring off Nina. Had she overhead me talking to Tatum earlier? Stifling a groan, I hoped not.

11

"Would you rather I prepare you a cup of tea instead?" Alex asked me, looking me over with concern.

My brows drew close. *Son-in-law?* Did I hear correctly when I overhead Alex and Tatum talking? He hadn't mentioned that tidbit last night. As if that wasn't bad enough to ratchet up my nerves, Tatum had given him a blatant *watch yourself* look on his way out.

Turning to Alex, I replied, "I love coffee."

Did he assume I didn't like Turkish coffee? If only he knew that Tasa prepared it every morning for us.

He cleared his throat as his hand caressed down the side of my neck before cupping it at the base. "I used your pretty mouth rough last night. Thought you might need tea with honey. The grounds of Turkish coffee can be hard on a tender throat."

Good God. Heat shot up my cheeks, and I swallowed around the light band of his fingers, inadvertently testing the soreness. While touched by his concern, it was a pretty ballsy thing to say, first thing in the morning. But that was Alex. Alpha all the way.

"I'm good... It's not really *that* sore," I managed to rasp out, dizziness taking hold of me.

"Good," he replied, his hand slipping off my throat. My skin turned cool at the absence of his touch, and the urge to follow him and burrow into his chest dogged me, but I forced myself to remain where I was.

Reaching for a pan, he said, "I'm fucking ravenous. I can make an omelet. You hungry?"

Oh, I was ravenous alright. Ravenous for him. But I refrained from saying as much, although the way his gaze lingered on me told me he was referring to more than physical hunger. Warmth pooled in my belly, spreading outward to heat up every cell in my body.

Approaching the fridge, I opened it and asked, "What do you need?"

As he rattled off the ingredients, I pulled them out and set them on the counter beside him. It was like a fantasy come true, helping him with Sunday breakfast as if we were a couple. A family. Taking a seat by a kitchen table overlooking a large window, I watched as he efficiently sliced up vegetables and ham. Needless to say, I was a little surprised at his quick and competent movements, as if he'd been making omelets all his life. With the traditional way his mother talked about gender roles, I hadn't expected Alex to be comfortable in a kitchen. A part of me assumed he had a live-in chef who prepared his meals.

Settling onto the bench, I relished the sight of the deeply masculine male moving around his kitchen with smooth effortlessness. I had been a ball of nerves waking up alone in his huge bed. Not only was it the first time, but the man in question was nowhere to be seen.

There were no sounds coming from the bathroom or anywhere nearby. I half thought he'd abandoned me, and I'd find a note telling me how to leave the apartment. Turning my face into his pillow, I'd taken a moment to inhale his male musk mixed with the woody scent of his cologne. It was such a hedonistic fragrance that I could've stayed there all day. There was no telling if I'd have another opportunity, so I took my time.

A whirlwind of images from last night had assaulted me. My back curved like a bow as he positioned me on my hands and knees. Alex licking my pussy from behind, nipping at my clit with his teeth. A blinding orgasm. Screaming until I was hoarse. Him mounting me from behind, his fingers around my throat just as they had been a few moments ago, although much tighter. Alex thrusting into me, letting out grunts that had me coming again.

After luxuriating in those thoughts long enough to make me wet, I'd thrown back the sheet and stared down at my nakedness. Not wanting to retrieve the discarded dress on the bathroom floor, I threw on the first thing I found in his chest of drawers. Creeping into the bathroom, I quickly brushed my teeth and did my business. After a little one-to-one pep talk with my reflection in the mirror, I quietly ventured out. Creeping softly out into the hallway, my ears picked up two deep masculine voices, which I followed to the kitchen.

My heart had seized with panic when I peeked around the doorjamb and found Tatum there. He was Alex's right-hand man. Tasa called him, "the voice of reason." I didn't mean to eavesdrop, but I couldn't help hearing him warn Alex not to think with his dick. That didn't bode well for me.

I melted when Alex replied that it wasn't only about sex with me. That my presence *soothed* him. A swell of gratification burgeoned from deep within me. This was exactly what I wanted to be to this man. I wanted to give him peace. He seemed to have so little of it in his life.

But that talk about being Nelu's son-in-law...maybe it was an off-the-cuff comment. *See, that's what happens when you eavesdrop*, I chastised myself.

A second wave of relief came when Alex took me into his arms. Wrapped up in the warmth of his big body, his woodsy musk had my head spinning for a moment.

Now, I lounged back and gazed out the floor-to-ceiling window, sipping from my small cup of coffee while he finished the omelet, imagining this was our life. Just another lazy Sunday morning, maybe with little kiddos running circles around out feet. It ticked off all the boxes. I gave a longing sigh.

He slipped a full plate in front of me, along with silverware, before taking a seat. Calm silence reigned as we ate. The food was as delicious as anything Tasa or her mother had prepared. Hints that this was a Romanian meal abounded in the sliced tomato and cucumbers, or the slices of bread and pieces of farmer's cheese that were found at every meal I'd ever had at Tasa's home.

"This is amazing," I praised him.

"Surprised that I can cook, aren't you? Don't try to deny it. I saw it on your face."

Giving a little shrug, I remarked, "I assumed you'd have a live-in chef or something."

"I have someone who comes in several times a week, but I like my privacy. I don't want to have to cohabitate with a staff of maids, chefs, and drivers. Work and family rules my life. People are always around me." He gave a small shrug. "Not everyone can be trusted either," he divulged.

My hands paused in the middle of cutting. "I'm honored you've let me in to your apartment."

"I'm letting you in even further, Nina. You'll live here until everything gets settled. I thought I made myself clear on that point yesterday."

"Um...I wasn't sure you meant it. Yesterday was yesterday. Sometimes, people change their minds the morning after..." I explained haltingly. Even though Alex had said some kind things about me, my insecurity over Tatum's comment and his parting look to Alex stayed with me. And then there was Alex's "son-in-law" comment.

He carefully laid his fork and knife down. Piercing me with a heated look, he said, "I'm a man of my word. My word means something. It carries weight and that's why I don't give it lightly. Anyway, it makes more sense for you to stay here. I live closer to your school."

Relief swept over me as I confirmed, "I know you're a man of your word, and I'll stay as long as you want. I have to get clothes from my mother's house and explain to her that I'm moving back into the apartment because the commute to school is too much. That would be the simplest way to go. She wouldn't understand otherwise."

My mother was as traditional as his mother, so he'd see the necessity in lying.

"Are you okay with that?" I inquired. "Will you tell your mother, or will this be a secret thing?"

"I won't need to tell her anything. I'm a grown man, Nina. She'll see what she sees and come to her own conclusions."

"Of course," I agreed quickly. Heat seared my nape. We were of different genders, ages, and statures. He had no reason to hide any part of his life. For me, it was simpler to keep my mother in the dark, especially if Alex and I fizzled into nothing. He'd made no promises. Despite the uncertainty though, I was willing to take a risk and follow this to its end.

His eyes lifted from his plate and locked on me. "Your mother wouldn't understand now, but what if this were to become a permanent thing between us?"

Permanent? As if he has to ask. Sharp hunger flared in my chest. My appetite fled, but I forced down a bite of omelet.

With a nervous laugh, I said, "That would be different. While our mothers aren't exactly friends, they're super friendly. They respect each other. As things stand right now, my mother would feel like she lost face. She doesn't understand hookups or flings. She'd only see this as tarnishing my reputation. Her pride would be bruised if she thought you were using me. That's not what this is about," I hurried to add, "but that's how she'd see it."

While this was a difficult conversation, it was surprisingly easy to talk to Alex. I was generally reserved about my private life. Maybe it was because Alex was tied to Tasa in my mind, and I shared everything with her. A pang hit me in the sternum as a wave of longing for my best friend crashed over me.

Scraping my hand through my hair, I let out a short exhale. "Things are tense at home. Very tense. I moved back after Tasa left because Yo-Yo needed me to protect him, not just because I couldn't stand living in the apartment without her."

"You won't be there, though. You'll be here," he reminded me.

Pressing my lips together, I stood and crossed over to the refrigerator to pull out a bottle of orange juice. I poured some into a glass and guzzled it down, savoring the pulpy tangy-sweet juice. Holding up the bottle with a questioning look in his direction, I waited for his response. He shook his head, so I returned it and sat back down. "I'll stop by every couple of days to do what I can. I don't know how long Yo-Yo can take it. They're screaming at each other every day. It's horrible."

Alex crooked his index finger at me and ordered, "Come here."

Oh, God. Was he going to try to comfort me? Bouncing my knee, I hesitated.

"Come *here*," he insisted.

I wasn't used to being physically attended to for my emotional needs. Feeling awkward, I rubbed my legs before rising to my feet and approaching him tentatively. He turned in his chair and spread his thick thighs. He was bare-chested, with a smattering of dark hair along his pecs. The thin strip of hair going down the center was enticing me to trace it with my tongue. His wolf's head shifted as his muscles flexed, the emerald eyes winking at me.

Biting my lip, I paused in between the V of his open legs. Ever so slowly, I took a seat on the hard muscle of his thigh. The instant my butt hit his lap, he looped an arm around my waist, bringing me into his chest, and closed his legs to pin me between them. I was enveloped in his sandalwood scent, and that, while wrapped in all those chiseled, hard muscles, made me feel protected. Coveted. Precious.

While the juncture between my thighs was getting moist, especially knowing I was completely nude under his simple sweatshirt, I knew this wasn't sexual. Alex couldn't change the circumstances of my family dynamics. But by giving me a hug, he was giving me comfort. He was a protector at heart. His instincts were to shield, comfort, fix. My body melted into his chest. We sat together quietly, him cradling me and rocking me a little. It was a balm to my aching heart. To my soul.

We stayed like that for some time, him nuzzling my hair. Breathing me in. And I did the same to him.

Eventually, his cell phone rang in the distance.

Not hurrying, he said, "I should get that. It's almost noon. I'm surprised it's my first call of the day. Everyone must be hungover."

Nodding, I forced myself off his lap. He gave my butt a playful little swat as he went in search of his phone. Hearing his gravelly voice in the distance, I set about cleaning the dishes and putting the kitchen to rights.

He'd finished with his call by the time I was done, but the energy had shifted; gone was the sexy man I had cuddled with before.

A muscle in his jaw ticked away.

Something had happened.

"What is it, Alex? Did you learn something about Tasa?"

"No, but Nelu has. He found out she's gone. It'd be an understatement to say that he's not pleased. I have to prepare for a meeting with him in a few hours."

The tension permeated the air. The son-in-law comment he'd made about Nelu earlier popped into my head. What if he was pressured into taking Tasa's place? Of course, since I overheard it while eavesdropping, I was powerless to bring it up.

Wiping my hands dry, I said, "I'll get out of your way. Would you like me to get my clothes and come straight back here, or should I stay in Queens until the evening?"

"Stay until late. I'm going to be busy with this. Stegan will take you home. He'll wait in the café until it's time to bring you back."

"You don't have to do that," I insisted.

He gave me a hard look. "You're not taking the fucking subway, that's for sure. Don't argue with me, Nina. I've got enough on my plate as it is."

"Sorry," I muttered, my eyes batting away. Even though his tone was hard, the worry behind it was undeniable, and I didn't want to add to his burden.

His finger tucked under my chin and raised it. "That's my good girl, firefly."

"Firefly?" I coughed out.

He grinned. "Yeah, well, in the dark of the night, you're my light."

"That...is so sweet. *Cheesy*, but sweet," I couldn't help but say. Grabbing his forearm, I shook my head. "I meant to tell you this earlier. Not sure if this will help you find Tasa, but I figured it couldn't hurt."

His green eyes turned crystalline sharp. "What is it? I have no leads, so anything would help."

"I don't know if you know this...if anyone knows, but Tasa's minor is modern dance." I was almost certain she'd switched it to her major, although I had no proof of it so wasn't going to go there. "A few weeks ago, she received something in the mail. From a highly sought-after experimental dance workshop that's very popular among the dance students. Everyone knows about Madame Pierrette's dance troupe and her spring workshop in Canada. It's a big deal, so I was surprised when I saw mail addressed from her. Long story short, Tasa was accepted, which shows what raw talent she has. It's in Montreal in May. That's a few months away, but I can't imagine Tasa missing this opportunity," I finished breathlessly.

My grip on his forearm had tightened at the thought that I might be betraying my closest friend. But if Alex was afraid for her, then that was enough for me. If he didn't want me to take the subway, only a day after hooking up, what kind of danger might Tasa be in? His one and only little sister.

Pressing a kiss to my forehead, he murmured, "You haven't betrayed her by telling me. You're helping me find her before someone else does. Someone who could hurt her, kill her even. Especially now that Nelu is in the know. Who the hell knows what he'll do if I don't talk him off the ledge."

Wrapping me in his arms, he gave me a tight hug. "Come on, let's get you dressed and on your way home," he advised as he walked me back into his bedroom. I nodded and quickly put on the icky dress from last night. I could only imagine what would happen at his meeting. He didn't want to marry anyone related to the Popescus, but would he have a choice in the matter?

I let out an anxious breath.

I had no answer, and I didn't think he was any closer to one, either.

12

Once I put Nina in the elevator, making sure that Stegan was in the lobby to guide her to the car and drive her to Queens, I quickly texted Tatum, Nicu, and Luca about the new development with Nelu, ordering them to come over as soon as possible. Since I'd made the decision to release Tasa from her obligatory marriage to Cristo, it didn't much matter whether I found Tasa before Nelu found out. Now that he had, though, I had to deal with him.

The backlash of pulling out of the contract was going to be hefty unless I found a suitable alternative, and for that, I needed my brothers. Having finished taking a shower, where images of Nina on her knees, sucking my cock, assailed me at every turn, I was in the middle of putting on cuff links when Luca sailed through my bedroom door. Even though Nina wasn't there, my body tightened at the thought of another male in my bedroom.

Even if that male was my brother. Apparently, I was losing my damn mind.

Confusion crossed my middle brother's face as I waved him out of my bedroom.

"What are you? A prude, all of a sudden?" he asked with a snort. "You're not even naked."

"Just get out, will you," I snapped, gesturing toward the door. "I'll be out in a minute."

"The fuck?" was all he muttered as he turned on his heel and exited my room. My family wasn't known for their privacy. Back home, we walked in and out of one another's bedrooms without knocking. None of the rooms, besides my father's office, had locks. The only door we ever knocked on before entering was Tasa's, and that was because we didn't want to run the risk of walking in the middle of her changing.

Shrugging on a jacket, I strode out into the living room as Nicu came out of the kitchen with coffee, which he served with *Bunică's* shortbread made from crushed walnuts, rose hip jam, and meringue.

"You went home?" I asked, although it was obvious when he came back with such bounty.

Nicu merely shrugged. He was the closest to our mother in many ways. For a brute, he was also a mama's boy to the core. It was ironic, to say the least, considering he was the most bloodthirsty of us all.

"Just shut up and eat," he grumbled, turning his back to return to the kitchen. Tatum entered as Nicu returned with glasses of water.

Now we could start.

"As I texted earlier, Nelu called me this morning," I began. "He knows Tasa's gone."

"Cristo must've guessed. That was probably the reason for his little party at The Lounge last night. He must've gotten a good laugh, listening to our song and dance about Tasa working late as an intern. God, I want to punch that fucker in the face. How pissed was he?" asked Nicu.

"His tone was cold, which is worse. A hot-blooded Romanian screaming at the top of his lungs is easier to deal with any day," I remarked. Turning to Luca, I updated him on my recent decision. "We're still going to find Tasa, but I'm not giving her over to that bastard of a son he has."

Sipping calmly from the intricate small porcelain coffee cup, he asked without surprise, "What's the sudden change of heart?"

"Nina," Tatum and Nicu responded simultaneously, darting glances at each other.

"I assume you found her in his bed this morning," Nicu said to Tatum.

"Yup," Tatum replied succinctly.

I rolled my eyes. "Shut up and stop acting as if you know what my every move is."

"It's my job to anticipate your every move," Nicu declared calmly.

"Yes, the good brother. The *best* brother," taunted Luca with a little vicious smirk on his face.

"Shut up," snarled Nicu. Proud of the work he did for the family, he was quick to react to Luca's judgment of him as my lackey.

They may share the penthouse floor in the other tower, but they were more competitive than Luca and I ever were. Probably because Luca had never coveted my place at the top. Far from it, in fact. Luca was the rebel. But unlike Tasa, he didn't go off script. He was a cynical loner who never agreed to anything without a fight first. Fistfights between us were never off the table, even as adults. Which was why

Tatum was so crucial to our crew. He liked things balanced and stuck up for Luca. With three brothers forced to work together, the pieces were complex indeed.

"Can we not argue right this moment? We have a bigger issue to deal with," I intoned.

"So. Let me get this right. You fucked Nina, who convinced you to not force Tasa into a marriage with that upstart of a family," Luca summarized.

"In a nutshell," Tatum agreed with a smug grin on his face.

Although Tatum was my oldest confidant and *consilier*, he and Luca were brothers at heart. Tatum was the closest Luca had to a friend, which was quite a feat since Luca was philosophically against getting close to anyone. Trust wasn't something that came easily to my younger brother. Tata didn't do right by him, designating him as the black sheep of the family. I tried to eradicate those patterns after his death, but the scars ran deep. Part of me shied away from looking too closely. Tata remained my idol, but if there was one blemish on his otherwise faultless record, it was the way he'd treated his second son.

"Whatever. The point is we're required to create a bond with that upstart family," I reminded him.

"Why?" he growled, leaning over his lap and stabbing me with a stare that could wither flowers pushing out of the ground. "Because our precious *pater* demanded it? The fucking ground he walked on was sacred. Everything he wanted, he got. Unquestionable loyalty for a plan that was, and continues to be, madness. Nelu will betray us. He doesn't have an honest bone in his decrepit body. He's evil personified, and as a result, any of his offspring are as putrid as he is."

"You mean besides the fact that it's good for business? Then, yes, because Tata demanded it. On his deathbed. It was an oath I made to him, and I'll be damned if I don't do everything in my power to bring it to fruition. While I may agree with your judgment of Nelu, after all these years we finally have a contract—"

"One which you've already violated. If you think he's going to do right by you, you might as well get drunk on cold water," he snapped, using a Romanian proverb to suggest I was grasping at straws and being unrealistic.

"Ha, ha, fucking funny," Nicu mocked.

"What makes you think he'll follow anything in that contract when you can't bring the bride to the altar?"

"Because," I answered calmly, "I'll bring him a groom instead."

"A *groom*?" Luca spat out.

"For Nelu's precious young daughter. Tasa's age, I believe." I snapped my fingers, pretending I didn't remember her name for Luca's sake. "What's her name, Nicu?"

"Cătălina," he helpfully supplied.

"There you go. Cătălina. A good Romanian name if I've ever heard one. She's a looker, too. A blonde, and we know how much you like blondes. Unlike her father and brother, she's as pure as the driven snow," I noted, arching my eyebrows at Luca expectantly.

After a beat, realization dawned on his face. "Romanian, yes. But good? Never. Oh fuck no. Hell. No. I know what you're thinking, but there's no way I'm getting married. Ever. And if I was ever insane enough to do so, there's no way I'd marry a Popescu. Pure, my ass. I'd bet my balls she's a whore. There's no way you can expect her to be a virgin with that cocksucker as a father. He'd fuck the virgin out of her himself, as retribution for the dishonor of Tasa's running. And without virgin blood to shed, there'd be no bond. Not that you could do anything about it, without adding insult to injury. We don't check the sheets anymore, so it would be my word against Nelu's, and you'd have to side with him or insult him and risk starting a war."

I expected a fight, of course. Luca never went down without one, but this would clearly be a bad one.

"Calling the poor girl, Popescu or not, a whore is going a bit far," I chastised. "You're so fucking cynical. If he says he'll produce a virgin, he'll do it."

"Doubt it, but even so, I'm not a fucking stud to mate with any bitch you put in front of me," he sneered.

I spread my hands wide. "So much drama over nothing, Luca. You know you'll have to marry eventually. For the good of the family."

"I know no such thing. Sure, I'm a Lupu, but I'm not a fucking ass licker like this one," he jutted his thumb at Nicu, seated to his left. "I'll do what's required to protect this family. Within limits. I have a fucking brain of my own, Alex. Don't take the fact that I went to graduate school or followed any other of your directives as signs of weakness. I did it because I believed it was the right thing to do, not simply because you said so. You know nothing about me if you don't know that."

"I do know it," I replied slowly because keeping my calm was paramount and I could feel my blood starting to boil. "Just as I know you will agree in the end because if I don't produce a groom, it *will* trigger a war. And war is bad for business. Not only would it fuck up the contract we have with him, but we'd be forcing his hand to retaliate."

"Surely, he wouldn't dare go to the Bratva," supposed Tatum.

My head swung toward him. "Do you want to risk it? You know his pride. If he feels like we've insulted him, there's no telling how far he would go. And if he were to turn to the Bratva…"

"It'd be game over," Tatum finished. "There'd be no getting back from that. It would make the skirmishes of the past look like child's play."

"Oh, fuck no," rumbled Nicu. He hated the Bratva the most, and that was saying something.

"Why not you, Alex? Why don't you marry the little bitch, since you think she's so precious? Or do you think you're above it? Are you holding out for a girl from a better family? Sacrifice the black sheep to that wretched family of trashy newcomers and preserve the bloodline of the chosen heir."

"Certainly not, I'm not a snob like you," I said dryly, leaning back into the leather seat.

There was no way I was spilling my feelings about Nina to Luca. While Nicu was physically rough, Luca was emotionally harsh, and Nina was too precious to carelessly place in his brutal grip. I loved my brother, but we didn't relate to each other in a way that allowed for weakness. And Nina was my weakness.

Was I wrong to ask this of him? Perhaps. Then again, I was şef. I'd sacrificed my entire life to them; left college and my plans for law school to take over the family. In comparison to what I'd given up , the least Luca could do was accept this marriage. Hell, it's not like he cared who he married.

Placing my elbows on the armrests, I steepled my fingers together. "I have my own reasons for not choosing her for myself, but you're not privy to them."

Tatum leaned over as if he was about to speak, but I gave him a short nod, and he pulled back. He might be Luca's closest friend, but his loyalty was to me first, if for no other reason than that I was the *Lupul*.

"Why not? Don't you owe me that much?"

"No," I finally snapped. "Just as you keep most of your life hidden from us, I deserve a modicum of privacy."

"Touché," murmured Nicu because we all knew how protective Luca was of himself and his life. Even though he maintained his apartment in the city, he spent most of his time at his secluded house in the country, living a solitary existence. Not having spied on him of late, I didn't know what he was up to. Perhaps he had a mistress holed up in there with him and that was the reason behind his adamant refusal. This could be more than mere stubbornness and his tendency to automatically deny every request.

"Do you, though?" he challenged. "I never envied your position, because your life is not your own, but you chose to pick up the crown our father tossed your way. That's on you."

"Perhaps, but there are limits, and I'm drawing one now," I returned.

Nicu snuck a worried look my way, and Tatum turned his face away, both signs they silently agreed with Luca that my life wasn't my own. Well, fuck them. Boundaries had to be drawn, and they were going to be drawn by me. Today.

"My head isn't on the chopping block, and that's my final decision," I declared.

"Good luck with that," retorted Luca. "Nelu may not give you much of a choice."

Nelu could go fuck himself. I wasn't his dog.

"Luca, you'll be the groom." I pronounced. "Let me worry about Nelu."

"I. Won't. Do. It," he growled. "Don't try forcing my hand, Alex. You won't like how I react."

"I have to force your hand every single time, Luca. Every fucking time because you won't simply do what you're told," I snapped in exasperation.

"Like your good little solider right here?" he shot back, gesturing toward Nicu. "Fucking take him. He's willing to do anything for you. He has no soul. No feelings. He doesn't give a shit who he marries. Use him."

"Wow, talk about throwing your brother under the bus," drawled Nicu, taking a sip of water, completely unperturbed.

"Don't be such a child. You know Nicu is the youngest. Nelu will take that as an insult."

Since Luca always said no, I was going with the assumption he'd capitulate in the end. God, I prayed I was right...I had to be. Otherwise, it was my head that was going to tumble, and that couldn't happen.

Luca slapped his hand on the glass top of the coffee table, rattling the glasses, cups, and plates. "I'm not fucking joking, Alex. If you can't get your little fuck toy here to do your dirty work, then you'll have to marry the girl yourself. I'm not doing it."

I stroked the prickly bristles of my chin, recalling the red rash I'd left on the inside of Nina's thighs when I went down on her and licked her delicious honey last night. Outbursts were so common with Luca that I didn't even twitch.

Watching my brother carefully, I noted the flush on his pale skin. The man rarely went out, choosing to entomb himself in that mausoleum of a mansion he lived in, in the north of the city. While we'd returned to our family's home in Queens, he'd escaped to a fancy suburban neighborhood in Westchester County, as far from the city streets of the borough he was born in as he could get.

Clearly, we'd reached an impasse for today. He was an obstinate bastard. It was what made him so good at what he did for our family. Luca liked to fuck with other people's money, especially rich people with dirty money. He was our Robin Hood. But when he stole, which he loved to do, he filled the Lupu coffers.

Flicking my wrist, I checked my Greubel Forsey watch.

"Time's ticking, and I can't waste it arguing with you, Luca. We can return to this discussion later. Scurry back to your marble mansion while I get my hands dirty with Nelu," I taunted.

"Better you than me," he mumbled, not taking the bait. "We can discuss this all you want, but I'm not budging. Not this time. There's no negotiating or haggling our way through this."

Rising to my feet, I made a scoffing noise in the back of my throat. "You know better than to say something as stupid as that. There's always space for negotiation. And you're not Tasa. I don't have to worry about your sensibilities or that you'll run..." *Like a coward.* I left the words unspoken, but they hovered in the air between us. I didn't say them, because I wouldn't want them paired with Tasa's act. She hadn't run out of cowardice. For her, it was an act of strength and willpower, but that didn't mean it'd be the same for my brothers. She was a girl. Right or wrong, in our world, that made a difference.

I ignored Luca's low growl. It was best to act from a position of strength, which was to assume I'd get what I wanted in the end.

Nicu and Tatum rose to their feet as I did. Luca could stay. He rarely attended meetings, and he'd refrain this time to avoid suggesting he'd tacitly agreed to my demands. Days like today, I questioned my sanity for taking on the role of *şef*. On top of having a runaway sister and a difficult brother who rarely did as he was told, I had to face Nelu. Holding him off would be no easy task.

13

The meeting with Nelu was scheduled in neutral territory, a French restaurant in Tribeca owned by a Frenchman of Romanian descent. He owed both of us for helping get his business up and running, which meant he was Switzerland.

Nelu was seated at a table in a cramped backroom office of the restaurant, which was packed with families on a Sunday. Small glasses and a bottle of *ţuică*, traditional plum brandy, were waiting for Nicu, Tatum, and me on the wooden surface of the antique desk.

As always, Nelu was wearing a silk suit, which left him looking a little too shiny and a lot greasy. It certainly didn't take away from making him look like a crocodile in a suit, but I supposed he'd never know better. Cristo sat on one side while his *consilier*, Simu, was at his other shoulder.

Checking on us nervously one last time, the Frenchman quickly closed the door behind him, drowning out the bustling noise from the kitchen outside the office door.

"*Bună ziua*," Nelu greeted me, Nicu, and Tatum.

"Good afternoon," I returned.

"I'm glad you were able to meet on such short notice," he began in his heavily accented English, all too insincerely. Of course, I could respond in Romanian, the more polite option, but I didn't want to give him the advantage of speaking in his mother tongue. I certainly wouldn't have cut my time with Nina short to look at his ugly mug on my occasional day off. Whatever. This was a game of chess, and what better way to while away a Sunday afternoon, if not inside Nina, than to play psychological games with a vicious opponent.

"Of course," I replied smoothly as I took a seat across from him.

Lifting the bottle of brandy, he poured the clear liquor into shot glasses.

"*Noroc*." He said the traditional toast before throwing back the shot.

Every man repeated the toast of good luck and drank their shot. It was a gut-tearing drink I'd never much cared for, but that was the way of things. A negotiation didn't begin without a drink of *țuică*. If anything, I preferred the twice distilled *palincă*, another strong spirit from the old country, most popular in Transylvania. If I confided as much to Nelu, he'd mock me because my mother's family came from there, even if Tata's family originated in the capital. That kind of regional snobbery was to be expected from a *bucureștean*, a native from the capital, Bucharest.

Slamming his shot glass down with a hard bang, Nelu eyed me and said, "So, the little bird has flown the coop. Is that not how the saying goes, my friend?"

"That is the saying, yes," I confirmed, leaning back nonchalantly, as if I didn't have a care in the world.

Here we go.

"And when were you going to tell me your sister has *fled*

the marriage with my son?" he asked, his tone edged in shards of broken glass.

"When I felt it was necessary. That time had not yet arrived."

"It's been more than a week since she's been gone, no?" he gritted out between his perfectly aligned teeth. They clenched so hard together that what he thought was a smile came off as an ugly grimace.

"True, it has, but I am close to finding her." *Lie number one.* My shoulders slouched back against the wooden spindles of the chair as I pretended to inspect my nails.

He made a grunting noise of approval. "Good because, otherwise, I would have to go and track down the little minx myself."

That got my attention, and my entire body tensed. Nicu stiffened behind me as well. Forcing myself to relax, I straightened slowly and languidly placed my forearms on the table. "She's not yours," I stated tightly.

"The contract was signed."

"Perhaps, but that would be overreaching, and I could not allow for that. They are not married. There is no blood bond. Therefore, she is and remains 100 percent Lupu."

He raised his hands in a gesture of acquiescence. "It would've been as a form of aid, to bring back the wayward child."

"Nevertheless, unacceptable."

He tsked softly. "But really, Alex, I don't know what to make of you. You are the *Lupul.* You cannot control a small female such as her? It's unbecoming of your family."

"Perhaps, but it is what it is. Unfortunately, when I bring her back, there will need to be an adjustment made."

Nelu's entire body stilled, his ears almost pricking up in alert. His beady eyes narrowed as he went through the possible meanings behind my words. He should be the one with the advantage, yet I was suggesting he would be making a concession of some kind, in the near future.

"And what would that be, Alex?" he asked in a deadly cold tone. "I want the girl."

"You may want her, but after what I've found out, I'm not sure that is in the best interest of my sister." I shook my head, feigning disappointment. "It was after she found out about Cristo that she fled." Now, it was my turn to *tsk* softly as I turned my attention to his son.

I only had to say one word.

"Una."

Cristo's face turned pale.

I smirked internally. *Good, I've got the little bastard.*

"Yes, your mistress. Side piece. Love. And now what? Mother of your child, Cristo?" I tutted him. "Reckless. So very reckless. There is such a thing as contraception, my friend."

Cristo leapt to his feet and swept the glasses and bottle of *ţuică* from the table. Glass crashed everywhere, shards flying in every direction. One shot glass hit the wall and shattered. Liquor splattered across the tiled floor and pooled beneath the table.

Nicu shot to his feet, gun whipped out and trained on Cristo.

"*Destul!*" bellowed Nelu, backhanding his son in the mouth. "Enough. I told you to control yourself with your woman. Now look what you've done."

"It's not true!" Cristo shrieked.

"Oh, but it is. Pity your *dearest* hadn't chosen to tell you," I mused aloud. I waved to Nicu to put his gun away. I was never at risk of Cristo attacking me. This was a little show of his displeasure, but Nicu was always quick on the trigger. Literally.

Cristo didn't know it, but I'd had that girl followed. Straight to the health clinic. She'd made an appointment for an abortion. It didn't seem right to not let the father know. Cristo having a woman was never an issue. Cristo having impregnated a woman, regardless of what she chose to do in the end, was more of a problem. It would've become a nonissue again, if she had gone through with the procedure, but why waste a perfectly good opportunity to save our asses? I'd had her appointment erased from their system as a precaution until this issue was resolved. Was it heartless of me to take the choice away from poor Una, whose most stupid choice was falling for Cristo? Perhaps, but I did make sure to see she wasn't so far along that it compromised her ultimate decision.

From Cristo's reaction, I'd guess he didn't know.

"She'll terminate the pregnancy," Nelu declared with a wave of his hand like he was ordering lunch. Cristo's face drained of all color, and that told me more than I had ever wanted to know of Tasa's fiancé. He'd foolishly allowed himself to fall in love. It made me want to punch him, and it certainly strengthened my determination to cut Tasa loose from him.

"Look at him," I said in disgust. "Get a chair. He looks like he's about to faint." My head snapped toward Nelu. "And you would simply dispose of your grandchild so easily? Quite a head of family, you make."

"What would you suggest I do, then?" he spat out, rage turning the edges of his eyes red.

"I don't know, but I can only imagine you would do the same for my nephew if such an alliance were to go forward. It's not a good look for you, Nelu. We are a family-friendly clan. First off, there's no way she can abort prior to a marriage to my sister. It would implicate us, making it seem as if we sanctioned it. Secondly, Tasa ran away *because* she found out about the baby." *Lie number two.* "I mean, really, it must be common knowledge if someone as innocent as Tasa found out."

"We don't know for sure if that's why she left," Cristo pleaded, wiping the trickle of blood from the corner of his mouth.

It was my turn to rise from my chair. I did so slowly, pushing the chair back with a screech against the tiled floor. Deliberately placing my palms on the surface of the table, I leaned in and sneered, "What other possible reason could there be, Cristo?" I spat out his name like it was a curse. Fuck, I wanted to smash his face on the floor and grind it beneath my shoe.

"She's a good girl. Too good for you, apparently. She was willing to turn the other cheek about Una for the sake of the families, but she's a naïve virgin. How could she turn a blind eye to an *infant*? I can assure you that the possibility of an abortion never crossed her mind. That's not the kind of upbringing she's had. And it's the type of scandal the Lupu clan simply cannot ignore. We're not so desperate for an alliance that we leave our morals at the door."

Breaking eye contact with Cristo, I switched back to Nelu. "He's unsuitable."

"*Futu-ți pizda mă-tii,*" he grumbled under his breath.

"Such profanity is unnecessary," I replied instantly, but I was fucking smiling on the inside. I got him. I got the bastard.

"Oh, please," said Nicu with a chuckle from behind me.

Nelu scratched his chin, his clever brain flipping through different scenarios like the good chess player that he was. When he was done and realized he had no get-out-of-jail card to play, his gaze returned to mine.

"How do we fix this?"

Time to introduce Luca as a substitute.

"You have a daughter, right?"

His jaw tightened. Even Cristo, the moron, tensed beside his father. As did Simu, interestingly enough. So Nelu and his family were protective of his daughter, huh? Oh, I was going to have fun gutting this fucker.

His hands came up in a pleading gesture. "She's but a child."

I slammed my palm down on the table. "I gave you my sister. How old is she?"

"Soon to be eighteen."

"Then she's old enough. Don't act as if this girl is any more pure or precious than my own little sister, who's only two years older."

"Can we not hold off a year?"

Oh, she was very precious indeed if Nelu was already asking for mercy. I took my time, slowly unbuttoning my jacket, spreading it out, and easing myself back into my seat. Eyeing him dubiously as I rapped my fingers on the table-top, I said grandiosely, "Fine, but it's going to cost you. You want to hold it off a year; we'll hold it off a year. If it's one year you want, then we'll have a discount for a year."

"And who will marry Cat?"

My brows gathered. "Who the hell is Cat?"

"Cătălina. In the family, we call her Cat. She's a real beauty and a sweet, gentle soul. I'm unenthused by the idea of her marrying so young, but I suppose we owe you..."

"I'm leaning toward Luca, but I'm undecided as of yet. Quite honestly, Nelu, I was unsure whether we would continue down this path, but Nicu here kept reminding me of my father's wishes. Money alone would never be reason enough to pawn off my blood in the midst of a scandal that would bring shame to my sister and our name. You should thank him for having me stay the course under such trying circumstances."

Lie number three. Nicu had done nothing of the sort, but if he was the one who would marry Cat should Luca prove to be difficult, I had to start making him look good.

Nelu gave a chin lift to Nicu as acknowledgment for his role.

"I'm thinking something in the range of a 30 percent discount," I suggested.

"Have you lost your mind? I might as well take my chances with the Taliban, if that's the case," he countered, referring the fact that if he didn't use my routes out of Afghanistan, he'd be forced to transport his product through Taliban territory.

Ah, now came the haggling. Nelu was back on solid ground. We went back and forth until we settled on a fair price and shook hands over it. Cristo gave me a glare, leaving my hand hanging for a long moment before Nelu nudged him in the back, finally prompting him to shove his hand into mine. Swear to God, seeing Cristo get protective over his little sister was the first good thing I'd ever seen him do. She must be quite something. Hell, maybe Luca would like her, after all. One would never know it, but he was sensitive underneath his rough outer crust. I assumed he didn't care who he married, but perhaps he was holding out for love. A ridiculous notion in our world, but wasn't it that very notion that was driving me?

Crunching the broken glass strewn on the floor, I made my way out of the office, Nicu and Tatum at my heels. We

weaved through a narrow path between crowded tables and
went out the door.

Once in the car, Nicu congratulated me, "Bravo, you did
the right thing, brother."

Did I? Or did I not have much of a choice if I wanted to
keep Nina? I wasn't proud that I was forcing my sibling into
a marriage with the Popescu clan. "Right. Wrong. Such
words are meaningless. The only thing that matters are
results and I always get the result I want."

"We got away by the skin of our teeth," Nicu remarked.
"How did you know about Una?"

"I know everything. That's why I'm the *Lupul*. You
already know I had someone on her tail from the moment I
found out about them. Nelu may be crafty, but his son's an
idiot. It was only a matter of time before something came to
the surface."

"Would you have brought it up if you wanted the
marriage to go forward?" he asked, curiosity lining his face.

"I would've certainly allowed Una to go ahead with the
abortion if that's what she wanted. I'm not one to get in the
way of a woman and a plan, but would I have told Tasa?
Certainly not. Would it have changed my idea about Cristo?
Honestly, no. Tasa forced my hand by running away. I didn't
realize how much she was suffering over this marriage, but I
had a chance for a do-over and I took it."

"What about Luca? You're basically doing the same
thing to him," noted Nicu with a wry smile on his face. He
wasn't one to hold back from busting balls, so he'd enjoy
Luca's discomfort.

"That's different, and you know it," I replied succinctly.

Luca was a man. He couldn't afford to have such sensibilities. Whether misogynistic or not, women were allowed
a bit more flexibility in that area. This world of ours was

archaic as hell when it came to many things, including gender roles. We arranged marriages in the twenty-first century, for fuck's sake. Tasa got out of that marriage because of a combination of the leniency given to women, and the fact that I cared for her and that she'd run away.

"Yes, but Luca's a stubborn bastard."

"And he can continue to be a stubborn bastard. Just one that's married to Nelu's daughter," I stated with finality, turning my gaze out of the car window and effectively ending our discussion. Although I spoke with conviction, I had no real idea of whether or not Luca would do what he was told, and that thought scared the hell out of me.

14

Waving to Stegan from the stoop of my family's brownstone, I unlocked the door softly, hoping to sneak into the house without much fanfare, when I heard a crashing sound coming from the living room. My mother's accented voice crept higher and higher with every word coming out of her mouth. By the time I stripped off my coat, placed it in the closet of the foyer, slipped off my shoes, and made my way to the living room, she was shrieking at the top of her lungs.

Pressing my index fingers into my ears, I stepped inside to find her waving a porcelain figurine in her hand, the kind my grandmother collected, about to fling it across the room.

Rushing up behind her, I whisked the object out of her hand and demanded, "What is going on, Mother? I could hear you shouting from the street."

She did a double take. So intent on deriding my brother, she hadn't notice I'd entered the house.

With a trembling finger pointing at Yo-Yo, she accused in a shaking voice, "He's going to be the death of me! I'm going to die of unhappiness because of him! Die, die, die!"

Yo-Yo rolled his eyes at me. Dramatic was an understatement when my mother got on a roll. Coming home to this after the time I'd spent with Alex was mentally exhausting. The weight of it pulled on my tired muscles.

"Mother," I said to her in a calm but firm tone as I carefully placed the figurine back on the small end table by the couch. Finally, her gaze broke away from Yo-Yo and flicked over to me. "Leave these alone and tell me what's happened. There's no way you're going to die."

My mother's face was drawn tight, deep wrinkles digging into her forehead. Her eyes were bleak with fear. For a moment, I almost pitied her, but she constantly revved herself up over small things. Her life was one big ball of anxiety, and even things that weren't problems could trigger a screaming fit.

Looking around, I asked, "Where's Dad?"

"You're father left to do groceries," she muttered as she plopped down onto the couch, wringing her hands. "But him!" she reproached again. "I woke up early and checked in on him. He wasn't in his bed. He wasn't anywhere in the house. Slipped out the window and was doing who knows what in this city. He doesn't listen to me. He doesn't follow the rules of my house. He's going to be the death of me, that child."

"If you were normal, I would've told you where I went, but you freak out about every little thing," began Yo-Yo.

"Normal? Your life is going to hell, and you call that normal? Do you know what I went through to get to this country? I crossed through one of the most dangerous jungles in Colombia, crawling with bandits and bad men, wearing only the clothes on my back. I walked and walked and *walked* through the Darién Gap—"

"Not with the Darién Gap again," grumbled Yo-Yo, and I sent him a quelling look.

Talking over him, my mother rambled on, "...Mexico and into this country to escape the poverty in China so that I could give you what I didn't have. A future. I had two children, not only one. That was all that was allowed under the One Child Policy. But I had two. One girl and one boy. Everything I've done in my life was for you, but you want to throw it away to *rap* on a stage in a dangerous neighborhood, where you might get killed." She lifted back up to her feet and shook her finger at Yo-Yo. "*Over my dead body!*" she bellowed out.

"She exaggerates," Yo-Yo turned to say to me. "I was at a club, hosting battles for new talent by a record company."

Waving at Yo-Yo to leave us, I grabbed my mother's hand and dragged her back down to the couch. "We know what you went through too," I assured her. "We understand. Yo-Yo is not taking for granted the sacrifices you made to come to this country, but he's almost eighteen. And you know, he's a boy," catering to her notions of gender. "They have lots of energy. He was just blowing off steam."

"It was hard enough with you, but it's even worse with him. At least you got into Juilliard. But what am I going to tell everyone back home, Nina? I can't tell them he didn't go to college. I can't tell them he decided to throw his life away by singing music that sounds like he's cursing. He's so angry when he does the rapping thing."

"Mother, you don't have to tell them anything. He will go to college," I tried pacifying her.

"It won't be a good college with the grades he's been getting recently," she griped.

"As if they would know the difference," I said.

"Nina, there's the internet now. Everyone is on it, and

they will go and look at the standings for the college he goes to," she chided me impatiently.

Keeping up appearances was supremely important to her, especially with her father's side of the family. After my grandfather died, my grandmother came to live with us and intense competition erupted. His side of the family took every opportunity to subtly scorn her. While I sympathized with her, I didn't think Yo-Yo should be a slave to her ego and a family rivalry with strangers from halfway across the world.

"The most important thing is that he goes to college," I reminded her. "While I know you have high expectations of him, Mother, pushing him will only make him rebel more." Yo-Yo would only push back against pressure. "As long as he's not hurting anyone, it's okay to give him a little bit of space. Screaming at him will only drive him away, and he will stop listening to you completely."

Squeezing my hand, she looked at me with desperation in her eyes and pleaded, "He listens to you. Nina, you have to speak to him about this."

"I do already, and I will continue to, but you have to ease up on him, Mother."

"There is no way he can succeed with this plan. There is no future in this music. It's not an honorable profession, and it does not have the stability of a doctor or a lawyer. What about health insurance and a 401k? These are things you have to start with early."

Patting her hand, I replied, "Let's get him enrolled in college first, okay? We'll worry about the rest later."

Guilt gnawed at me because Yo-Yo diverted my mother's attention away from my upcoming graduation. So anxious about him, she didn't have the energy to get on me or my lack of a solid future plan. Truthfully, with Alex suddenly in my life, all I could think about was him and the possibility of what lay before us. It lit a fire under my dream of having a family, especially with college ending soon.

The lock of the front door rattled. Glancing over my shoulder, I watched as my father came in, weighed down with several bags of groceries. Rushing over to him, I took a couple of bags off his hands. Following him into the kitchen, I told him about Mother's earlier explosion and asked him to go calm her down as I put away the groceries. I was grateful that I was moving back into the city because I needed a break from the drama.

Taking the stairs up to the second floor, I passed Yo-Yo's room. Sounds of Pop Smoke's deep voice blasted through the thin walls. Hoping to relax, I took a shower but my mind kept spinning. My best friend had run away, I lost my virginity, and I may or may not have a boyfriend. *Oh, and don't forget you're going to move into his place behind your mother's back.*

I had to snatch up this chance with Alex because the reprieve I had with my mother would end at some point. She hadn't approached me about my plans because she was wrapped up in Yo-Yo, but she would, and soon. After graduation, I was expected to move back home, unless I went off to a graduate program or got married. There was a small window of time to see if there was any future with Alex. That was my real dream, not another degree or starting a career, but I could never confess that to her.

Since showering did nothing to clear my mind, I threw on a pair of tight running shorts, a sports bra, and a long-sleeved running shirt. Trekking down the stairs, I slipped on my sneakers and grabbed the key to the front door. My father's head snapped up from their deep conversation and looked at me from above my mother's bent head. Gesturing down my body, I pointed to the door and slipped out, locking it behind me.

At the top of the stoop, I took a deep breath of air and exhaled slowly. When I finished a series of quick stretches, I hit the pavement and went on a run.

※※※

I WAS in a groove as I ran through my neighborhood toward the park alongside the East River in Long Island City. The skyline of Midtown Manhattan, with the Empire State Building and the United Nations building, always did the trick of calming me down. And a relaxed mood was more imperative than ever. My concerns about Yo-Yo and my mother, about Tasa and Alex receded into the background. Although that left space in my head for guilt that I might have violated Tasa's trust by telling Alex about the dance workshop in Montreal. It was so hard to know what was the right thing to do, but I figured it was best to put my trust in Alex since he knew most about any potential threat to Tasa. The scary-looking knives I found in his chest of drawers when I went looking for something to wear hadn't escaped my notice. It was the knives that had tipped me over to disclose my knowledge about Madame Pierrette's dance workshop. By the time I passed the ginormous neon Pepsi Cola sign along the river, I was feeling lighter than I had all day.

While pounding the pavement, I was focused on my breathing when a black car flew past me on the street and screeched to a halt a dozen feet in front of me. The back door flung open, shuddering from the force used to open it. As I passed by, I rubbernecked to see what was going on when I was snared by a pair of livid green eyes.

Fear sliced through me.

Skidding to a stop, I breathed heavily as Alex unfolded his large body from the car. Fury vibrated off him in tsunami-like waves.

Pointing to the ground in front of him, he commanded, "Come. Here."

Flustered, I squeezed between two cars parked at the curb to stand in front of him. "What happened? Did anything happen?" I rushed out, my chest heaving.

"In the car," he demanded. His voice was stone-cold, but his eyes were blazing hot. Tripping a little, I slipped past the bulk of his body and slid onto the seat. He instantly came in behind me, slammed the door shut, and ordered the driver to go.

Blood rushed to my head from stopping so suddenly and panic slinked through my chest.

"What's happened?" I repeated. Why wasn't he telling me what was going on instead of staring at me silently? He looked furious, but it couldn't possibly be with me...though his nostrils flared wide with barely restrained rage and all his intensity was focused on me.

"Fucking really, Nina?"

"What?" I cried out, my nails digging into the leather seats.

"You fucking go running out in the open. *Alone.* Are you out of your mind?" His hand motioned up and down to encompass my body, as he spat out, "You don't even have your phone on you."

"I was running. I don't take my phone running. Only my key. See," I unzipped the little pocket of my running shorts and took out my key to show him. While I knew his world was dangerous, I hadn't thought anything of going running like usual. Although, I'd witnessed the limitations put on Tasa, it would definitely be an adjustment for me.

He gazed down at me as if I'd lost my mind. "A key? That's it? I texted and called you and got no answer. *Nothing.* Panicked, I finally went to your house. Your dad told me you went out running. Thank fuck he knows the circuit you usually take." He looked like he was about to throttle me as he said in a low, pained tone, "Nina, if I didn't want you to take the subway alone, what in God's name would make you think it'd be okay to go running without a bodyguard in the middle of Queens?"

My breathing should have returned to normal, but I was still panting, anxiety bubbling in my chest.

"Christ, woman, I thought you had better sense than this." His voice turned guttural, "Violence, blood, death. They're a regular part of my life. At fifteen, I killed my first man, making me the equivalent of what you might know of as a made man."

"What happened?" I asked, dying to know more about him.

Alex gave me a sharp look. His eyes flickered away and then slashed back to me. "Fine, you want to know? It was in Romania. We were driving from my grandmother's village to the capital when our car was run off the road. There was a shoot-out. We held tight until we managed to pick off enough of the attackers and then the rest ran for a nearby forest. My father was shot in the leg, so he shouted at me and Luca to go after them."

His face grew still, a mask of serenity sliding over his features as if he wasn't discussing the killing of men. His voice turned eerily calm, almost monotone, and his eyes emptied of life. He was torpedoed back to that day as if the events were playing out before him. My heart ached, imagining Alex not much younger than Yo-Yo, living through the fear and panic of an attack.

"It was only me and Luca. We were out there for hours, creeping, stopping to listen for signs of them hiding, circling back and forth until we slaughtered them, one by one. An hour later, we captured the last one standing." There was a long pause. My breath faltered in my chest. Rapt by Alex's face, I saw the killer in him. Another creature stirred beneath his civilized suit, and it was not a pretty sight. Should I have been scared by that revelation? Probably, but life wasn't black or white. I'd also been on the receiving end of his protective, caring side. Seen him go to great lengths to care for his family, over the years. Witnessed his concern for Tasa. Those qualities compensated for the other, darker side of him.

Alex shook his head, breaking the spell. His eyes refocused on where he sat, in the back of his black Mercedes. "My father almost bled out that day. The wound was bad, and he had to wait until we came back with our quarry. Do you know why we kept the second man alive?" he asked in a wry tone.

I shook my head, fear slithering down my spine. I sensed I wouldn't like the answer, but if I was to be part of his life, it was time to woman up.

"Because we needed to torture him to find out who he worked for and who had tried to dispose of us."

"Who was it?" I squeaked out.

"The highest Roma gang in the country. A simple vacation to the old country, and they thought it was a prelude to us returning home to rule. That vacation turned into a bloodbath. It wasn't the only kill Luca and I would partake in for the next two weeks." He let out a weary sigh. "My life is brutal, Nina."

His hand shot out and captured my chin. He'd moved so fast I barely registered it until his fingers were griping me tight. "If you want to be with me, if you want to be part of my life, then you need to follow the rules. Starting today. You have to start thinking. While we might not be out as a couple yet, there are spies and snitches everywhere. *Everywhere*. Do you understand me?"

I nodded solemnly. I was touched that he was taking my safety so seriously. In truth, I hadn't even thought of him, or whether people knew about us when I stepped outside to run. While I had watched Tasa being trailed by a bodyguard most of my life, I had always done my own thing. Another pang of missing her reverberated through me. If she were here, she could've guided me through the pitfalls of her world. Instead, I'd have to navigate them on my own. And make mistakes, like the one I'd made today. Embarrassment burned through me. But I was determined to be with Alex, and I'd do whatever he asked of me. I certainly didn't want to complicate his already demanding life. My goal was to ease him of stress, not increase it.

"Good," he stated simply before his lips found mine. Dragging me over his lap until I straddled him, his tongue claimed and mated with mine. His erection grew until its hardness prodded my stomach, and I moaned, taking in his reassuring scent as I rubbed my belly against it.

Ending our kiss, he grabbed my ponytail and tugged my head back until we were at eye level. "Since I may not have been clear about the rules, let me define them now. You do not go anywhere outside alone. Ever. If you break that rule, you will be punished."

"Punished how?"

He groaned. "I'm a creative thinker. I'll come up with something, little girl." A twinkle entered his eyes as his hand landed a swat on my butt. "I'll start with paddling this sweet ass." His expression grew sober again. "I won't be the reason you get killed, Nina. I don't want to let you go, but if you don't follow my instructions, you won't leave me with a choice."

My heartbeat skittered in panic. I'd wanted him for so, so long, and for once, things were going my way. He was in my grasp, and there was no way I was letting him cut me off.

"Either you walk away now or you agree to take the consequences if you violate one of my rules. It's going to be a big adjustment for you, but this is nonnegotiable. I don't hide the way I live, and soon everyone will know who you belong to. So Nina, are you mine or not?"

"Yes," I hurried to respond. "Yes, I'm yours, and I'll do what you say."

There it was. My answer. My commitment. Even though I knew more than most what mafia life was like, this was still a huge change. But it was worth it to sit on Alex's lap and rub my mound against the underside of his cock. Not that this was only about the sex. Fantasies of Alex had populated my head for years. A little freedom in exchange for safety and to belong to this man seemed more than fair to me.

"Hmm," he hummed, his eyes dipping down to my splayed legs. "I've seen you go running over the years. I welcomed your outfits in the past, but I'm not so sure I appreciate them quite so much now. If this is what you wear in the winter, the summer months will drive me insane."

His finger dipped down the V of my shirt and traced the outline of my sports bra. An Alex-induced languor fell over me, like it always did.

"I get hot when I run, and I sweat," I explained.

"I have other activities in mind that will make you build up an even better sweat," he reflected aloud. He leaned forward, nuzzling into my hair. "I'll make you very sweaty, and then I'll lick it off. Taste you and consume you."

My heart pounded against my rib cage as if it were a trapped bird, wings beating against it to be set free. His lips grazed over mine before deepening the kiss when the car's forward movement stopped.

Ugh. We were home.

"I'm going over to the office and then my mother's for Sunday dinner. Get your stuff ready and text me. I'll have Stegan meet you at the door to take your luggage. Then stay with your family for the day and come over for dinner," he ordered.

I looked at him in horror. "What will your mother think?"

"I'm a grown man, Nina. I don't give a fuck what my mother thinks."

My fingers fiddled with his tie before smoothing down the long expanse of his chest, appreciating the fact that I could touch him whenever I had the urge. Appreciating the hard, defined muscles flexing under my hand. "Things are tense in my house right now. Yo-Yo and my mother are at each other's throats, and I'd rather avoid more drama, if possible. If your mother learns about us, she'll call my mother right after we leave."

He expelled a resigned sigh.

"It'd be different if we came out as a couple, but while we're doing this testing-period thingy…"

His fingers around my waist tightened as if he didn't like the reminder about our uncertain future, but I wasn't about to forget and allow myself to fall for him completely. It was bad enough that I was halfway there. It would be a knife to my heart to lose him after years of hopelessly pining away for him, especially when we barely began.

"Fuck," he muttered under his breath. Nodding tightly, he acquiesced with a question, "What do you suggest we tell her?"

"We could avoid dinner, and you can pick me up after you're done," I suggested.

"No," he clipped out. "I'm busy enough as it is. Sunday is the only day I take off, and it's already been marred with work. Normally, I'd say 'fuck it,' but none of us miss Sunday dinner unless we're on our deathbeds."

"Why don't you tell her I'm lonely and helping you find Tasa?"

"Fine," he agreed. "You know we sit down at seven, so come a little earlier." He took hold of my butt cheek and licked up the side of my throat. "How sore are you, firefly?" he asked, his tone hoarse with need.

I squirmed a little on his lap, eliciting a groan from him. "Not too bad. You can be quite gentle when you choose to be."

"What can I say? I'm a man of many talents."

I threw my head back and laughed. When my gaze returned to his face, his eyes were a smoldering hue of deep green.

"Now you can add deflowering a virgin to the list," I teased him.

He buried his face into the crook of my neck. "God-damn, it was hot as fuck taking that tight hole. Can't wait to get back in. Stretch it out a little more every time until it's molded to the size of my cock."

"That's going to take some time and lots of hard work," I rasped out. "Are you sure you're up to the challenge?"

"Oh, I'm up for it." He lifted his hips so I could feel just how *up* he was. "You tease, but this isn't a cock you want to do that with, firefly. I might have to wield it like a weapon and give you a lesson on who you belong to."

I swallowed around my suddenly dry throat. God, I loved it when he talked dirty. "How do you plan to do that?"

"I'll use everything I have. My fingers." His hand trailed up my thighs to the juncture. "My tongue." He opened his mouth and laved the sweat off my collarbone. "My cock." His palms wrapped around my upper thighs and dragged me closer until his cock dug deeper. Oh. God. I melted against him, getting wetter by the second. His touch was so affecting. Heat scorched every inch he grazed with his fingers or the tip of his tongue.

"Yes," I begged in a moan. "Please."

He laid kisses up my throat and along my jawline. "Soon, baby girl. Let's get through this evening, and I'll bring you home to my bed and tie you to it. Spread those firm thighs and lick into that honeyed pussy until you scream my name."

My chest swelled as I leaned into him, scraping his cock back and forth against me.

"Şef," came a voice through the intercom. "People are looking outside the window."

I pulled back with a long groan, quickly rearranged my clothes, and stumbled out of his car. The curtains flicked back into place, and I figured my mother hadn't seen enough to know what was going on. Giving Alex a saucy little salute, I jogged up the stoop and let myself into the house.

The thought of tonight's dinner rattled me. How was I going to make it through dinner at his *mother's* house after last night? His mother was lovely, but I'd never had to lie to her before. I'd just hooked up with her son and, after dinner, was returning to his penthouse where I'd sleep with him again, God willing. I had to remain stoic and keep my hands to myself, lest I slip and give anything away. Another horrifying thought popped into my head. What if she thought I had helped Tasa plot her escape? I groaned. This was going to be stressful. By the time I made it to the top of the stairs, my bouncy step had turned into a drag.

15

I was in my bedroom, gnawing on my thumbnail as I reviewed the dismal array of clothes in my closet, when I heard a soft knock at my door. Like a special ringtone, I knew it was Yo-Yo. My mother never knocked. She just entered, regardless of what I was doing. Sauntering in, my brother fell into the office chair at my desk and sprawled out his long legs like an overgrown colt.

"How can you stand sleeping in this room anymore? You're drowning in pink," he remarked with a shudder of his broad shoulders as he surveyed the pale-pink-and-white duvet, the matching pink of the curtains, and the pink pillows bordered in ruffles. While it was no longer my taste, I hadn't changed the decoration since high school, because Mother liked it. Both Tasa and I bemoaned our mother's horrid tastes in decorations. An additional reason for wanting my own home and family.

Giving him a light shrug, I said, "I live with Mother's taste here and Tasa's mom's decorating aesthetic in the city. Of the two, this one is more cheerful."

"Good point," he conceded.

Taking a pen from the penholder on my desk, he twirled it between his fingers and said, "I don't get it. He's as controlling as Mother. You're about to graduate and finally be free of every responsibility she's thrown at you and you go shackle yourself to a man? Especially him. Not only is he dangerous, but he screams control issues."

"Spying on me, were you?"

Putting aside my hopeless struggle to decide what to wear, I dragged out my suitcase and flung it open on the delicate pink-and-cream floral rug. Influenced by Tasa's mom, Mother went through a phase of investing in nice rugs. Which no one was allowed to walk on. Half our childhood had been spent skirting the rugs on the floor of the living room, even though we didn't walk with our shoes in the house. It was a huge moment when Mother had rolled out this rug for my sixteenth birthday.

He shrugged. "You're my sister. I knew something was up when you came in earlier, but what with the volcano downstairs, I couldn't bring it up. You're moving back into the city, aren't you?"

"I need a break. You're not totally wrong about Alex," I conceded, "but the difference is that he listens to me. He's not irrational. Quite the opposite, in fact. Getting him to embrace human emotions in his decision-making process is a challenge. Maybe I'm attracted to the controlling part of him, having grown up with Mother. But the big distinction is that I hold a degree of power. I've seen how my words impact his decisions."

"He makes you think you have a voice, but you don't," he countered in a grumpy tone. Like most almost-eighteen-year-olds, Yo-Yo thought he knew everything. I didn't bother to correct him. This wasn't his life; it was mine, and I didn't have to justify myself to him.

"Yo-Yo, you barely know him. When it came to Tasa, he listened to me."

"That only strengthens my argument. She ran away because he was so controlling of her. He lost his shit just because you guys went to a club."

"To be fair, we were two virgins at a sex club," I quipped.

He made a dismissive gesture. "Please, he managed every part of her life. Jesus, Nina, he was going to force her to marry some guy she didn't even care about."

"I regret telling you anything," I muttered.

He halted in the middle of twirling my pen and fixed his gaze on me. "Hey, you're not only my sister. You're my friend." Dropping my pen, he stood up and paced the length of my room. "He's not a good man. He's definitely a criminal, and he's most likely a killer. I mean, I might've been a kid, but I remember seeing the news after his father was gunned down on Queens Boulevard in broad daylight."

If my brother only knew the extent of the violence. Only moments ago, Alex had confided about his first killing. Or rather killings. My heart almost broke for him. A wave of protectiveness swept over me. He was just a kid, and he'd had to survive a shoot-out and hunt down the guys who tried to murder him, his brother, and his father. I shuddered. I couldn't imagine the kind of stress he lived with.

I plucked shirts and dresses off the hangers and dropped them on my pink bed. Canting my head to the side, I gazed down on the bedspread. Yo-Yo was right. It really was too much with the pink and ruffles and frills. I'd be embarrassed to have Alex in this room.

"Listen, I appreciate what you're doing, but you don't know Alex like I do. He'd never let anything happen to me."

Yo-Yo stood up, crossed my room, and flicked the curtain open. Taking a long moment to stare out the window, he disclosed, "There's a guy standing near our stoop. Is that the kind of life you want for yourself? You're so close to freedom. You can do whatever you want. Follow in Tasa's footsteps and get out of here instead of latching on to a guy who's going to keep your life small. Or worse, make it smaller than it already is." His head twisted over his shoulder, gaze burning with frustration. "Why would you do that?"

"For love."

There, I said it.

Yo-Yo's eyebrows hit the top of his hairline. "L-love?" he sputtered out.

I threw my hands in the air. "God, you're so thick sometimes. Love. I love him. I've loved him for *years,* and it was awful. I didn't have the guts to do anything about it while Tasa was here. I was loyal to her, so I pined away for him, watching from the corners and shadows. You talk about a small life? My life is expanding." I spread my arms wide to demonstrate how I felt. "I have a chance to come out of the shadows and live in the light. My life will grow. I will grow. And I want a family. My *own* family, based on love and mutual respect, not twisted control and manipulation like in our family."

His jaw dropped, his mouth hanging open. Walking toward me, he stumbled on the carpet. Righting himself, he plopped down on the edge of my bed and stared at me like I'd sprouted two heads and about half a dozen arms.

Carefully pulling out the delicate gold necklace from around my neck, I held up my grandmother's pale-green jade pendant for him.

"This." I shook the pendant at him. "This is why I'm certain of him. It wasn't long after his father was murdered that *Nana* died. He found me crying on the stoop after her funeral, holding on to her good-luck necklace. I was only his little sister's friend. He had no reason to come over and sit beside me on the stoop, but...he did. He held me as I cried into his shoulder and asked me what I was holding. When I told him she wore this necklace every day of her life, that she never took it off, he took it from me, told me to turn around and placed it around my neck. He made me promise to wear it in her memory and live like she would've wanted me to live. 'Don't let one day go to waste,' he said, 'and make sure to let her love guide you.'"

I'd been distraught that day. *Nana's* death had been sudden and Mother had fallen into a deep depression. Our grandmother was the heart of our family in many ways. She understood her daughter and comforted her when she became overly emotional. She also served as a buffer between our mother and us. Where my mother pushed, my grandmother soothed. Perhaps she and I got along so well because our personalities were similar. Her loss was deeply felt by everyone in the family, except maybe Yo-Yo, since he was still so young when she died. But my father and I definitely felt her absence, especially when Mother's anxiety ratcheted up.

"That had to be one of the most painful days of my life, and he was there for me. His words gave me strength and I fell in love with him that day. I've never taken this off since."

In my mind, it was as if *Nana* had willed his fingers to latch the thin, delicate chain around my throat. At the same time, latching my heart to him, years before lust made an appearance.

"I know this sounds weird, but it's as if *Nana* is guiding me even now. I may have lost Tasa, but I've gained something in exchange because I've wanted him for a very long time."

"Aww, fuck," he cursed, swiping his big hand over his face and tugging at his chin. "I had no idea."

"No one did. Not even him. Tasa was the only one who guessed, and she tried, in her own subtle way, to suggest that I do something about it, but I couldn't. Her arguments with Alex were epic, and I was afraid she'd feel betrayed."

"They couldn't be as horrible as the fights that go on in this family," he said with a snort of disbelief.

My lips twisted in a wry smile. "No, maybe not. Our fights are legendary. Pretty sure the whole neighborhood has heard the shouting coming from here."

"Fuck," he said again. Coming to stand in front of me, he placed one of his now-oversized hands on my shoulder and squeezed. "Be careful, girl. I won't survive if anything happens to you."

"Nothing's going to happen to me," I assured him, making a funny face and sticking out my tongue.

"Better not, or I'll hunt him down and kill him myself," he warned.

"Yo-Yo, you don't own a gun and wouldn't know how to use one even if you did."

He raised an eyebrow. "You doubt my skills? I'm a gangsta when I wanna be. I'll be his worst nightmare, his public enemy number one if he touches a hair on your head. Anyway, who says I need a gun? This is a lean, mean fighting machine," he said playfully, smacking himself in the chest. Yo-Yo had been taking tae kwon do for years, it was true, but he was no match for a grown man with the kind of strength I'd felt on Alex.

Not wanting to bruise his ego, I agreed, "Fine, you can be my avenger. Satisfied?" Testing one of his biceps, I made a little scoffing noise and joked, "You better get back to those weights if you plan on any one-on-one combat anytime soon."

"Funny. So fucking funny," he retorted as he sailed out of my room.

"Shut the door," I called after him. That boy always left the door open. This was the first time Yo-Yo had seen me with a man, and I was touched by his protectiveness. Even though I was usually the one looking out for him, it made me realize how lucky I was to have him. Tasa might love her brothers, and they certainly treated her like a princess, but she didn't have that kind of relationship with them. Not even Nicu, and he was her twin. In a more hopeful mood, I turned back to the closet to figure out what to wear for this dreaded dinner. *You know what they say...fake it till you make it.*

16

I t took a special kind of willpower to let Nina off my lap and watch as she traipsed up the stoop like a slim sprite, in her too-short shorts. Entering my family's home next door, I first stopped by the kitchen to let my mother know Nina was joining us for dinner. For Nina's sake, I gave her a vague excuse that she was helping me with Tasa. My mother gave me a startled look, but I didn't care. I wasn't about to pass up the opportunity to spend time with Nina, especially after the scare she gave me earlier.

Bunică shot me a too-perceptive look from the stove, where she was stirring something in a big cast-iron pot, but I purposely ignored her and marched out of the kitchen. My family could have left Sunnyside years ago, after my father established himself in the Romanian *mafie*. While Sunnyside was the center of Romanian immigrants on the East coast, it was an average middle-class neighborhood, and most families moved out as soon as they could. If they couldn't afford the Manhattan prices, they moved to Jersey, at the very least.

But Tata wanted to stay at the heart of his people. He

remodeled the existing structure of this house, giving my mother the massive kitchen she'd always wanted and adding a few bedrooms on the second floor. Buying the building next door, he'd converted it into a commercial space and opened the Dacia Café, settling his headquarters above it. That was the office I took over after his death. Even though I had the opportunity, I didn't move out. He always took pleasure in hearing Romanian intermingling with other Eastern European languages spoken by the old men and families that patronized the place. The café's baked goods became popular in the neighborhood, and there were always kids running in and out to buy sweetbreads, a couple of *papanași* donuts, or a slice of *Joffre* cake.

I trudged into the family room, where I ensconced myself to work. Normally, I used the office upstairs, across from Nina's bedroom, but that would've been too distracting. The family room had the added benefit of being located off the foyer, so I could hear the doorbell when it rang. Later, Nicu and Luca showed up and joined me on the couch to watch a soccer game. Just as I had commanded, Nina was at the front door before seven o'clock.

I went to open it myself so I could get a moment with her before dinner.

Fuck, but she was stunning. Peeling off her coat, I smoothed my hands down the sides of her formfitting black crêpe dress and buried my face in her shoulder, drawing in the decadent vanilla-jasmine fragrance that was quintessentially Nina. Just one whiff, and I was an addict. She probably thought I was insane, earlier today, when I'd pursued her like a madman as she finished her run. But when I watched her from the car, alone and exposed, all I could see was my father getting mowed down by bullets. After catching her, I'd reigned in my fury because I knew she hadn't countermanded my order on purpose, but fuck if it hadn't been a close thing.

"Goddamn, you smell so good," I murmured into her skin before taking a taste. Her head fell back, and she bared her throat to me like the good girl she was. I wanted to sink my teeth into her supple flesh, silky and smooth for the taking. "I can't wait to be inside you again, baby."

A throat cleared behind me, and I threw a glare over my shoulder at Nicu, who gave me a pointed look as he walked past. My mother and *Bunică* couldn't creep up on me like my brothers, so I wasn't too worried about them. I wasn't too worried, period. I was doing this for Nina, and Nina alone. Like I'd told her, I was a grown man, and a *șef* to top it off. I didn't do hiding.

"It's going to be a special form of hell, this dinner. How am I going to keep my hands off you," I confessed, my fingers digging into the flare of her hips from her small waist. "Or my mouth," I added, nuzzling her petal-soft skin, giving it a little nip for good measure. She jerked against me, which had me groaning against her when her ass pressed into my hard dick.

"For fuck's sake, will you stop," grumbled Luca as he turned away.

Suddenly, the only thing I wanted to do was get Nina back into her coat, whisk her right out the front door, and hustle her into the car parked at the curb. I was desperate to get her alone. I was ready to strap her to the bed and get back into that tight, hot clutch. Even more than the pleasure of fucking her, she settled my ruffles. When I was around her, something unexplainable filtered through me in a place deep down and brought me calm. That, in itself, was priceless.

What I felt for her was something I'd never felt before, suspiciously resembling love.

Love?

I should scoff at the notion. Hell, I couldn't afford that kind of sentiment. My family, my *clan*, required my undivided attention, not to mention arranged marriages to solidify alliances. Even if I managed to wiggle out of marrying Nelu's daughter, assuming Luca played nice, I was expected of marry someone from a consequential family. Again, frustration snapped at my heels like a snarling mongrel. I loved my position as *şef*. I was born for it. Was molded into it. It had always been my calling. I took the sacrifices I had to make in stride, like dropping out of Columbia University after Tata's death or starting a blood feud with the Bratva over it. Neither of those things were as hard as the possibility of giving up Nina.

"Like I said, a special hell," I murmured against the curve of her ear before pulling away and hanging her coat in the hallway closet.

My mother hustled down the wainscoted hallway from the kitchen, wiping her hands on her apron. Clasping Nina to her chest, she made soft cooing noises. My mother had always had a soft spot for Nina, and she wasn't one to suffer fools gladly. While she happily shared her role of matriarch with *Bunică*, she was a force to be reckoned with. She didn't wield her power often, but she was fearless when necessary.

In many ways, Nina conformed to her notions of how a girl should behave much more than her own daughter did. More than once, she'd chastised Tasa and thrown Nina in her face as an example of how a proper lady should act. And more than once, she'd taken Nina aside to get her to influence Tasa. Not that it did much good.

Watching them together, I was doubly glad I'd insisted

Nina come over. Her presence was a balm for my mother, and watching them together spread relief through my chest.

Pulling back to stare into Nina's deep brown eyes, my mother said, "I should've called you, checked on you, but I've been beside myself with worry over Tasa. How are you, child?"

"I-I'm managing," Nina stuttered. It pleased me to see how she struggled, knowing she was keeping something from my mother. If that was as good as she could do, I'd have no trouble catching her in a lie. Not that I expected her to lie or give me trouble. She ached to fulfill my wishes, to please me. One of the reasons we were so compatible.

Nina grasped my mother's arms and redirected the conversation, "How are *you* holding up?"

My mother wiped her brow wearily. "Oh, you know, I toss and turn throughout the night, thinking about what she must be going through. She's only twenty years old, and she's been pampered her entire life. What does she know of the dangers of the world? Nothing, that's what." Peering at Nina closely, she declared, "You didn't know anything about her plans, did you?"

"I did not," Nina confirmed. "You know I would've tried to talk her out of anything rash. That's why she hid it from me. If I thought she was going to do something like this, I would've told someone. She didn't want to put me in the position of betraying her." Nina's eyes dipped down, obviously disturbed by the idea that she might have had to make such a choice.

I stepped in and placed my hand on her upper arm, "But you didn't. You didn't betray her trust."

Her eyes lifted to mine, holding them. I read the dismay in them. The urge to bring her into my chest and kiss away her worries rode me hard.

"Didn't I, though?" she countered in a soft, hesitant voice.

"No," I replied firmly. "You did the right thing, Nina. Without you, we'd have no lead until it was far too late."

"What have you found out, Alex?" My mother's head whipped toward Nina. "Nina?"

"Come, let's get out of the hallway and sit down," I suggested, knowing that by moving us into the living room, my mother would go straight into hostess mode and back off from her interrogation. Nina already harbored enough guilt, as it was. She'd done the right thing, but she was loyal to a fault.

"Of course, of course," my mother said, ushering us into the living room. "Dinner will be ready any moment. Would you like a glass of something? Wine, perhaps?"

I gave my mother a warning look, but she ignored it. The European in her didn't factor in Nina's age when handing her a glass of wine, especially with a meal coming up. My parents had insisted on letting us take a taste of whatever they were drinking for as long as I could remember.

Nina glanced at me for permission. Pride bloomed behind my sternum. Choosing to be magnanimous, I turned to my mother and conceded, "Your house, your rules."

It's not as if it were the first time she drank in my mother's home.

"Good," she agreed, and hustled away for the kitchen.

Leading Nina to the sofa, I sat down beside her.

Turning to me, she said, "I thought you said I couldn't drink until my birthday."

"That was at my club. In public. Here, we're in the heart of my family. You'll be safe."

"Are you saying I wouldn't have been safe in your presence last night," she teased.

I leaned over and rumbled into her ear, "Baby girl, there are parts of you that will never be safe in my presence." Inching closer, I murmured, "Like that sweet pussy of yours. If I were to take you someplace and check on that delicious cunt, would you be primed for me?"

Her breath hitched, and a small shudder coursed through her.

I had my answer.

Pulling away to leave a decent amount of space between us, I laid my arm across the gilded wood of my mother's overwrought couch. The living room leaned toward the ornate baroque style. She always had a penchant for expensive old-world things, and it showed in the royal blue velvet and white damask couch on which we sat. Across from it stood a matching love seat and two upholstered chairs. The gold threads in the heavy brocade matched the gold of the carved legs of the marquetry-topped coffee table, the ornate credenza, and a set of intricately carved bookshelves. Then there were the heavy blue velvet curtains that contrasted with the exaggerated golden pattern of flowers, leaves, and cherubs of the wallpaper. At least the living room wasn't as bad as her decoration of Tasa and Nina's place or our house in Romania. Those were positively atrocious.

My mother came back, holding two large glasses of red wine and balancing a plate of appetizers. I rose to take the plate and one of the glasses from her.

"Here you go, the new Beaujolais Nouveau," she singsonged. Perching on the edge of the chair closest to the couch, she watched carefully as Nina took her first sip. She made a noise of pleasure that shot right to my balls. Christ, I swore to elicit the same exact sound from her beautiful throat when I got her alone.

My mother leaned back in satisfaction. "Good, isn't it? I

thought this year was particularly flavorful. Light and fruity."

"Delicious," Nina agreed.

Delicious, indeed. Fuck the Beaujolais. If only she knew how delicious *she* was. How when I dipped my tongue between her inner folds, her honey tasted *light and fruity.* How was I going to get through dinner?

My mother leaned forward and cupped Nina's cheek. Patting it gently, she murmured "At least I still have one daughter with me." Turning her eyes to me, she said, "Thank you for bringing her, Alex. You know my heart."

Nina shifted in her seat, uncomfortable again. She gave me a side-glance with an apology on her face. I took her hand and squeezed it briefly.

Nicu sauntered in at that moment, his gaze fixed on our joined hands. It darted over to my mother, who was watching us with soft eyes. I shook my head slightly to communicate that it wasn't what he suspected, reluctantly withdrawing my touch.

Noticing him, my mother stood and asked, "Would you like an aperitif?"

"Sure," he answered, taking a seat in an armchair.

She prepared him a small glass of Kir at the bar, placed it in his hand with a peck on the crown of his head, and left, reminding us that dinner would be ready soon.

A moment later, *Bunică* hustled in on her short legs, giving Nina a kiss on each of her cheeks. Although my grandmother was Tasa's number-one champion, she was also a great fan of Nina. She sat with us, assuring Nina that everything was fine with Tasa, until we were called to the dining room.

Luca wandered in at some point, stopping to give Nina a hug before getting his own drink. How had I not realized how loved she was? How established she was in my family? Of course, I noticed her in the past few years because of her beauty, but I suppose I had taken her for granted. Until now, I hadn't appreciated how much she was part of our family. It was an impressive feat. We were a fiercely private family. While we were model hosts with visitors, we didn't open our hearts easily. Yet she'd already captured them. She was certainly close to capturing mine.

During dinner, I had to suffer under *Bunică's* glare as I relayed to my mother the information about Tasa's dance workshop and the steps I was taking to search for her, both in Montreal and along the corridor leading from the city to Canada.

I was almost done summarizing my meeting with Nelu, avoiding the subject of offering up Luca as the groom, when my mother suggested, "Why don't you take Nelu's girl as your wife?"

Nina stiffened beside me, at the long wooden table. My stomach pitched. I slipped a hand underneath the jacquard tablecloth and wrapped my fingers around the curve of her knee.

"*Mama*," I started in warning.

The woman was obsessed with marrying us off.

"What? You're almost twenty-nine years old, Alex. I already had you and Luca by the time I was your age."

"The family needs me," I replied, my fingers tightening as Nina's thigh trembled beneath my touch. Visceral disgust smoldered inside me for putting her through this. Nina didn't deserve to hide. Although it had been her suggestion, the cause behind it was my inability to claim her outright. It was because of me that she was being placed in a position of disrespect, a position which both my brothers were keenly aware of.

I'd apologize later, but the point was to protect her from such things. I already knew she'd reply that there was no need to apologize, that she trusted me implicitly, but that would do nothing to assuage my guilt.

"Hush with that excuse. The family also needs you to marry a good Romanian girl," she replied firmly. "I need grandchildren, especially now that Tasa's marriage is in the gutter."

Nina cringed at the words *good Romanian girl*. And for good reason.

Nicu attempted to divert my mother's attention, but she was like a dog with a bone when she got onto the subject of marriage. Jesus, this was what Tasa had to put up with constantly. I was getting but a small taste of what my sister dealt with these past years.

My skin crackled under my mother's criticism.

"Mama," I replied sharply, "I'm a man and head of this family. I'm not Tasa. I will not be spoken to as if I'm some child."

My mother took in a quick breath, and I shifted my eyes off her. Focusing on the pale-green vines of the wallpaper, I worked to regain my temper. Nina froze underneath my touch. Her eyes swung and stayed on me. She'd never heard me raise my voice. Each of us had that infamous Balkan temper, but I rarely lost it, outside of arguing with Luca and Tasa.

"Let the boy alone, Marina. Tasa is gone. I know what an embarrassment this is for you, but you cannot turn on the boy. He's doing the best he can to fix this, and he's already dealt with Nelu, which is a miracle in itself."

Bunică, thank fuck, swooped in to save the day. Her eyes pierced me before shifting to Nina and then back to me. That wily woman knew something was up, and every cell in my body urged me to take ownership of Nina in front my family. My muscles tensed, as if poised to go into battle, but *Bunică* defused the tension by tutting my mother as if to chastise her gently.

Shuffling over to me, she patted my hand and then scooped out *mămăligă*, or polenta, from a big pot cradled in the crook of her arm.

Leaning over, she shoved a dish of feta closer to my plate, knowing I always added some crumbles to my polenta. "He's a good boy. Lots of pressure on his head." Waving her hand to encompass Luca and Nicu, she asserted, "They're all good boys. They'll get married when they're ready, and I bet it will be faster than you think." She cast a glance at my hand on Nina's knee just as I forced myself to drag it away. "You'll have the big wedding celebration you've been dreaming about. Don't *worry*."

"Of course," mumbled my mother, her gaze back to the meal as she slowly resumed cutting into her sausage.

Christ, I hungered to scoop Nina into my arms and whisk her out of there. My family was always a mixture of push and pull, comfort and irritation, but at that moment, the disappointment oozing out of Nina and my mother, although for different reasons, was suffocating. I'd made many difficult decisions during my time on the throne, but this was by far one of the more challenging ones. On one hand was the duty to my clan. The duty to use marriage as a way to consolidate power or solidify a strategic position. Love had nothing to do with it. On the other was Nina. My heart was tied to her. I imagined her sitting beside me, as she was now, at a family dinner but with my hand publicly displayed on her swelling belly. My brows drawing together, I shuttered my eyes. What kind of choice was I being forced to make, between family and love?

※※※

AFTER WHAT FELT like a never-ending dinner, I finally managed to hustle Nina out of my mother's house. Back in my apartment in Manhattan, I carried her suitcase straight into my bedroom, so there would be no misunderstanding about my intentions, and deposited it near my walk-in closet, where I had made space for her.

She'd followed me silently, hands clasped behind her. Nodding attentively, she listened while I showed her where to put away her stuff.

Pulling her into my arms, I said, "I know what you're going to say about dinner. That you understand my reasons for not claiming you in front of my mother. Believe me, I fucking *hated* seeing you in that position," I emphasized. "Not only did it hurt you and put you in an untenable position, but it made me feel less of a man."

Her head flicked up at that, brows drawn together in the most adorable expression of confusion. "Why would you feel that? You're beholden to others. You don't live solely for yourself and what you want."

"Fuck that," I persisted, my breath picking up a bit. "A man makes choices and stands by them. I don't give a damn about marrying a good Romanian girl."

"You felt differently, not so long ago," she reminded me.

A burn of shame crashed through me. Yes, yes, I did. It was one of the rationales I gave Tasa to press her into marriage. That she had to follow tradition and marry within our society. It wasn't only about being Romanian but being

Romanian *mafie*. Tasa could never simply marry an average Joe. She had to marry someone who could protect her from the dangers of our life. My father was gunned down by the Bratva, which was the motivation for my deep hatred of the Red Mafia. And he'd been a *şef*. A boss. If that could happen to him, then an innocent girl like Tasa was vulnerable.

I tried to explain to Nina, "With Tasa, it was about protection, and I suppose I trust a Romanian *mafie* before any other kind of made man."

"You're backtracking," she chided softly as she pulled away gently and sat on the edge of my large bed.

Not liking the distance between us, I took a seat beside her and brought her into my arms again. "Yes, I pressured her into an arranged marriage, but my primary motives were her security and marrying someone who'd fit into my family. Not only my nuclear family but the entire Lupu clan."

Folding one leg beneath her, she shifted toward me, "And what about for you?"

Time for the truth. I owed her that much, at least.

"For me? I want you. But until I'm sure we can be together in the right way; my hands are tied. Believe me when I tell you I feel like a man in chains. A captive to my family and my world. Despite the perks of being in charge, I resent it deeply. It's the first time the expectations of my family have conflicted with my own desires over something serious," I confessed.

"I understand," she replied softly, her gentle hand cupping my cheek.

A cheerless laugh escaped. "I knew you'd say that, and it makes me want to punch a wall. You shouldn't have to settle for less, Nina. Christ, look at you. Not only are you drop-dead gorgeous but you're perfect. My family fucking loves you. And," my voice dropped an octave, "you gave me your virginity. That bound me to an oath, and I don't break my oaths."

"There's the oath you gave to the Lupu," she prompted.

"And that's the rub, but I will figure it out, Nina. I swear, if you afford me a bit of time, I will find a solution."

"I trust you," she replied.

"Christ, don't say that. I don't deserve your trust so easily. I'm a ruthless bastard in every other aspect of my life."

"But not to me. You've only shown me kindness, and that's what I'll base my decision on. I'm not wrong, I know it," she replied with a vehemence that took me by surprise. If she trusted me to find a way for us, then dammit, I'd find it. I was already close, so close. Once Luca agreed to marry the Popescu girl, we'd be golden. But what if he didn't? Unlike Nicu, Luca couldn't be counted on. Where would that leave Nina and me? Nowhere I wanted to dwell on tonight.

It'd been a long and trying day, and I was done talking for the night.

Standing from the bed, I took a step back and commanded, "Pull up your dress."

Her gaze flickered away for a half second and came back to me. Like a scent in the air, she felt the shift between us. We had gone from her consoling me to me preying on her. She was right to sense danger because I was in the mood to dominate this little girl. Bravely, she swallowed before rising to her feet. Taking a firm hold of the hem of her dress, she slowly dragged it up to show me a stunning view. The sexiest little scrap of emerald-green silk and lace contrasted sharply against the glowing pale smoothness of her skin. Along with the matching set of garters and a pair of see-through black stockings, she was quite a sight. Christ, this woman was conjured from my dirtiest fantasies, with her oversized tits, trim waist, and slim hips, encased in brilliantly colored silk. I liked that she had a penchant for sexy, luxurious underthings, and I'd make sure to cover her in silk, satin, and lace.

"Take it off," I rasped out as I stripped off my jacket and let it fall to the floor. I began to unbutton my shirt as she swooped the dress up and over her head. Clutching it tightly to her chest, she watched as the buttons of my dress shirt flew open, exposing more and more of my chest.

"Down," I demanded roughly, signaling to her hands.

Stretching her arms out, she dropped the dress to the floor.

A matching set. She was wearing a matching set; the bra of emerald silk and lace cupped her full tits.

"The bra. Off."

She unclasped it. The straps slid down her arms and tumbled to the plush dark-blue carpet at her feet, leaving her only in her emerald-colored panties and shoes. Feeling awkward perhaps, she cupped her elbows and hugged herself, which pushed those lush breasts up. That elicited a deep moan from me. I was starting to feel feral. Her gorgeous tits did it for me every time.

Stalking her, I walked her backward until the back of her legs hit the edge of my bed. She sank down onto the mattress, her arms flying back to catch herself.

Stripping off the rest of my clothes as if they offended me, I returned to her, my hard, demanding cock vibrating just inches from her mouth. Dragging my knuckles down her cheek, I relished the light flush creeping up her throat and down her rack. Each time we've been together, her responsiveness had been an aphrodisiac.

Head tilted back, her eyes flared wide with excitement

and a tinge of fear. To distract her, I began to stroke my cock. Nice, hard strokes. Captivated, her eyes followed the movements of my hand. I caught drops of pre-come bubbling up from the slit of my crown and lathered my shaft on a down swipe. She squirmed her tight ass on the bed beneath me.

"Open those beautiful legs for me," I urged her.

Obeying, she promptly showed me the few dark curls she had above her mound. The dew glittering on her lips made her pussy seem more innocent than it had been since its initiation to my cock.

"Touch yourself."

Her fingers slipped down, trembling slightly, but her glazed-over eyes fixated on my cock told me she was more than ready for me.

"Stroke in," I directed.

Two slim fingers swirled around her little nub a few times before sliding in deeper between her pussy lips, and swear to God, I almost came right then and there.

"Do you pleasure yourself, firefly?"

"A bit."

"With your fingers or with toys?"

"Both."

I groaned, deep and low.

My eyes shot to her suitcase. "Did you bring them with you?"

A husky laugh slipped past her lips.

"No," she said with an edge of shyness.

"Oh, but you will. Next time you go home."

Her fingers stopped.

"Did I tell you to stop stroking, sweetness?"

She immediately resumed her movements, but a small notch developed between her delicate dark brows.

"What is it?" I demanded.

"I don't think they will impress you. My toys. You're bigger than they are."

"Maybe I'll use them to take that virgin ass," I mused.

Her eyes shot to mine, and I chuckled. "I'll be taking everything, baby. If...you choose to be my good girl."

"I'm not sure I want to be your good girl, then," she countered, peeking up at me with a mixture of shyness and greediness that drove me insane. Did she have any idea how she tortured me?

"Oh, but you can't help it, firefly. You crave to do my bidding. Crave to please me. Look how well you take directions," I said with a chin lift toward the fingers in her cunt.

Her head dropped back, baring the long column of her throat to me. "Alex, stop teasing me," she whined softly.

She was right, of course. Building up anticipation, I was keeping her suspended. Lying down on my king-sized bed, my back resting against the white leather of the headboard, I patted my lap. "Come and take what you want."

Twisting around to follow me with her gaze, she inhaled sharply. "I don't know how."

"Time you learn." Patting my thigh again, I said, "Saddle up."

Her eyes sparkled with interest. The shy little minx was intrigued, that much was obvious. Crawling over the bed, the soft curves of her hips swayed from side to side like a sleek feline. Fuck, but she was sexy. I'd had many a woman. Many of them were beauties. But Nina, with her sultry body interlaced with innocence, made for a heady combination. Now I understood why people mixed more than one drug, like cocaine *and* heroin. Her body was the rush of coke, but her soul was like an opiate to my soul. There was no going back because, having tasted the combination, I was addicted to both.

Rising to her knees beside me, she gracefully swung one leg over my hips, until she was hovering above my stiff shaft. Her hands came to either side of my head, palms against the headboard.

"Show me your moves," I commanded. My tone was unnecessarily sharp, but I couldn't help it. My inner dominant had been let out of its cage. Although my instinct was to slam her down on my cock in one fast plunge, I was determined to give her the space to learn on her own, so I refrained from touching her. This was her move.

And show me, she did.

First, it was her lips on mine. She tasted sweet from the after-dessert liquor she'd sipped from my glass. Her hands speared into my hair, twisting strands between her fingers and yanking on them as she pressed her slick opening onto my rigid cock, her mouth gaping in unadulterated lust as I thrust gently into her. Her back arched as she shifted this way and that, attempting to adjust to my thickness. Fuck, her sheath was tight. Watching her wet cunt struggle to take all of me edged me close to delirium. As she slipped down another inch, I gave her a swift slap on her ass, a quick little reprimand for making me feel so good.

She jerked forward, her thick breasts swaying in front of me, and I buried my face in between those pillows of flesh. My tongue came out in fighting mode, shooting this way and that, tasting the sweet saltiness of her skin until it found a nub and sucked. My ministrations were an incentive for her, and she took a big plunge, impaling herself on my cock.

Crying out, her nails scraped down my flanks, urging me to grab her by the waist and fuck her down on me. I reeled it back just in the nick of time, taking out my frustration on her nipple. Her punctuated pants blew across my shoulder as she caught her breath. This couldn't be completely comfortable for her, feeling as full as she did, but my heart filled with pride. She resembled a beautiful nymph above me, perspiration dotting her skin, long strands of dark hair cascading over her shoulders.

Popping off her nipple, I leaned back to get a good look at her flared pussy lips stretched wide around the base of my cock, a sight I knew I'd never tire of.

"Ride me. I wanna watch you ride me," I gritted out in a voice rough as gravel.

And she did. This untried, inexperienced woman drew herself up, leaving my cock slick with her juices and seated herself back down. Up and down, in slow, luxurious movements, she took me in, her tits bouncing in my face. I sucked one nipple into my mouth and moaned around the taste of her tight bead. My body shuddered as I rocked my hips slowly upward with each of her downstrokes. Goddamn, the tingling at the base of my spine and the pressure in my balls were both a revelation and supreme torture.

She kept that leisurely pace, teasing, testing, goading me to break. I held on as long as I could, even after she figured out how to grind down on me, drawing a tortured groan out of me every time. Testing her myself, I plucked her nipples and nipped at her throat, but she held steady, the strong girl. The notion crossed my mind that this woman's willpower could very well outmatch my own.

Finally, finally, it was too much. The charge at the base of my spine ignited. My balls felt like they'd burst at any moment. Finally surrendering to my inner beast, I exploded into a flurry of moves.

Taking her by the waist, I slammed her down as I thrust upward, hard and fast. I set a relentless pace, giving us the friction we both needed. Head flung back, she desperately screamed out my name, more guttural than language. Her pussy clamped down on me, sucking me off, that tight little cunt demanding every last drop of come. And I gave it to her. God almighty, but I made it my mission in life to do so.

In a sudden move, I brought her down on her back and pistoned into her sweet heat. The tight pulse of her flesh wrapped around mine was too much as she milked me, and I thrust hard as I emptied myself. Her sweet body gave little jerks and twitches.

Breathing heavily in the crook of her neck, I clipped a sliver of skin to mark her. She tried moving away from the sharp pain, but I stayed on her, laving it soothingly. I was a greedy bastard. It was never more evident than at that moment, knowing that my brand would be nice and dark by morning. But my anxiousness over our future drove me to fuck her hard, mark her, and leave whatever imprint I could.

17

Two weeks had passed since I moved in with Alex, and I was in paradise. The days flew by as I attended school, with a bodyguard discreetly following me to my classes, and studied at the library afterward. He went to work, doing whatever it was he did during the day. Weekend nights were spent at his club, and Sunday dinner was at his mother's. Outside of that, the time was our own. It would've been perfect if I didn't volley back and forth between two different realities, torn between dreaming of a future between us and fighting with myself to smother any unrealistic hopes.

Stretching in his large and luxurious bed, I woke up with aching muscles after another vigorous night. It was particularly hard, waking up surrounded by his scent, not to succumb to imagining that this could be our life. Beams of sunlight seeped through the chinks in the Venetian blinds. Lifting my head, I found Alex, wearing a pair of perfectly fitted pants that tapered slightly down to his ankles. His naked, broad back was to me, and he spoke softly into his cell phone. The lilting sounds of Romanian, a

Romance language similar to Italian and Portuguese, danced in the air like dust motes on a lazy Sunday afternoon.

Shrugging on a crisp light-blue shirt, he buttoned it up and strapped on a holster before bending down to a safe hidden in the bureau beneath the plasma TV hanging on the wall. There was one thing I could say about that TV. I'd never watched more soccer in my entire life than I had in the past two weeks. There was always a soccer game humming in the background, whether on the TV, a laptop, or coming from his phone. He pressed his thumb on a small pad, and the door swung open. Crouching, he slipped a gun out and tucked it into his holster.

After a few bouts of sex last night, he'd left me boneless to take care of business, armed to the teeth with guns and knives. While I didn't like him leaving in the middle of the night, I cuddled into the warm covers he'd tucked around me and fell back asleep, not even hearing when he returned.

The man didn't seem to need much sleep. From what I'd gathered, he rarely slept more than five hours. Six, tops, if I'd really worn him out. He was a machine, constantly fielding calls, working throughout the day, coming in and out during the night. He was so capable and responsible. Pride filled me that I was with someone who took care of things, including myself, so thoroughly.

By the brightness from the thin rays of light coming through the blinds, it was already midmorning. I shifted and flinched at the twinge between my legs, quickly followed by the chafe on my backside from the little spanking I got yesterday. Our playing in bed had gotten rougher. Not that I was particularly surprised. Alex oozed dominance, and while I hadn't heard about his tastes before, I was sure that was partly what drew me to him. Everything we did, even when it elicited a frisson of fear, left me in a puddle of need at his feet.

Seeing me awake, he came toward me. My gaze dropped to his strong hands, and I felt...swoony thinking about how they'd pummeled my behind. God, I was getting wet. Seeing his strength, I only thought of when he'd next get to use it on me.

It was times like these when I missed Tasa most. We'd gab about my situation with Alex, sifting through the range of conflicting thoughts I had. Of course, I understood why she'd left the way she did, but she was my person. There was a dull ache left behind at her absence. Several times a day, my thoughts drifted to her, wondering where she might be, how she was doing, or thinking of something I'd talk to her about.

In the end, I knew the advice she would've given me about Alex. Not to blindly follow society and its stupid rules. If it made me feel good to be with him, then I should enjoy myself and not overthink it. She'd remind me I was strong enough to stick up for myself if he did something I really didn't like. What she wouldn't need to remind me of was that Alex would never intentionally hurt me. Only for play and in the name of the game when we gave each other mutual pleasure.

Taking a knee at my side, he brushed his lips against my temple. "Who's the birthday girl today?" he crooned.

I blinked up at him, swallowing hard.

He'd remembered. We hadn't spoken of it since the night I lost my virginity to him, and I hadn't brought it up. While our intimacy had deepened, nothing about our relationship had changed on the outside. I'd still lied to his mother the last two times I went to Sunday dinner. No wanting my birthday to become a flash point, I'd refrained from bringing it up. It was painful, but I wanted to be realistic, if nothing else, so I went on the assumption that I would celebrate it with my family alone that evening.

"Thank you," I mumbled. Afraid to bring up the subject of "us," I watched his face carefully for any clues as to what he was thinking.

Opening the nightstand of bleached wood framed in lapis lazuli, he pulled out a flat velvet box.

My eyebrows lifted in surprise, and I struggled to prop myself up against the headboard.

"What is this?" I asked in a hushed tone, somewhat cowed by the gesture.

"Open it," he said with a nod.

I gently creaked open the velvet box and tilted my head to snatch a peek.

My gaze jumped to his, and I smacked the lid down.

"You can't be serious."

He gave a light chuckle, as if he hadn't just offered me an unbelievable rare luxury. Sitting on the bed beside me, making it dip to one side, he placed his large warm hand over mine. *There's no way... He couldn't possibly...* My thoughts flew away like wisps of smoke in the air.

Tugging the jewelry box out of my tight hold, he snapped it open. Shards of light fell on a jade cabochon shaped in the head of a Lupu wolf dangling from the center of a thin gold neck cuff.

"Th-that's imperial jade," I stammered out. Anyone who knew jade knew it was the most valuable form of jadeite, it was that recognizable. Its color and transparency rivaled the finest emeralds and was highly prized in China. The thing cost tens of *thousands* of dollars.

One of his eyebrows tilted up. "You know it?" he asked mock-innocently.

"Yes, of course, I *know* it."

"Then you like it? I want you to like it," he murmured.

"Of course, I like it. It's gorgeous, but it's too much—"

"Don't say it's too much for you. If you don't accept my gift, it will hurt my feelings. My ego will be bruised," he said with a playful pout although his gaze pinned me in place, hinting at his unwillingness to compromise.

I could never deny him the pleasure of giving me a gift. Lowering my gaze, I took in the splendid hue of green. It was unbelievably beautiful. More than that; it was an incredibly thoughtful gesture. He already knew I loved jade, and this was the most exquisite jade available, aside from the fact he'd personalized it.

Yet, it did nothing to settle the many questions running through my mind about us. He'd given me a stunning and meaningful present, yes. To wear this cuff, with the Lupu wolf, was a kind of claiming, and I should be relieved by it.

But...I knew what few others did. To be genuinely accepted into his family and clan, a woman would've had that same exact head *tatted* on their skin. Permanently. The ultimate gift, the one that eluded me most, was for him to brand me as his forever.

While the necklace was striking, it fell short of his true mark of ownership.

I tried my best to take our time together day by day. *Don't focus on what you can't change,* I reminded myself. *Focus on the time we have together.* It was undeniably a step in the right direction, but it left me feeling a bit empty. It was as much a reminder of what I wasn't as it was a statement of what I was. I knew he cared for me. But did he love me? It was too soon to expect so much, but I longed for it. I yearned for it *all,* dammit, and the Lupu wolf inked on my skin would've been the absolute answer I wanted.

Swallowing around the tightness of my throat, I smiled up at him.

"It's the Lupu wolf," I said, holding back the silly tears that burned behind my eyes. "I love it. Would you put it on me?"

I turned around and heard clinking sounds as he lifted the necklace. Then the cool weight of the jade and gold settled around the base of my throat. I kept very still for him to clasp it behind me, my fingers tracing the delicate indentations of the jade wolf head.

"You'll wear it tonight," he said matter-of-factly.

Shit, he assumed we'd be celebrating together, but not wanting to assume we would, I'd told Mother I'd stop by.

Glancing over my shoulder, I muttered, "M-my mother has something special planned at home. It's family tradition. She makes *mee sua* from scratch. It's a traditional homemade noodle soup she only makes on birthdays."

It hurt to not invite him, but how could I when nothing was definite between us? He could feel my tension, and his warm fingers gently kneaded the tight muscles of my shoulders. The woodsy scent of his cologne, combined with the underlying hint of musk that was all him, wafted into my nostrils and I inhaled him deeply into my lungs.

Now I wished I hadn't been a coward and had brought up my birthday earlier. In an ideal world, I'd bring him home with me, the way normal couples would. But we weren't a normal couple, and that reminder was like a knife slicing through my heart. *This* was why I avoided thinking about my birthday. The more time we spent together, the more I yearned for something permanent. Like the wolf tat, like celebrating milestones. *Fuck!*

His warm breath by my ear brought on a shudder as he

said, "You go to your mother's house. Afterward, we'll have a special celebration. Just the two of us."

His fingers reached up and tangled with my hair. Fisting it, he pulled my head back as he slid his warm, moist lips up my throat and clipped my earlobe. "Make sure you don't overindulge because I'll be filling your belly with something special. Something that's all me."

I think I had a mini orgasm right then and there, just from his scent, from his hold on my hair, and those filthy promises falling from his lips.

With that, he released my hair and moved off the bed, leaving me feeling bereft. He walked into his closet and came back out, shrugging on a dark-colored jacket that was a perfect match for the blue of his shirt and tie.

"Stegan is on another assignment, and Nikki is off, searching for Tasa, so Tomas is with you today. Text me toward the end of your birthday dinner. I'll be at the office, waiting for you." He dropped a kiss on my lips. "We'll go from there," he finished, and was out the bedroom door in the blink of an eye. I flipped the bedcovers off me and padded after him, watching as he collected his laptop and slipped it into a briefcase.

I followed him to the front door and gave him a final kiss.

"Be my good girl and lock it behind me. I don't want Tatum wandering in," he ordered, and then, *poof*, he was gone.

Before stepping into the shower, I tried taking off the cuff, but it had a strange mechanism that was impossible to maneuver. Rats, I was stuck with this luxurious necklace around my throat for the day, and I had a sneaking suspicion he'd done it on purpose.

18

Fuck, *it was hard leaving her.*

The warmth of her supple body, unconsciously leaning back into me when I fastened the cuff around her delicate neck. The little hiccup in her breathing when I laved her throat, and the tiny gasp when I nipped her earlobe. Everything about her screamed at me to take, take, *take*. Yesterday should've been an all-nighter, what with the first shipment of Nelu's product coming in, but I couldn't stay away.

Nina in my bed had to be the most enticing fucking temptation I'd ever had to deal with. Spending the evening with her, fucking her tight clutch, then forcing myself out of the warmth of our bed to drive over to the port in Newark and make sure everything was running smoothly was sheer fucking agony.

Leaving Tatum to keep watch, I'd returned to Nina for a few hours. And now I had to leave her once again, after seeing the Lupu wolf dangling from the cuff at her neck. Fuck, but the image of my family crest swinging from her throat was almost too much. It reared up my most possessive traits. I wanted to watch in the mirror as I mounted her from behind and gave her a hard fuck with my hand wrapped around her throat, the wolf banging against her from the power of my thrusts.

Instead, I forced myself out the door and made my way to our warehouse underneath the Brooklyn-Queens Expressway, near Calvary Cemetery.

I saw the sadness coat her eyes when she looked at the cuff. The disappointment. I'd given many presents to many women over the years, but unlike any of the others, Nina knew about our tat and what it meant. She knew too much about our ways in general, so there was no hiding from her.

Still, I had hoped to make a point with the jade piece carved into the symbol of our clan. Although we had yet to acknowledge what we were to each other, there was more between us than three little words like "I love you." It was deeper than that. Our souls spoke to each other. Not only did I want to cuff her with the Lupu, I wanted my tat inked above her heart. I wanted her draped in clothing with the Lupu emblem repeatedly stamped on it, like Coach or Gucci. I wanted to see her fitted in the Lupu from head to toe.

My mouth twisted in a smirk as I reached the parking lot underneath my building and strode to my Porsche. She was going to have a little surprise when she tried to take the cuff off. It wasn't coming off without my help. I hadn't missed the way she'd assumed I wouldn't show up at her family's birthday party. She wasn't wrong, which had pissed me off even more. There was no doubt I wanted to claim her publicly, which was why she would be unable to take it off. She'd have no choice but to wear it to her parents' home. It'd be interesting to see how she handled it. Would she attempt to hide my mark or give in to me and flaunt it?

"*Mee sua*."

The foreign sounds fell from my lips as I slipped into the driver's seat. Another thing I loved about Nina was that she was a first-generation American, like me. We both straddled the demands of more than one set of cultural expectations, but our lives were also richer for it. Suddenly, I wanted very much to be there and slurp on her mother's noodles. I wanted to know every little thing about Nina. In my hubris, I'd thought I knew most everything there was to know, what with her being present on the sidelines of my life for so long. Those two little words made me realize that there was so much I didn't know, and that—that was unacceptable.

Driving out of the underground parking lot onto 59th Street, I headed east toward the Queensboro Bridge to get to the warehouse. The first shipment had gone off without any glitches, establishing the partnership with Nelu. After siphoning off half the product straight out of Afghanistan to my suppliers in Europe, I tried a new route to move the rest of the load through North Africa, from where it was shipped to Jersey. Considering everything went as planned, I was satisfied.

The only thorn in my side was Luca, who was still holding out on me with respect to Nelu's daughter. Nelu had upheld his part of the contract, so time was running out. I felt like a convicted man being led up to the electric chair. Fucking hell, that brother of mine better come through. His behavior was frustrating on a good day, but now my life depended on him, and the sense of powerlessness was grating.

I checked the crates stocked with burlap sacks filled to the brim with the small sticks of the grayish-green ephedra shrub. I had plans to set up meth labs in Romania and Moldova to turn it into crystal meth and then distribute it to the Russian Federation and Western Europe. But first, I wanted to have some brought to me. We'd cook it up here so I could better understand the product.

I supervised distribution to the RVs and vans used as cook labs that traveled around rural Jersey and Pennsylvania to avoid detection and capture by the DEA.

Done with my responsibilities at the warehouse, I drove to the Dacia Café to finish paperwork and wait for Nina. Nicu stopped by for a game of chess. I had a little table set up with an antique chess set that had been in the family since the 1800s. We usually played at least once a week, leaving the pieces in place if we had to pause and take care of business. When he was younger, Nicu had once tried to trick me by switching up the pieces. It was the first time I'd laid my hands on him. Not only was it a dishonorable act, but it was an act of betrayal specifically directed toward me, the *şef*. I remembered his young tearstained face, staring up at me with dismay and regret, but I couldn't show pity. I had to take Tata's place.

Many people envied my position. Coveted it. But they rarely delved into the difficult aspects, which included disciplining my siblings or pressuring them to make decisions for the good of the family.

In the waning light of the setting sun coming through the windows, we launched into a new game. Nicu glanced up from the chessboard and grumbled, "Do I really have to finish college?"

"Did you really ask me that? Organic chemistry with a minor in chemical engineering will come in handy for the business, you'll see. You're lucky I'm leaving it at an M.A. after you're done with college and not pushing you to go for your PhD. This concession is for you. I'll have to forgo my dream of calling *someone* in this family 'doctor' before I die."

"You're not going to die anytime soon," Nicu quipped, standing to click on a floor lamp I had placed nearby. The artificial light flooded the room, glinting off the ivory pieces of the chessboard.

"I will die one day. It's the natural course of life that I should die before you, but hopefully, I'll manage to live a little bit longer. At least until you graduate with a masters in hand."

"You don't have one," Nicu accused.

"Only because when Tata died, I couldn't head the family, keep the businesses afloat, and keep our enemies at bay while completing a degree. We're not like made men who drop out of high school and can barely write their own names. Why do you think we play chess?" I gestured to the half-emptied chessboard. "And not bocce like the old Italian men?" Not bothering to wait for an answer, I continued, "Because living by your wits and savagery isn't going to cut it in this day and age. What sets us apart is our strategy and sophistication. It's what will *always* set us apart. We have the high skill sets of the Russians with the undying familial loyalty of the Latins. We represent the best of both worlds, forged into something quintessentially unique. And what is that, Nicu?"

"Blood," he rasped out.

"Exactly. We make the blood oaths of the good fellas and the Red Mafia look like paper cuts. We live and die by blood. It's the Dracula in all of us that the Romanians tapped into in the fifteenth century. Dracul the Impaler was the cruelest ruler because he took whatever punishments his enemies dealt him and returned them tenfold. He understood the power of blood, the symbolic energy of shedding blood for acts of disloyalty and disrespect."

Waving a knight he was about to move, Nicu expelled a

heavy breath and interrupted, "Come on, Alex, enough with your twisted history lesson. I get it, I get it. I'll finish my degree."

I cracked a smile and chuckled lightly as I moved my rook and swiped his knight off the board. "Bedtime stories is all they are."

"What about Luca? Are you any closer to convincing him to take the daughter for his wife?"

I stood up and stalked to the credenza that held bottles of liquor and poured myself a glass of bourbon. Lifting the bottle, I silently asked Nicu if he'd like one, but he shook his head. Returning to the oxblood leather seat, I swirled the liquor a few times before bringing it to my lips. The taste of vanilla and caramel, mixed with charred oak, flooded my tongue.

"That stubborn bastard. He's a pain in my ass, but at least he's useful in other ways. The one thing Tasa had to offer this family is now in the gutter, and she might get herself killed for it."

My jaw clenched tight, the muscles at its base pulsing away. Was I upset about her dismissal of her obligation? Hell yeah. Was I more worried about her safety? You bet. I was nowhere closer to finding her. The Montreal tip had been a dead end in terms of actually getting my hands on her. Luca had broken into the dancing company's internal records and found Tasa was indeed registered for the workshop. That was a good sign, but it was more than two months away. Anything could happen to her from now till then. I let out a grunt of frustration.

I'd failed her, which was why I was trying to handle Luca a little differently, despite our spat when I first told him of my plans. The thought of Luca not bowing down to my demand had the expensive bourbon roiling in my spasming stomach. Fuck, no, I couldn't marry the Popescu girl. I simply couldn't. The grip around my glass tightened like a vise. I didn't even want to recall her name. The less I knew about her, the better.

It was bad enough that Nina and I were hiding. That I couldn't show up to her twenty-first birthday party at her home. Christ, I didn't even want to know what kind of pussy Yo-Yo thought I was. It was telling that I was worried what a seventeen-year-old boy thought of me. I was a man who didn't hide my life and certainly not the woman I wanted, but I'd conceded to Nina's request. I wasn't about to make her life more difficult than I was already making it. But the thought of another woman like the Popescu girl? Hell, that only made me want to smash my glass against the wall.

"Luca's loyal, there's no question about that," declared Nicu, sliding his pawn forward.

"He is, but his understanding of loyalty is not the same as yours and mine. Tata treated him differently, and his resentment runs deep."

"How are you going to convince him?"

"I can't bribe him. The man wants for nothing, and he has no desires I can fulfill. Nor is he a soldier who simply takes orders. He's my brother, and after Tasa, I'm hesitant to push too hard."

"He knows it, too," observed Nicu. "And he's taking advantage of that. You might be better off if you act decisively."

"That's what I thought with Tasa after I caught her going to that sex club with Nina. I thought she'd settle down if I took her in hand. Instead, she rebelled, and look where that's put us. I already have one sibling on the loose. Can't have a mutiny with Luca, as well."

"You might give him L.A.," Nicu suggested.

"Have him move out of New York? Across the country? Mama will have a fit."

"He wants to be his own man," my brother elucidated. "He's a loner. Stays away from the family as much as he can. You can't please everyone, but if you find Tasa and bring her back, Mama will be satisfied. Let him get married, go to California, and take over for you there. That's a carrot you can dangle in front of him."

"How do you know this?" I asked, absorbing his argument.

"Besides the way he acts, you mean?" Nicu replied, casting me an incisive look. "We practically live together when he's not isolating in his Westchester mansion. He talks enough that I get the gist of what drives him, which is to get away from us."

Leaning back into the chair, I studied the chessboard as I stroked my chin. It could work. At this point, it was the closest I had to a solution. That was assuming I found Tasa. After that ridiculous little workshop, if she wanted to pursue this bizarre form of dance, she could do that just as well at the center of the dance world in New York City as in little Montreal, Madame Pierrette notwithstanding.

Waving to the chessboard, Nicu returned my attention to the chessboard and challenged me, "Come on, let's see if you can checkmate me this time."

19

I t was past nine o'clock by the time Nina skipped down the stoop of her parents' home and slipped into the passenger seat, her eyes glistening with excitement.

"Hey, baby, how was your mother's *mee sua*?" I asked before leaning over to give her a searing kiss with the dark promise of what I would do to her later.

"Delicious, as always," she replied breathlessly, dropping back against the leather seat and buckling up. "My mother's a fantastic cook. Every evening, she comes home from work, and no matter how long it takes, she makes two or three different dishes for dinner. She comes from the southern Fujian province, so lots of seafood, noodles, and soups."

"Do you know how to cook those dishes?"

"Some of them," she replied as she peered out to try to guess where I was taking her.

"I'm guessing you're full, but I promised you a drink on your twenty-first birthday, and I never go back on my promises. We have reservations at a place in Midtown. You can have that dry martini I promised or your first lesson in champagne."

Her eyes melted on me for remembering my promise of a martini the night I took her virginity, an adorable expression that made me want to take a bite out of her. "How about both?"

"Hmm, we'll see. Have you had champagne?" I asked, curious as always about every aspect of her life.

"At Tasa's eighteenth birthday-slash-high school graduation party," she said, coughing into her fist as she turned three different shades of red. I chuckled. How could I forget when she caught me getting oral from one of her classmates, and I'd taunted her. It had been hot as fuck seeing her touch herself, but she was only eighteen and my sister's closest friend, so when she ran away, I decided it was for the best.

It would've taken me a few minutes to get out of that particular situation, but if it had been anyone other than Nina, I would've pursued her. Relentlessly. Instead, I had to push the image of her fingering herself while watching me thrust inside another woman's mouth out of my mind and keep going as if I didn't rage with lust for her. Damn, I'd forgotten how much she'd turned me on with that special sauce of shock, fear, and intrigue on her face. And desire. So much desire for me it'd fanned the flames of my own need. Funny how life worked out, because here she was, sitting in my car, with my hand on her thigh.

We drove to one of my common haunts where I could find good French food, even better alcohol, and enough privacy. Handing my keys to the valet, I prodded her through the doors of the restaurant attached to the hotel not far from my apartment. We followed the hostess down the long center aisle. There was a long bar on one side and small, intimate tables on the other, both filled with customers. Walking over the black-and-white-checkered parquet floor, we passed beneath huge glittering Baccarat chandeliers before taking a right at the far end of the aisle to a small nook, off to the side. Nina slipped into the high-backed banquette. The silk-covered wall behind her exhibited a range of gilded-framed paintings stacked one on top of the other like at the Paris Salon.

Her wide eyes skipped from place to place, taking in the sumptuous surroundings, before returning to the hostess, who offered her a menu.

"Which should we start with?" I asked.

"Champagne," she replied breathlessly with glistening eyes.

"A bottle of the Louis de Sacy Brut Originel," I ordered without bothering to look at the menu. "And two dozen oysters."

My gaze rested on Nina. Her eyes bulged out.

"Have you ever eaten oysters before?"

"I've eaten fried oysters, and my mother makes a killer oyster omelet, but the oysters are much smaller...and cooked."

"Good, then, you'll experience your first raw oyster from my hand," I said as I took her palm in mine.

Our waitress came over soon after with a silver vasque, showed me the bottle to inspect, and efficiently popped it open. A busser placed two intricate crystal champagne flutes on the table, and the waitress filled them with the bubbly. Moments later, two plates of oysters were swept in front of us.

"To your twenty-first birthday, Nina," I toasted, holding my glass high before clinking it lightly against hers.

"To my birthday," she murmured back and took a small sip.

Licking her bottom lip, she hummed and gave me a

bright smile that almost brought me to my knees. "Delicious."

"No, you're delicious," I replied.

Her eyes knocked from right to left, pink flagging her high cheekbones. "Shush, you're so loud."

I threw my head back and laughed. "I don't care who overhears me. You taste better than the rarest champagne on this menu."

"Oh my God. You did not just say that," she hissed.

I loved it when she got flustered by my forwardness. Touching the jade wolf head, I said, "You're still wearing it."

"Ugh, I couldn't take it off." Her eyes narrowed on me. "You did that on purpose. Were you testing me?"

"No, but I'll admit that it was possessive on my part. I want everyone to know who you belong to. What did you do at your mother's?"

"She was very admiring of it, so you chose well but I couldn't admit that I got it from my sugar daddy." I barked out a laugh at that. She continued, "So I lied and told her that Tasa lent it to me."

"Hmm," I replied, expecting as much. While I felt a small pang of disappointment, I had achieved my goal, which was to make sure *she* knew who she belonged to. If Yo-Yo had figured it out, that would've been an added bonus.

"Come," I urged her as I squeezed a bit of lemon juice into the shell of an oyster, picked it up, and held it up to her. She bit into her plush bottom lip, two pearly white teeth making slight indentations into the plump flesh. I wanted to drag her over my lap and lick it all better for her, but there would be time enough for that later.

Tipping her chin up, she finally opened, and I let the

oyster slide into her mouth. She chewed on it thoughtfully and then looked up at me.

"It's not bad. Salty."

"Good girl," I complimented.

Following my lead, she squeezed a little bit of juice from a sliver of lemon and picked up the oyster. "Now it's my turn."

I took the oyster she offered, flicking the tip of her fingers with my tongue before allowing her to slide the oyster into my mouth. Afterward, I took a sip of champagne.

"Oysters, champagne, *you*. Three of my favorite things."

The vein at the base of her throat, just below the cuff, pulsed wildly. I watched it appreciatively before lifting my gaze up to hers. She took another drink from her flute, this one more of a gulp than a delicate sip.

"Watch it, or you may get tipsy," I warned.

Batting her eyelashes, she teased, "Wouldn't you like me just a tad bit tipsy?"

I stifled the groan coming up my throat. "Fuck, you know I would, little girl."

Needing to be closer to her, I moved from my seat opposite her, and she shifted to give me space beside her on the banquette. I unbuttoned my jacket and wrapped my arm around her shoulders. Instantly, she leaned into me, her floral scent drifting up to me and grabbing hold of my balls. I was glad that she was so receptive to trying new things. I wanted to experience more with her, like showing her my little house in Capri, on the Amalfi Coast of Italy, or my penthouse in Paris. I'd search out the best southern Chinese restaurants so she could initiate me to the things she loved.

My fingers crept beneath the hem of her red knit sweater dress, my thumb swiping back and forth over her bare skin above her garters. It hadn't escaped my notice that under my firefly's demure clothing, there were garters and silky jewel-colored underthings. A collection I would definitely be adding to. Getting a peek of ruby red, I bit down on my groan and refocused my attention on our conversation. "How was it at your parents' house? Any arguments?"

She shook her head, long tresses of dark hair tumbling over her shoulder. "Birthdays are special, so we try to keep the peace. Or rather, my mother does, and she's the source of most arguments. During special occasions, she's able to contain herself." Her forehead puckered. "Mostly."

I petted her silky hair, silently urging her to continue.

"My mother," she began with a sigh. "I mean, I love her. She's sacrificed so much, but her ideas of what's right and wrong are super rigid. If we deviate just a little bit from what she thinks is safe, she stresses out. I'm better at managing her anxiety, but Yo-Yo's dreams of being a rap star are a nightmare for her. I'm trying to convince him to at least go to college, but even that's an uphill battle," she finished, her eyebrows pulling tight in worry.

I huffed out a small laugh. "I had the same conversation with Nicu this afternoon in my office while I waited for you," I replied. As if I didn't already know she was perfect for me, her commitment to her family and her love for her brother were yet more proof.

Bringing her into my chest, I raised her glass and fed her a healthy sip. Her hand came to my chest, stroking it gently with a little scratch now and again that had me wanting to grab her and pull her over my lap to straddle me. I thanked my lucky stars that I'd convinced her to live with me. That at the end of this meal, I would take her home, spend the entire night, and then wake up to her in the morning. That could happen day after day, and I'd never get tired of it.

Hopefully, that right would become legally mine, and I could keep her forever.

We'd polished off the champagne, along with some other light fare, when my cell phone vibrated in my pocket. I was highly tempted to ignore it, but my phone didn't usually ring after ten o'clock if business wasn't on the agenda. I'd specifically cleared off this entire night, alerting everyone that I wanted to be left alone tonight.

With an irritated sigh, I pulled out my phone and checked the number.

Stegan.

He was on an assignment to follow Una, Cristo's girl. Although I had gotten the information I needed, it was important not to let up on anything relating to Nelu.

"What?" I started with a growl in my tone.

"Sorry to bother you, *Şef*, but we have a situation. I'm so sorry, Alex." He sounded genuinely apologetic.

"Explain," I demanded.

"Una. The girl."

"I know who Una is. Go on, man," I clipped out.

"Cristo, the fucking bastard, beat her up. It was bad. Real bad. I was afraid she was gonna die. I couldn't let that happen, so I busted open the door to her apartment. There was blood everywhere, coming from...you know... Anyway, I shot his bodyguard. Dragged Cristo off her. Then, he went ballistic on me."

Silence reigned as I tried to process what he was saying, and what he wasn't saying. "You beat him up."

"Yeah," he confirmed, a harsh exhale of breath rattled through the phone.

"The girl okay?"

"She lost the baby. He k-kicked it out of her. She's a

fucking mess, Şef. I couldn't stand by and let it happen. I'm sorry—"

"Enough," I cut him off.

Was I pissed? Damn right, I was. His job was to hide, watch, and relay any important information, not barge in and create a fucking mess for me to clean up. Not to let them know they were being watched, and not to get caught. You certainly didn't bust in a door and get involved in a fucking domestic situation. At the same time, it must've been bad for Stegan to violate the carnal rules of spying. My men weren't angels, by any stretch of the imagination, but I would never blame him for protecting an innocent woman about to be beaten to death. Which was where it was going if he'd felt compelled to get involved. And there had been a bodyguard present, watching over and doing nothing? Typical shameful behavior from the Popescu clan.

"I called his father from his cell phone. The idiot didn't have it password protected or anything. Figured it was better for Nelu to handle it the way he saw fit. He ripped me a new one and told me to tell you he'd be in touch to deal with this. Then I carried her to my car and brought her to the hospital."

"How is she?" I gritted out. I didn't want the girl hurt, but whatever injuries she'd sustained might help during my inevitable negotiation with Nelu. As much as I disliked the man, he was Romanian. Our common enemy was the Bratva. Regardless of what Stegan did to Cristo, we were better off sticking together. There was no way in hell I'd deal with Russian scum, and a bonus of Nelu of partnering with me was that he couldn't work with them. Not without crossing me. Considering they'd killed my father, this was a given.

Which meant I'd have to make this up to him. *Fuck!* The

more this nightmare unfolded, the more it was imperative I remain calm on the outside. But on the inside? I was burning up. With the marriage still up in the air, this was bad timing. God only knew what he'd extract from me to make this right. I didn't want to consider the worst scenario. I couldn't, or I'd lose my shit and go into a rage. And I never ever lost my shit.

"The hospital staff wouldn't tell me anything 'cause I'm not a family member. I didn't want to reach out to anyone on her behalf until I got the okay from you. Boss, I panicked. I broke protocol, and I'll accept the necessary punishment."

Nina's fingers wrapped around my wrist, distracting me. My gaze flicked over to her and found her worried eyes glued to me. Christ, I needed to get her in a secure location ASAP.

"I'm in public. Let me get Nina home. Where are you?"

"New York Presbyterian in Flushing," he answered.

"Stay there and keep an eye out for Una. How was Cristo when you left him?"

"Bad. I..." There was a long pause. "I lost my temper," he admitted.

"The hell, Stegan? Is there something going on that I should know about? Never mind, don't tell me now. I'll be—"

"Aww fuck, *Şef*, they just brought Cristo in through the emergency room doors."

Fuck, fuck, fuck.

"Get the hell out of sight," I growled. "Keep your phone close, and I'll call you when I get there."

As I disconnected, I pulled out my money clip and dropped several hundred dollar bills on the table.

"What happened?" Nina asked softly, clearly rattled by whatever she read on my face.

"A clusterfuck, that's what. I'm sorry, firefly, but it's time to go. I need you safe at home. This may be war."

"With Nelu?" she replied in a hushed voice, her plump bottom lip pushing out into a little pout of worry.

"Yeah," I affirmed, waving to the waitress. Nina's safety was my first priority. Always attentive, the waitress came over immediately, and I told her to keep the change. Helping Nina into her coat, I shielded her from patrons as we walked out, just in case someone came out of the wood-work. While the chance of an attack in public was slim, my nape pricked in anticipation of chaos.

The days of public shoot-outs were a thing of the past, but there were always exceptions, like what had happened to my father. His death had occurred in broad daylight. While that had been the work of the Bratva, and I didn't expect a backlash like that from Nelu anytime soon, I was on the alert. Nina brought out my inner beast. Currently, it rose tall, on its hind legs, scrapping for a fight.

Nestling her sweet curves into my body, we waited near the entrance in the lobby. Once the valet threw me the keys, I swiftly whisked her into my Jaguar.

On the way to my apartment, I called Tatum and briefly explained to him in Romanian what had happened, ordering him to be downstairs in the lobby by the time I arrived. He was to stay the night in my apartment. Then I told him to call and alert my mother to go on lockdown until further notice.

Driving into the semicircular driveway near the lobby of my building, I put on the brake and dragged Nina close to me. Scenting her throat, my eyelids shuttered as I drew in her delicate fragrance and let it wash over me for a brief moment of calm before facing the storm. I was going to need every ounce of patience and cunning for whatever awaited me in Queens.

Clawing at my shirt, her eyes clung to mine. "Are you going to be okay?"

"Yeah, baby. Nothing's going to happen to me, but I need to know you'll be guarded tonight." My eyes flicked past her to Tatum, who'd exited the building and was waiting under the awning. The first thing to do was secure those I loved in case Nelu or anyone in his cohort tried to exact revenge. "I don't want you going out for any reason. Tatum is going to sleep in one of the other bedrooms. You need anything, and I mean anything, you ask him."

"Shouldn't he be with you? He's going to be unhappy, stuck with me instead of being part of the action," she pointed out.

Yeah, that's not how it works in my world.

"Tatum will do what I require of him, and that's making sure you're safe. It's an honor to protect those I love, baby girl, and he knows that. He'll do what's necessary, without a word of complaint. That's why he's my right-hand man," I assured her.

Pressing my lips to hers, I sucked on her tempting bottom lip. "I'll be back late, but I *will* be back." *If it's the last thing I do, I'll be back*, I silently swore to her. The only thing keeping me sane was knowing I had her to come back to.

"Promise," she uttered.

"Listen to me. Nelu's furious, but he's not a madman. He won't touch me. He'll make me pay, but he won't hurt me," I insisted.

Her concerned eyes found mine. "And Stegan?"

So sweet. This woman didn't know Stegan well, but he'd shadowed her often enough in the past few weeks, and she knew he was an important member of my family.

"Stegan did what any man of honor would've done in the situation. There will be retribution to pay, but he's under my protection. No one can hurt him but me," I intoned.

She inhaled sharply. "W-will you hurt him?"

"I don't know yet," I answered. "I have to get more facts before I make a decision. A prince's blood was spilled. Regardless of what a sniveling little asswipe he is, that wrong has to be made right, and money can only go so far. Nelu is a greedy bastard, so who knows? He might be satisfied with a large enough payment." *I doubt it, but one could always pray.* "Enough money and certain other benefits might possibly resolve this without bloodshed," I finished.

I very much doubted this would pass without bloodshed. Stegan was a good soldier to me. Had never failed me. Not once in the eight years he'd been with me. That was quite a record, and I would do everything I could for him. He'd certainly keep his life and his position as a family member. Beyond that, it was too early to tell. But there would be difficult decisions to make.

From the corner of my eye, I saw Tatum step out from under the awning. It had started to rain, and the *plink, plink* of raindrops hitting the windshield was starting to come down.

After delving in for one last deep kiss, I held her shoulders and put her away from me. "Come on, out with you. Text me when you're safely in the apartment," I commanded.

A brief nod, and she turned her anxious face away from me. By the time she opened the door, Tatum's hand was on the top of the frame. He bent down, and we exchanged a look in which I communicated how important his task was before he assisted Nina out of the car. Slamming the door shut behind him, they ran through the rain coming down in sheets.

Too soon, they were gone.

Facing ahead, I clenched the steering wheel, focusing my energy forward. I put the car in gear, rolled out of the driveway and drove toward whatever the fuck was going down in Queens.

20

W *hat the hell is Nelu doing, bringing Cristo to the hospital?* That was the pressing thought at the forefront of my mind as I raced across the Queensboro Bridge toward the scene. *Mafie* never went to the hospital unless it was a life-or-death situation, and even then, it wasn't common. Hospital visits brought police attention, and that could lead to questions directed toward Nelu and his business. Which was now also *my* business. It's not like we were invisible to the police, which is why everyone had a hand in bribing them, but that didn't mean you waved a red flag in front of a bull.

Nicu was waiting for me near the front desk of the hospital. He briefed me on Cristo's condition in the elevator. The fucker had come in unconscious, but he'd be fine. Nicu told me his face was fucked up, but other than that, he only had a few bruised ribs. *Really, Nelu? You brought him here for busted ribs?*

I stepped into the sterile private waiting room, where one corner was filled to capacity with Cristo's family and soldiers. Seeing me, Nelu rose from his seat and charged at me with hands curled into fists at his sides. "How dare you come here? My son, my heir is in a hospital bed because you have no control over your people," he spat out.

He pulled a gun out of his jacket and placed it beneath the curve of my jaw. Staying Nicu with my hand, I allowed the little show of force. Breathing calmly, I stood still and waited until he grunted in exasperation, digging the muzzle in deeper before shoving it off me.

"You don't pull a gun on the *Lupul*," Nicu snarled from behind me, but I cut him off with a slashing motion of my hand.

Nelu glared at Nicu and fired back, "Then don't fucking put my only son in the hospital."

"Why'd you bring him in, Nelu?" I asked in a cool, detached tone. Every cell in my body shrieked at me to pummel this bastard to the ground, but I had to remain levelheaded. Maintaining my unflappable mask was an absolute necessity, especially with Nelu losing his shit.

"That little bitch is going to suffer for what she did. Cristo is going to tell the police everything, and she's going to be locked up," he threatened. Ah, that was his reason for bringing Cristo to the hospital. Counting on the police to show up, he could take revenge on Una, and possibly me.

I rolled my eyes. "Christ, you're acting like an idiot. First off, Una didn't do anything, so I'm not sure what you're punishing her for."

"No, it was Stegan," he sneered. "Your man."

"Exactly."

"But that bitch is going to pay," he promised darkly. "And if Stegan's name comes out, so be it. He can join her in jail."

"How do you see that happening, Nelu? It was a domestic incident. Cristo beat her till she lost the baby. Under New York State family law, both actors are considered perps. The police are required *by law* to arrest them both. Cristo will be behind bars as soon as he's deemed fit enough to get out of bed. Is that what you want?"

Being prelaw at Columbia University came in handy for moments such as these. Nelu's head snapped up, his eyes burning into me.

"I suggest you go into Cristo's room and tell him not to say a thing. Knowing him, he'll end up incriminating himself. He's not clever enough to deal with the police, even with an attorney at hand," I counseled smoothly.

Nelu caught the eye of one of his captains and jerked his head toward the exit, telling him to do what I said.

"You owe me," he grumbled, his voice scratchy with anger.

Gesturing to the far corner of the large waiting room, I walked in that direction, knowing Nelu had no choice but to follow me. If we were going to going to negotiate now, then I wanted as much privacy as possible.

Once I reached the corner, I pulled up two chairs, took a seat, and invited him to take the one facing me. After a moment of hesitation, Nelu collapsed into the chair. I noticed the deep grooves stamped into his forehead. He looked tired. For the first time, he looked old and tired. This life of ours didn't go easy on a man. He was about the same age as my father was when he died, but I reminded myself that the similarities ended there. The man was a conniving snake who'd slit his own brother's throat if it gave him an edge.

"What happened exactly?" he started. "I couldn't get the whole story from Cristo. He sustained a nasty hit on the head. The doctor said it was a concussion and made me back off."

"From what I've gathered, he beat up Una. Kicked her in

the stomach until she miscarried." I paused for a beat before continuing, "Your grandchild. A boy, I believe." There was probably little chance that she was far along enough to know the sex of her child, but I banked on Nelu not knowing that fact.

His eyes hardened; the silver-gray turned to steel. "Fuck."

"My man came in and stopped him from killing her. Had to shoot your bodyguard to get to her. He did Cristo a favor. Your son could have a manslaughter charge hanging over his head right now."

"Don't fucking think you're getting a thanks from me," he snarled. "Even assuming anyone found the body, I would've gotten Cristo off."

I gave a nonchalant shrug. "Perhaps. Perhaps not. My man would've been a witness. Then it would've been *my* decision whether he stayed quiet or not. Besides paying off the police, the judge, and the jury, you would've been indebted to me for eternity, so, yeah, I'm pretty sure I did you a favor."

"Your father was always soft when it came to women. Seems that weak trait has carried down to you and your men."

Mention of my father had my hands balling into fists, but I wasn't about to fall for his little taunt.

"Fuck, Nelu, don't say things to make me hate you more than I already do. I get that Cristo wanted her to have an abortion, and for whatever reason, she hadn't gone through with it yet. But to kill her unborn baby with his own fists? Thank fuck my sister ran away."

"He would've never touched your sister," he hurled out.

I gave him an incredulous look. Jesus, did he think I'd turn a blind eye to this? Having a mistress was one thing.

Beating a woman half to death was an entirely different matter.

"After what happened tonight, there's nothing you can say to convince me of that. Honestly, knowing what I know now, I would've terminated the condition of Tasa's marriage in our contract."

"Well, you can pat yourself on the back for saving Cat from my family, you sanctimonious prick," he snarled, his eyes snapping with fury. It was his way of saying that, regardless of what happened, I wasn't off the hook for his daughter.

"One of my best soldiers is dead," he continued, "with a wife and snot-nosed kids I've got to feed for the foreseeable future. My heir is in a goddamn hospital bed. You owe me in blood." He took a dramatic pause before demanding, "I want Stegan."

"That's not happening," I clipped out. While I was willing to give him some leeway since Stegan had worked Cristo over, that didn't give him the right to dictate to me.

He leaned back against the chair, folding his arms across his protruding belly that pressed against the buttons of his shirt.

Eyes narrowing, he ground out, "I. Want. Retribution. How are you going to make it right? And don't for a second think this is about money. Fuck the money, and fuck you if you bring it up. Money's off the table until the issue of blood is dealt with first."

"Isn't it enough that you lost your grandson?" I'd made that up. I didn't have any actual proof the fetus was a male, but in our regressive society that made him worth more, bastard or not.

He laughed. A false, brittle noise, like the clacking of window shutters let loose in the wind. "Sure, it's a tragedy, but another grandson can be produced in the future. It's not like Cristo is dead. I have a reputation to uphold, especially to my own kin. They want proof that you understand we lost a good man and my son's been injured for no good reason. And don't tell me a domestic *incident* was good enough. We both know that doesn't mean shit to my people. Cristo may not have had the license to kill her, but shit happens between a couple," he ended.

What a cocksucking bastard. Then again, could I expect anything less ruthless from this prick?

I could see the blatant greed etched on his face. My upper lip curled. "What the hell do you want? Spit it out."

"You. I want you to marry Cat. You're the *şef*, not Luca. You control your family, and nothing's more prestigious for my only daughter than marrying the boss of the Lupu clan. *Nothing.* So either you marry Cat or hand over Stegan, and I'll make an example of him. I swear, I will drag out his death for days. That's the only thing that will make this right," he pronounced.

Fuck. Fuck, fucking fuck.

Stegan's life or my happiness.

My gaze flicked up to Nicu for help, but I couldn't step away from the negotiating table to discuss this with him. It would make me appear weak.

"Otherwise, it's war, Alex," he warned. He knew he had me where he wanted me. What I would pay to wipe that smug look off his face. "And by God, I will make you suffer."

He wasn't bluffing. If I didn't either hand over Stegan or marry Cat, I'd trigger a war because his demand was considered reasonable in our world. Dragging the Lupu clan into war would be a blatantly selfish thing for me to do to my clan. On a personal level, I could deal with the violence. I'd already coped with it once, to avenge my father's death. Of course, the difference was that I'd done it knowing he'd approve of my course of action. Not this time. This time, I could feel his disappointment bearing down on my shoulders. My oath to my father to make good with Nelu would go up in smoke.

And Nelu was not to be underestimated, ever. He could hurt us. We'd hit back of course, but it would be considered shameful when our clans had finally reached the tail end of a decades-long feud and entered an era of peace. To bring war so I could keep Nina, an outsider, would be seen as rabid, crazy by my people.

No, war was not an option.

That left me with turning Stegan over to this madman. Stegan was a good soldier who'd found himself in an untenable situation. I couldn't send him to his death for choosing to save an innocent's woman's life. That would be counter to the tenets the Lupu lived by, and my men would see it for what it was, forfeiting the life of a loyal member to keep an outsider in my bed.

Even if I made Nina my wife, Stegan's death would taint our marriage. Romanians were superstitious people. To them, our marriage would always be linked to Stegan's death. It would never be clean and good, which my wife should symbolize. In the filth that underpinned our lives, our women and children were our only vessels of redemption. Right or wrong, that was how it was. And while I didn't believe in ridiculous superstitions, my people did. Deep down, I couldn't deny that it might bring a dark cloud over our union. It had the power to taint the love we had for each other.

Nina was a woman who loved to please people, who needed to be liked and accepted. Scorned by my clan, I would be dooming her to a life of misery. All to be with me. I couldn't do that to her.

Leaning forward, elbows on knees, my fingers steepled together. There was also a much, *much* deeper problem. Black clouds brought black luck, and bad luck could end up getting Nina hurt or killed. If not by Nelu for revenge, then possibly by one of my own kin. Someone might take it upon themselves to purge the clan of such bad luck. Behind my back, of course, but that would put Nina in the line of danger.

It was bad enough that they'd never accept Nina under these circumstances, but to not be able to trust my own people with her life? To not know if I was sending an assassin to slit her throat? I'd never survive that.

Stegan would die for no reason, and Nina would end up getting killed. No, nothing inside me could allow that to happen.

My heartbeat pounded in my ears like tribal drums, and I felt a little light-headed. Shaking off the dizziness, my gaze slammed into Nelu's, and I forfeited my life.

Between clenched teeth, I spat out, "I'll marry Cat."

Triumph lit up his eyes in an unholy shade of silver.

He clapped my shoulder, and I stiffened under his touch as he said, "Good choice, son."

"I don't need your fucking approval," I snapped, but Nelu was too ecstatic to notice my wrath.

Rising up, he spread out his arms and shouted, "The *Lupul* will be our next son."

His wife, other family members, and his soldiers turned in his direction after pretending they hadn't been paying attention to every twitch of our faces for the last twenty minutes. Not for the first time, I noticed that Cat wasn't there. She was never around, off to boarding school, far from her family. I was glad I didn't have to pretend to care for her gentle sensibilities when my heart was cracking inside my chest.

Nicu rushed to my side, hissing near my ear, "What the hell did you do? We could've figured something out."

Yeah, right.

"No, we couldn't have," I pushed back. "He had me by the balls." It was all I could say in public. Every person in his family was approaching me to congratulate me on my nuptials and give me a kiss on both cheeks. I wanted to rage and thrash on the ground. I wanted to beat my chest, tear my hair out, and bellow in agony until the walls came crashing down around me.

Instead, I had to grit my teeth in the semblance of a smile as Popescus rejoiced around me. My neck muscles bunched together as someone patted me on the shoulder. Pain swelled in my throat to the point that I couldn't even swallow. I should've known better than to foolishly hope Nina and I had a chance. We were doomed from the very start. My life was never my own. My choices were never my own. Even if Stegan hadn't fucked up, the pressure to marry an appropriate bride would've eventually toppled us. There was no escape. And now? Now, I was a dead man walking. Shackled and bound, I was a slave to the demands of my clan.

Recognizing I was about to crack, Nicu took me by the arm, elbowed his way through the throng of joyful Popescus and spirited me out the door. Once in the hallway, he made a low whistling sound. Stegan came out of the woodwork, took one look at me, and braced my other arm. I was having trouble pulling enough air into my lungs.

Bypassing the elevator, Nicu turned us toward the stairway and threw the door open. It bounced against the wall and hit his shoulder as he hustled me down a few flights of stairs and into the parking lot. Rain slashed down on us, drenching us in a cold shower, as Stegan ran up ahead and clicked open the black Mercedes SUV.

Nicu tossed me in and slipped in beside me as Stegan started up the car.

"My car—"

"We'll get it later," Nicu cut me off, checking all sides for a possible ambush.

The instant we were in, Stegan gunned the accelerator and we were off, tires skidding with a squeal.

"What the fuck, Alex? What have you done?" Nicu heaved out, disbelief in his eyes.

Stegan remained silent, but from the tightness of his jaw, he was angry as well.

"I had no choice. It was either Stegan or me, and he made it clear they'd torture him to death."

"What about Nina?"

"Dammit, Nicu. You know as well as I do that if I gave Stegan over, which I would never do, on principal"—I glanced at Stegan, but his jaw was as tight as ever—"that Nina would never be accepted by the clan. Not by the men or women. They'd see it as a sacrifice of a good man, a good soldier, in exchange for an outsider. Some might see it as a weakness and challenge me, not that I give a shit. I have no issues with fighting to keep my place, but I'd never be able to live down their judgment that I put my desires above the needs of the family. And that would ultimately put Nina's life in danger."

"I'd rather you gave me over," brooded Stegan. "I knew the moment I touched that bastard that my life was forfeit. I prepared myself."

"Then you're lucky you're not the one with the decision-making power here," I huffed out, passing a hand over my forehead. The feeling of loss was like a chasm in my heart, gaping wider and wider. "I'd thought you'd at least be happy about it."

"Not if you have to martyr yourself in the process," he replied vehemently. "I gave my life over to you—"

"You did, and I decided to keep you alive to continue to serve me," I cut him off.

"My job is to protect you," he insisted.

"Well, you can't do your job if you're not alive, now, can you?" I snapped. "What the hell, Stegan? I expected a little gratitude, not back talk."

He clamped his mouth shut, grinding down on his back molars so hard the sound could be heard from the back seat.

"He feels guilty. He never meant for you to suffer in his place," Nicu murmured.

"Either way, I was a fool to think it could work out between Nina and me. It was inevitable that my duty to this family would get in the way." Turning to my friend, I tried to alleviate his guilt. "It was doomed from the start, Stegan. You may have been the vehicle, but if it weren't you, it'd be someone or something else. It was a mistake to believe I could have more than was my due."

"Stop with this old-world doom-and-gloom bullshit," insisted Nicu. "The old 'don't expect too much or else you'll be taught a lesson.' We're in fucking America now. We get to dream big. That's why our parents suffered like they did to bring us here. Ripped away from their country, their culture, their language. At least, the upside should be that we get to have more than they did."

"We do have more," I argued. "We have enough food on our table. We have financial security. We're safe. But if you aim too high, you'll get your wings clipped, like Icarus. Nina was me flying too close to the sun. Now I'm crashing back down to earth."

Turning toward the window, I watched the rain pummel the deserted streets as we drove back into Manhattan. The hole inside me, the one only Nina could fill, was a gaping abyss of emptiness. I stared as the rain lashed against the panes, leaving rivulets of water behind. The world lacked color. Everything was subdued. Dark. The only sound I heard was the loud exhalations of my breath and the splashing of the car through puddles. My heart pounded against my ribs; the aching void spread like ice over my chest. I'd failed her. I'd failed us. How was I going to face Nina and tell her that we were no longer together?

21

I couldn't settle down, much less fall asleep, knowing Alex was in danger. He'd assured me he'd be fine, that Nelu wouldn't hurt him, but there was a nervous jangling in my gut that told me otherwise. One way or another, Alex was in danger, and none of Tatum's reassurances could convince me otherwise.

Despite the late hour, I stayed up with the television on in the living room to keep the silence from suffocating me. Tatum remained with me until I finally persuaded him to go to bed. There was no reason for both of us to lose sleep. After swearing to him that I wouldn't leave the apartment for any reason, he finally took me up on my offer and padded off into one of the spare bedrooms.

I squeaked in relief when I heard the click of the lock on the front door. Jumping off the sofa, I rushed to the entrance and threw myself onto Alex the instant he walked in, peppering him with kisses. Relief coursed through my veins at finding him in one piece.

That was...until I saw his face. It was stark. For a

moment, I thought someone had died, and I supposed that was what had happened.

"What is it?" I asked, helping him out of his damp coat and dragging his stiff, reluctant body to the sofa. Tatum stormed out of the bedroom, probably woken up by our voices. Alex gave him a chin lift and then nodded toward the door. His friend stared at him for a long moment, but Alex shook his head and muttered, "Tomorrow." Without another word, Tatum walked barefoot to the front door. There was the swishing sound of the door closing and the subsequent snick of the bolt engaging.

Taking off his shoes, because that's generally what he did when he came home, I placed them in the hallway closet and returned to Alex's side. His head was tilted back against the top of the sofa, eyes squeezed closed as if he was fighting off a nightmare.

Taking a seat beside him, I gently took his hand in mine and waited.

After a few long moments, his eyes flashed open and fixed on me. His irises embodied fiery flames of green. Grabbing me by the waist, he swooped me onto his lap. I straddled him, laying my chest against his. His heartbeat pounded against my own. As he often did, Alex nuzzled my throat the way I loved. Whenever he sought comfort in me like that, it turned my insides to mush.

"Fuck, Nina."

"What happened? Is Stegan okay? Is he alive?"

"Yeah, he'll live," he murmured into my throat, taking a taste of me before pulling away.

Silently, he stared at me. Again, his eyes were bleak. Inconsolable. Panic rose inside my chest, my throat cinching, tighter and tighter.

"Jeez, you're scaring me, Alex."

"He wanted my life for Stegan's," he blurted out and then shook his head. "I mean, the only way to save Stegan's life was for me to marry Nelu's daughter. It's what he'd been going for all along, and he pounced on this regrettable incident to force me into it."

My first reaction was relief because, for an instant, I'd thought Alex meant he was going to die. Then he clarified, and my heart sank. Dreams of happiness and everything precious burned away between those few words he'd spoken, leaving behind rubble and ash.

Not a whiff of hope remained.

Despair set in, deep in my bones.

I could do nothing but stare back at him. My brain was a jumble of conflicting thoughts, my heart a battlefield of warring emotions, but eventually, everything weaved together into one prevailing fact: it was over between us. It didn't matter that we loved each other. We hadn't used those three little words, but they weren't needed, because I knew this man. I knew his heart, and there was no doubt in my mind that he cared for me. Deeply. The agony I read in his eyes was real, and the regret churning in his green gaze wasn't only for me. It was for himself as well.

I'd had a taste of paradise, but the aftertaste of being tossed out of Eden was harshly bitter.

"Fuck, Nina, it was psychological slaughter, and the only thing that keeps me from imploding is you. I understand that you're disappointed—"

"More like torn apart," I interrupted.

"You must hate me. You *should* hate me," he bit out.

I shook my head, tears rolling down my cheeks. "I don't," I said firmly. "Part of what I love about you is your loyalty and your desire to do right by everyone. You're willing to sacrifice yourself for Stegan. You know it's the only option. Even if you had entertained the idea of turning him over, I would've never allowed it."

His hand cupped my cheek. His expression was bleak, cheeks hollow and clenched jaw jutting out. He twisted his head away, as if it was too painful to look at me, and I understood. "I've betrayed you for my family. If it were only me..."

"No," I intoned. "You took care of someone who you've sworn to protect. You're the only man between Stegan and death. *Death.* A man's life depends on you. If there had been any other choice, you would've taken it. You wouldn't have agreed to Nelu's demand."

I bit down on the inside of my cheek to stifle the whimper of despair, but I wouldn't add to his misery. I'd never seen him so stripped down before. No walls between us. No mask he could hide behind. His heartache was bare for me to see. Alex felt responsible for what had happened. He'd see this as his failure. Even with my own heart bleeding out, I only wanted to comfort him.

He bent over me, his thumb glancing over my bottom lip.

"You don't know what that pouty lip does to me. The way it constantly teases me," he confessed.

Under his riveted focus, I couldn't help but lick it, flicking over his thumb in the process.

His fierce emerald eyes sparked.

My hands reached for his shoulders. I wanted him closer. I just wanted *him*. For tonight at least, he was still mine. Tomorrow I'd be gone. Desperation clawed at me to drown myself in him one more time, like an alcoholic reaching for a drink on his deathbed.

His head dipped to mine and then his tongue was parting my lips. What started out slow quickly became desperate. Soon, his mouth devoured mine, our tongues tangling together. I gripped his nape to press him closer, as if somehow I could inhale him into me, make him mine. Greedy, I sucked on his tongue, as if I could imprint his taste on me, as if then I'd have him with me always.

His fingers slid down and fumbled with the belt of my robe. Parting it, he dragged the hem of my nightie up, baring me to him. Already, my arousal was there for his viewing.

"I need to taste you, baby. I need to taste the sweetness of your pussy," he begged, pushing my thighs apart as he moved me and slid off the sofa to the floor. At eye level with my pussy, his eyes glittered at my blatant need for him.

"Such a pretty pussy...so fucking pretty," he crooned before his tongue darted out and took a taste. I gasped, my thigh muscles tightening. "How am I going to do without this? Fuck, I should've made sure to eat you out every day."

"Um...you did. Practically every day."

"Fuck that, I can't believe what an idiot I was to miss out on every chance I had," he answered in a vexed tone. Settling in, his elbows were propped on the edge of the sofa as he buried his face in me. "I should've lived and breathed in this fucking delicious cunt."

"Oh my God," I breathed out as he took a long, deep lick from the back to my clit, which he instantly latched on to. My backside jumped off the couch, my spine arching like a bow. I grabbed for his curls, twisting them in my fingers. His hands held me down by the hips as he attacked me without an ounce of pity. There were no slow licks to tease me, no circling my engorged clit, no applying gentle pressure. There was none of that. Instead, Alex went on the offensive, tackling me to the ground and making me come at his instant command. I cried out, thrusting my pussy in his face, already so close to the edge when he withdrew his tongue.

Breathing heavily, his head rolled away. His deep exhalations, like faint whispers, prickled the sensitive skin of my inner thigh. Rolling his head slightly, he deliberately blew onto my pulsing clit, cooling me off and torturing me at the same time. There was something so intimate about a man going down on me, and the effect was devastating with Alex. He was so strong, so dominant. I couldn't help but feel a moment of utter vulnerability between us, as if our souls were staring at each other, recognizing their mates.

With a groan of desire, his masterful tongue resumed its skilled movements. This time, he savored me with expert flicks and licks, punctuated by hard thrusts and relentless suckles, until I was a trembling mess. Twisting my hips beneath his ministrations, I worked my pussy against his mouth until I fell headlong into one of the hardest climaxes of my life. Perhaps knowing this would be the last time made it so much more intense. My body knew to eke out every ounce of pleasure from these last moments together.

As I broke beneath him, so did my heart. Again, tears spilled out of the corners of my eyes. I shattered in more ways than one. After being wrapped in Alex's security and love, how was I going to do without? On top of that, knowing he would be with another woman, his wife. He'd be pleasuring his new wife, while I laid alone in my bed halfway across the city. Even if he didn't love her at first, how could I go on knowing his hands would touch another, his tongue would taste another?

Seeing my tears, he rose above me, tucked me into his arms, and carried me to the bedroom. Peppering my face with kisses, he lapped up my salty tears. His own eyes were wide and glistening with moisture. He was suffering, too. I knew that. I saw the agony bleeding from his eyes, but it hurt. It hurt so, so much.

"Let me help you forget. Please, Nina, let me help you forget for tonight," he croaked out. I nodded because, even though my heart was breaking, I knew he didn't want this any more than I did.

He laid me on the bed, and I reached for his belt, unbuckling it and freeing the length of leather from his trousers. Looming above me, he removed his cuff links, dropping them on the surface of the night table with little clinking sounds. Spreading his shirt open, he exposed his beautiful, carved chest with the trail of dark hair that unfurled between washboard abs to the opening of his trousers.

I shimmied out of my silk robe and short nightgown, moving to the middle of the bed to give him space. As his boxer briefs were peeled off, his strong, demanding cock jutted forward, pointing at me like a compass showing north. I craved the sensation of being stuffed full by him. I *craved* it.

My chin trembled at the thought that this would be the last time, but I thrust it away, determined to feast on the remaining moments of our last night together. Come morning, I wouldn't be able to stay, knowing this gorgeous, brave man was no longer mine. I already guessed that he would ask me to stay until the last bitter moment, but I didn't have the strength to drag this out until his engagement or his wedding day. I wasn't a prideful person by nature, but there was a shred of self-preservation left in me after all. Starting tomorrow, I'd have to cut off all contact with Alex. It was the only way.

He slipped in beside me, and I immediately went to him, rubbing against his chest until he flipped me on my back and braced himself above me. One hand on my throat, he stroked the underside of his cock against my mound, putting just the right amount of pressure to have me squirming beneath him.

Feeling achy and hot, I moaned, "Alex, stop teasing. Take me."

In that instant, he transformed from man to wolf. His lips crashed down on mine, taking me with a ferocity that stole my breath away as he pressed his thick cock inside me, stretching me deliciously. My inner muscles spasmed in response. Lifting himself on his arms, his muscles flexed and stood out in stark contrast to the darkness around us.

We both stared down to where our bodies were joined, as if memorizing the image for future use. Everything about this coupling was precious. Moments stuck out in sharp relief. The smoothness of his olive skin in the dim light. The flash of his emerald-colored eyes. Then, he began moving, his buttocks flexing under my palms as his hips snapped, building us up quickly.

"This is the sweetest cunt I'll ever have," he rasped, making a rough sound at the back of his throat. Needy and demanding. "So *tight*, so *mine*."

His control snapped. In a flurry of motion, he hooked my legs into the crook of his arms, spread me wide and pounded into me as if he could pin me to his bed, as if he could leave an imprint that would mark my spot long after I was gone. He drilled into me with brutal intensity, as if it was his last act on earth before expiring.

He fucked me with relentless determination, as if to brand me with his cock. It was almost cruel on his part, but I didn't turn away or try to shield myself. It was my parting gift to him, showing him that he had me. Body and soul.

Pulling out to rim my entrance with the flared tip of his

cock, he pushed in deep, to the hilt. With long, rough strokes, he claimed me. His hips rolled as he found the right spot, and when he did, he hammered it until I came apart beneath him. My fear, my anger, my sadness tore out of me as I keened out his name.

Our eyes clashed together, exchanging our mutual raw pain. Eyes wide, mouth gaping, I couldn't tear my gaze off him as my orgasm shattered my world. Then, I was milking him. My inner walls clamped down on his cock, demanding his release. His face twisted in bliss and agony as his large body shuddered above me. Tremors overtook him as his cock expanded. With one final jolt, he spilled inside me.

Internally, I screamed for this night to be different. Instead of it being the end, it would be the beginning. Instead of it being a breakup, it could be our wedding night. Instead of his seed going to waste, it would embed in my womb and bring forth life.

Shaken, I finally managed to rip my gaze away, focusing my blurred vision on the pillow beside me. I was completely spent, not an ounce of strength was left in me. I tried to be strong for him, but this had torn me apart. He released his hold on my legs and I shifted them downward, triggering spasms in him. Even as he pulled out, come sprayed onto my belly. Instead of cleaning it off, he rubbed it into my skin.

Overwhelmed, I tried to twist away, but I was stayed by his hand. It fanned across my belly, anchoring me in place. Maneuvering me like a rag doll, he positioned me to my side and spooned me from the back.

"I should leave," I said in the silence that weighed down on us, tears scalding the back of my eyes.

His fingers flexed, clenching my belly, pulling me deeper into his heat.

"Tomorrow," he breathed out, a fistful of gravel tossed

into the supplication in his voice. His jade cuff shifted, weighing heavily around my throat but exhaustion swooped over me and I didn't have the strength to ask him to remove it. My eyelids dragged closed, and I breathed back, "Tomorrow."

22

ell. My life is hell.

My work was spread out over a table in the back of my family's café. The clinking of porcelain and the hum of conversation were punctuated with the sounds of the espresso machine. When I was a child, my siblings and I would complete our homework in the back of the café, and I hoped to recapture that feeling of comfort from the familiar bustling noise, the copper ceiling, and the paintings of winding village roads, monasteries, and birch forests hanging on the walls. Once upon a time, it used to be a balm to my soul. Not anymore. Weeks had passed since I'd last had Nina in my arms, and I *ached* for her. Tilting my chair back against the bare brick wall behind me, my eyes were glued to the street beyond the large set of windows, waiting to see her lithe form pass by on the street.

The self-recriminations had come, fast and furious, after she left. She deserved better than me and the quality of life I could provide her. As an outsider, she had the opportunity for a normal life, and I had been selfish to take her. The blood bond, of course, complicated things. I snorted. Like I needed a blood bond when my obsession was spiraling. She would *always* be mine to protect.

I massaged my temples as I glared down at my laptop. I had a fiancée now. At least in theory. She was so young that I had to wait until she turned eighteen in the spring for the official engagement party. Why she was bundled off to a boarding school and far from her family, I had no idea. Not that I was complaining. Honestly, I didn't much care. My entire focus revolved around Nina. Each time I'd seen her pass by, every muscle in my body flexed, primed to run her down, tackle her to the ground, and drag her upstairs to fuck her like a madman.

Every time, I barely held myself back, repeating the mantra that I'd forfeited the right to touch her.

Fuck Nelu. Fuck my family. Fuck me. Fuck, fuck, FUCK.

The last time I'd felt this powerless, when my father died, I at least had a bloody war to wage. I had the ground beneath me to scorch to ashes. Now? Not one damn thing could mitigate my pain. Oh, unless one counted marrying a girl I cared nothing for while impotently watching the love of my life walk past me as if I didn't exist. To Nina's credit, she didn't know I was here, on the hunt to catch a glimpse of her. She purposely kept her gaze forward, and I'd seen her pass by enough times throughout the years to know she usually peeked in, either looking for Tasa or to get a glimpse of me.

Goddamn, I wanted to tear my hair out. Claw at my chest and carve out my hemorrhaging heart to make it shut the fuck up. Defying me, it continued to beat. Every one of those beats was a thundering bellow for my woman. I was sad. I was angry, murderously angry, and there was nothing to cool it, smother it, or suffocate it.

I thought back to the last moment I held her in my arms,

the last devastating smile she gave me before she left. I begged her to stay in the apartment. Told her I'd move out, either with Tatum, or if that was too close by, with Nicu and Luca in the other tower. Or back to Queens. Hell, I'd go anywhere as long as she stayed on my property. But she denied me, and I couldn't do a damn thing about it. She said it would be too painful because I was everywhere in the apartment. Which was the point. It made no sense, but the possessive, selfish beast inside me didn't want her to move on, to become someone else's. Even if I was the cause of her pain.

I'd done the unforgivable and torn us apart. She'd always have my protection, of course. She'd certainly always have my heart. It was only because she wasn't *mafie* that I could get away with not marrying her after the blood bond. That soul-tearing thought had me breathing heavily through my nose like a rabid dog. It was a dishonorable act, but did I have a choice? I was caught between dishonoring the blood bond, letting Stegan die, or starting a war.

Every day she was gone, I suffered from headaches. On good days, it was a niggling thing that harassed me like a swarm of gadflies. On bad days? Well, on bad days, it felt like my skull was being split in half, over and over again. It plagued me without mercy until I could finally shut my eyes at the end of the wretched day.

Turns out, I wasn't very good at staying away from her. She moved back to Queens, and I followed. I was currently in full stalker mode. The office in my family's house looked out onto Nina's bedroom window, and that's where I was posted in the evenings. Anything to get a glimpse of her through the mostly drawn curtains.

Same with the café. Instead of working upstairs, I spent

my days in the busy dining room downstairs, desperate to catch sight of her passing by on her way to the subway. As for Nina rebuffing my offer to continue having a bodyguard? I acquiesced to her face and immediately went behind her back and had her followed wherever she went. She'd lost her damn mind if she thought I'd allow her to take the subway to and from Juilliard on the Upper West Side without protection.

The sense of failure dug its claws deeper every passing day. It didn't matter that I was screwed, regardless of which decision I made. The fact that I had taken her virginity but couldn't have her drove me to the brink of insanity. As for the possibility of her being with another man? Yeah, I couldn't go there. And just the thought of having to touch, much less consummate the marriage with another woman, had bile rising to my throat.

And the only person who could console me, who could provide me with a modicum of peace during this hellish time, was the one person I couldn't have. Not only was she not of my world, but she wasn't even Romanian. None of that mattered in the least. She embodied everything good and pure. The opposite of me. I didn't deserve her, but she was as necessary as air to me. She filled the half that had been left empty, killed off by the violence I was forced to use to keep my family safe and prospering.

A part of me blamed Tasa. My unraveling began when she ran off. In an ecosystem like a family, when one person got out of line, it created a domino effect. Before then, I'd never second-guessed my decisions. I would've never entertained going after something I shouldn't want, like my little sister's best friend. But when Tasa, who embodied the soul of my clan, tossed her duties and commitments aside, it caused a fissure in my armor. That slender crack splintered wide enough to let in the possibility of taking Nina for myself. After having and losing her, everything came crumbling down.

I was brooding over this predicament, my finger tracing the rim of the shot glass before me, when a stranger entered the café and walked straight toward me. Stegan was out of his seat, a hand planted on the newcomer's chest before he could take another step.

"What do you want?" he asked bluntly, shoving his ugly mug in the man's face.

The man's eyes flicked over Stegan's shoulder and held my gaze.

They were eyes I saw in the mirror every day. Eyes the identical shade of green as mine.

I stood up and motioned Stegan to let him approach. I watched him closely as he stepped closer.

Same build.

Same gait.

His face was familiar, with an identical strong brow and angular jawline. There were differences, though. His mouth was larger and shaped differently.

Was he a long-lost cousin from Romania? We knew everyone there was to know within the continental United States.

"Alex, I presume," he began.

No accent, so not from the old country.

I cocked an eyebrow. "That's right. And you are?"

"Is there someplace we can speak alone? I have something to say that might be of interest to you, but I think you'd prefer to hear it in private."

I examined him closely. My gaze rippled down his body, checking out his clothing. He didn't look like *mafie.* Really, he came off like an average American male in a pair of jeans and a leather jacket. No expensive watch or other accoutrements that screamed money or *mafie.* He certainly didn't dress like a Romanian right off the boat.

"You'll need to be patted down," I warned.

He laughed. A deep throaty sound that snapped my head up. The last time I'd heard that sound was... *Who is this guy?*

"I'm not carrying," he replied. Spreading his arms, he said, "But go ahead. I'm not a threat to you."

I snorted. Yeah, right. Never trust a man who told you he was not a threat. There was no such thing as a nonthreatening male in the world I inhabited.

Stegan patted him down, and I tilted my head toward the staircase to my office. Leading the way, I watched from the corner of my eye as he followed me. Stegan, ever watchful, came in behind him.

Upstairs, I ushered him into my office and motioned for Stegan to stand guard outside. I figured that should be enough. Unarmed, the man's chances of killing me were slim. Besides the gun in my holster, I had another in the drawer and a couple of knives.

"Since you seem to already know my name, why don't you tell me yours?" I suggested.

"Sebastian," he responded promptly, leaving out his last name.

I motioned to a seat as I went around my desk and settled in. His eyes zipped around the room, taking in as many details as he could while he took a seat. Curious, was he?

"Sebastian what, pray tell?" I inquired. Family names were paramount.

His gaze returned to me. "I go by my mother's last name, Johnson, but I'm a Lupu."

"Are you?" I drawled. By his features, this didn't come as much of a surprise. Now, what did he want from me? After a beat, I hedged, "Listen, if you're looking for a job—"

"That's not why I'm here," he cut in.

"Then, why are you here?" I asked, hardening my tone a bit. I didn't have time to fuck around. I could be downstairs, hoping to get another glimpse of Nina as she passed by.

"I'm your half brother."

My head jerked back. "Come again."

He gave out a long-suffering exhalation. "I'm your half brother. By your father. *Our* father."

I blinked. This couldn't be real. "What kind of fucking joke is this? You think this is funny?"

"No," he answered smoothly, "and believe me, I wouldn't have come to you if I didn't have proof we share the same father. It's not a pretty story. Your father had a second family with my mother. Who's American, I'm sure you'd like to know. That's how we were able to stay off the radar of you and every other Lupu. You have a brother, Luca, who's twenty-six years old, one year older than me, and the twins, Nicu and Tasa, will soon be turning twenty-one. See? I know all about you."

Shock and recognition shuddered through my body. Followed rapidly by one thought. "Does my mother know?" I forced out between my pressed lips. This, I had to know before we went any further.

"I can't say for sure," he replied smoothly. "I believe a few of your older soldiers knew that our father was having an affair, but they didn't know about us. Răzvan, our father's *consilier* knew, but he took that knowledge to his grave when he died a few years back. He made sure to remind me of my duty before he died," he concluded, bitterness tainting his tone. "While I'm doling out the surprises, you should know you also have a half sister, Emma, who's two years younger than me."

Un-fucking-believable.

"Emma? Christ almighty, not another sister. I can barely contain the one I have," I muttered, more to myself than to him.

Sebastian chuckled. There was that sound again. An exact replica of my father's. Only one man laughed like that, and it hadn't been passed on to me or my siblings. I didn't even know I craved to hear it again until then, although it torqued my heart in a knot. That laugh, along with his features and the way he moved confirmed this man was indeed Tata's son. I'd get a paternity test, of course, but I already knew the truth in my gut.

"My advice is that you don't try to contain Emma. She's a wild child. Completely unmanageable."

"Normally, I'd say, if she's American, then that's not a surprise, but after what my sister did, I don't have a leg to stand on," I elaborated. Where did that come from? I didn't get chummy with complete strangers. Yet...there was something about Sebastian, an indescribable affinity and easiness that put people at ease. A charm that mirrored Tata's. He'd been the quintessential gentleman—except for this new discovery that he was an adulterer of the worst kind—that made people trust him and gravitate toward him.

"Assuming what you say is true, what do you want from me?"

"Dad gave me and Emma the option of living a life separate from the family. If we chose to tell you, he made me promise to wait until my twenty-fifth birthday. After some discussion with Emma, because I couldn't do this without her approval, I decided I wanted to know you. I'm aware this might complicate your life. I understand if you're upset. This discovery may cause pain to your mother and siblings, but I wanted to give you the option to get to know us."

Dad?   He   called   Tata   "Dad."   How quintessentially...American.

Spreading his hands in a gesture of harmlessness, he explained, "I'm not looking to become part of the family, take over your position as *şef* or anything like that. My mother recently passed, and since the moratorium on my silence is over, I thought it was time to expand our tiny family. Considering we share the same blood."

A laugh started to bubble deep inside me. This man was a level of naïve that was almost unreal, and...oddly endearing. It was obvious that he didn't have a dirty bone in his body. So very unlike me and my father. And yet, he knew about the inner workings of the Lupu clan by the way he casually mentioned *şef*, the Romanian word for boss.

Maybe my father had created an alternate reality with his other family. I could appreciate why he might be motivated to do that. Wasn't that what was so alluring about Nina? A vestige of purity and, with it, a hope of tranquility in the sea of violence that was our daily lives.

Should I be more shocked and offended in learning my father had a second family? Perhaps, but a few things mitigated it. He was an OG, a *şef* who'd built this empire in America from scratch. He'd done his duty to his clan by marrying my mother. Second families weren't unheard of in the old county, not that they were commonplace by any means. Maybe I was a bit unhinged after losing Nina, but discovering that my father wasn't perfect added another chink to the crack that began when Tasa left us.

Instead of disturbed, I felt...*free?*

A heavy weight was suddenly lifted off my shoulders. For the first time in eight years, except for when I was with Nina, I could breathe. I could step out of the shadow of the man I tried to replicate in every aspect of my leadership and life. This exemplar of perfection had a ridiculously huge stain on his soul. Learning that he had clay feet was liberating.

And it changed things in a fundamental manner. If I introduced Sebastian as my half brother to our clan, that would open things up in ways I could barely wrap my head around.

"This is quite something," I said. "If I understand you correctly, you don't want to usurp me, you don't want money, and you don't want a position in the family. Then what do you want?"

"Oh, you know, friendship. Brotherhood," he quipped with a little smirk playing on his lips, teasing me for my jadedness. "I'm aware that someone in your position doesn't trust easily, but I'm less of an outsider than you think. Dad didn't hide who he was from us, not even the fact that he had another family. We knew about each of you. There were photos of you guys around the house. My mother was a hippie. She didn't buy into bourgeois morality and hypocrisy. She accepted him for who he was. Didn't expect anything from him except honesty and mutual respect."

"Honesty?" I choked out. "That's rich considering they were both lying to my mother."

"Assuming your mother didn't know about us," he replied.

I swiped my hand over my eyes. This is where things could start to get dicey. My protectiveness over my mother was paramount. That could easily become a black or white issue, especially for Nicu. He was such a mama's boy.

He held up his hands. "I'm not saying I know everything about their relationship. Nor was it perfect, by any stretch of the imagination. It sure wasn't normal, but my mother was big into living your best life without the normal constraints that hampered people. Knowing her, I'm sure she tried to get Dad to tell your mother.

"Look, I didn't come to make trouble. Emma and I could've gone on as we were, but it seemed like a missed opportunity for everyone involved. Dad would've wanted us to come together. Family and children meant everything to him, and he wouldn't have wanted his faults to divide us. That's why he asked me to wait until I was older before coming forward. We wouldn't be so emotional and might figure out how to make the best of this."

Sebastian's description of Tata was eerily accurate. He would've wanted us to be together, especially Tasa and Emma. He always said that our lifestyle was hardest on Tasa because she didn't have a sister to commiserate with. I wondered if he had similar feelings toward Emma. And whether he'd dreamed of the half sisters coming together and becoming a support system.

My mind started ticking away in its efficient, businesslike manner. Opening up our closed society wouldn't be a bad idea, either. Eyeing Sebastian carefully, I wondered if he could be of use to us. We lived in a small, insulated society with a limited amount of trustworthy manpower. I could always use a good man. If he knew about Tata's activities, then I wouldn't be against integrating him.

Once I was sure of his loyalty. But there were ways to test loyalty and rituals to seal it tight. I should let him go on his way. Dismiss him and tell him to never grace my doorstep again, but already my brain was piecing together ways to make it work. It was obvious the man was intelligent and educated. I could do far worse than to bring him into the fold. As for his sister...

"And Emma?"

His eyes turned shrewd as if he'd already read my mind. "She's someone you might be interested in meeting, not only for the fact that she's your blood."

"Ahh. Why is that?"

"She's brilliant. She's a super nerd with a superior IQ, and she's a computer geek."

Hmm, interesting.

Beyond interesting.

"There's much for me to think about," I declared, already formulating the first step in my mind. "Ever been to a *baie turcească* before?"

"You mean a Turkish bath? Many times," he replied. "Although, I should warn you. I'm not fluent in Romanian."

I gave him a little shrug. "That shouldn't be a problem. Then our next meeting shall be at the Turkish bath. There's one in Queens that's part of the Lupu family businesses."

Let's see how you do, I thought to myself.

With that, I shook my new half brother's hand. He gripped it firmly, without making it a competition. Once I determined he could be trusted, I had work to do. This would be tricky.

But worth it, I reminded myself. It was worth it just to have a reminder of Tata's imperfection by my side. Unlike me, with an American mother, Sebastian was free from the bounds of the family. Perhaps he was a talisman of what my life might one day resemble. If I exposed this secret to the clan, which I would have to do if I introduced Sebastian and Emma, I'd *ruthlessly* pivot it to my advantage.

I waited until he was gone before hurrying downstairs to check if Nina had already passed by on her way home. Even if I'd missed her, this meeting almost made it worth it. For the first time, I had a newfound sense of hope. It reminded me of a Chinese proverb Nina had once told me. *If the winds of change blow, some people build walls, others build windmills.* There was a change in the wind, and I was determined to harness its flow for my own purpose.

23

I sensed it was morning from the brightness behind my eyelids. My puffy lids peeled back and my vision focused on the round pink clock near my bed. It had been weeks since I last saw Alex, but I still cried myself to sleep. No matter how much I did during the day, not matter how much I studied or ran, I still had enough energy to bawl my heart out at the end of the day. There was no running from the pain lodged in my chest. After everyone was in bed and the house settled for the night with creaks and groans, I pined for him. *Pathetic.*

Squinting in the dim light of my bedroom, I blinked as I adjusted to the land of the living. Turning onto my back, I stared up at the ceiling for a while. The clock blared that it was time to get up and plod through the drudgery of another lonely day.

No Alex. No Tasa.

I let out a weary sigh. At least I had Yo-Yo for a few more months. He'd decided to go to college, and even though he was only moving into Manhattan to go to NYU, he'd certainly move into the dorms, if only to get away from Mother.

While I stayed to rot away and die a spinster. I could move back to the apartment I shared with Tasa, but I knew I wouldn't. It would only intensify the loneliness that already enveloped me like a shroud. My eyes roved around my room, pausing on the various shades of pink here and there. Touching the fringe on the pink lamp, I decided it was time to change the décor. Considering this was my new normal, I might as well make it mine. Do something productive instead of moping around all day.

Pushing the covers off, I got ready for my day. Classes, study and practice afterward, go for a run, dinner with the family, then sleep. Over and over again, ad nauseam.

Throwing on a robe, I dragged myself down the stairs and followed the smell of brewing coffee. The sunlight glittered off the yellow walls and the chrome of the appliances in the kitchen my parents had remodeled recently.

Yo-Yo was at the counter, pouring himself a cup of coffee. When he saw my red and puffy eyes, a glower slid onto his face. Grabbing another mug, he poured me a cup, added milk and sugar the way I liked it, and slid it across the countertop toward me.

Wrapping my hands around it, I murmured a thanks and took a long sip. It was still hot enough to almost scald my tongue, but I was beyond caring.

"You look like shit," he remarked.

I snorted. "Wow, what happened to a simple good morning?"

His gaze pinned me in place, a scowl on his face. "Enough, already. It's been weeks, and you're still walking around like someone died."

I shrugged my shoulders. That pretty much summed up how I felt. "What do you want from me? I'm grieving."

"No one is worth what you're putting yourself through. Definitely not him," he retorted.

"Says the guy who's never fallen in love with anyone. Get back to me when your heart's been broken, Yo-Yo," I returned.

He clenched his mug and closed his eyes, taking in a long breath. "Is he really worth it, Nina? I mean, the guy dumped you so he could marry a chick he doesn't even know. If he loved you, he wouldn't have done that. The bastard was lucky you gave a fuck, and he threw it away without blinking twice. I know I sound harsh, but you've got to snap out of it already. He didn't deserve to be with you."

I placed the mug gently on the marble countertop. "He may be marrying a woman he doesn't know, but he's as much of a victim as I am. He's doing it because someone's life was on the line. Someone he cares for. Plus, this person is his responsibility. Agreeing to an arranged marriage with a stranger was his only option." My hands curled into themselves at my sides. "I'd do the same thing if your life was at risk, so I can't blame him for making the right decision."

Jabbing a finger in my direction, he said, "Ah-ha! See, right there! The fact that you're in love with a man who has to make those kinds of decisions is fucked. Can't you see that? Why can't you see that and find yourself a normal guy?"

"Whatever," I replied, feeling utterly exhausted. I'd barely had the energy to make it through the day before I even stepped into the kitchen. I definitely didn't have the energy to argue with my brother about Alex. Dragging myself to the small kitchen table by a bay window lined with pots of herbs my mother grew, I slumped into the nearest seat. "It's not like I chose to love him, Yo-Yo. It just happened. And it didn't work out for reasons that were out of his control." I gave a defeated shrug. "If you don't understand, then I can't help you get it."

Bringing me my coffee, he took a seat across from me.

"I wasn't going to have a man's death on my conscience," I explained. "I wasn't going to ask him to let people die so we could stay together. He might've done it, if I'd asked, but I couldn't." A profound sadness slid through me and settled like a heavy stone in my chest. My shoulders slumped forward.

"Your integrity is mind-blowing," he joked.

I gave him a small smile. It was the best I could do.

His hand reached out and clutched mine. "I can't stand watching you like this. You've never been depressed like this before."

"It'll pass," I stammered out, biting down on my lip to stop from crying.

"Are you sure?" He tipped his head to the side, doubt etched on his face.

"What do I know?" I rasped out. "I figure it will have to pass at some point. I had the choice to stay with him until the wedding, but it was more than I could handle. I'm sort of at a loss, right now. I'll be graduating in spring, but I don't know what to do next. Maybe get an MA in music therapy... I'd like to work with kids and have music be part of my life, but I don't know."

"Yeah? I could see you doing that," he said with an encouraging nod.

"I missed most deadlines to start in the fall, but I've been researching different programs. I'll stay here and find a job until I get in somewhere. But I'm warning you now, I will only apply to programs on the other side of the country. I need a break, and...honestly, I don't know if I can live here, knowing I might see him with her in the neighborhood. I mean, he's around all the time, at the café or at his mom's house."

"Fuck," he muttered.

"I'll go to Cali. You can move there after you graduate," I suggested softly because I'd miss him so much. I needed to start over and build a new life for myself, with new friends, but I'd miss him terribly.

"Maybe I'll transfer, depending on where you end up."

"You'd do that for me?" I choked out, my eyes and nostrils burning with unshed tears. After losing Tasa and then Alex, I was drowning. I felt as if I'd lost almost everyone important to me, and here my brother had thrown me a lifeline.

"Of course, I would. You're my sister, Nina. You've taken care of me your entire life. I know you stayed in New York because of me. I'm not going to pass up the chance to be there for you for once. And, it's not like it matters whether I'm a musician here or in L.A. So once you know where you're going, I'll transfer. Then we'll both get away from Mother and start our lives for real."

"That's...more than I ever expected," I said. "Most of the deadlines have passed, but I'll double check to see if there's any place I can apply to. Who knows, maybe I'll get in somewhere in the fall."

"If you do, then I'll apply for a transfer right away. Hell, I may drop out of college and head out west to meet you."

"Yo-Yo," I started.

He held up his hand. "Let's just see how it goes. Yes, I agreed to go to college, but I'm not giving up on my dream, no matter what. Get yourself into a program, and we can both leave this washed city and start new somewhere else.

Someplace sunny." He placed his hand on top of mine. "Someplace where we can live the lives we were meant to live."

The life I was meant to live was with Alex, but I bit my tongue. That life was dead to me. Instead, I nodded my head and gave him a watery smile.

It was a plan, which was more than I had five minutes ago. And my brother would be joining me at some point. That was more than I could've wished for after losing Alex. Because what I told him was true. I'd go insane if I had to see Alex with his new wife by his side. It was hard enough, doing everything in my power to avoid meeting him by accident. In the mornings, I went around the corner instead of passing by the café on my way to the subway. Knowing that in the afternoon, he was holed up in his office, if he was in Queens at all, I usually took my normal route back, but I only walked in the neighborhood when absolutely necessary.

He'd be married, and soon after, he'd have kids. I gulped down a large swallow of hot coffee, forcing the liquid down through the tightening muscles of my throat. The instant that thought dawned on me, I realized I'd better savor my time with my parents and brother in my childhood home because once I left, I wasn't ever coming back.

24

I let myself in through the back door of my family's home into the kitchen, where I found who I was looking for. *Bunică*. If anyone knew about Sebastian and Emma, it would be her. Standing by the large wooden table in the center of the kitchen, she was chopping onions, carrots, and celery for her famous meatball sour soup. I'd seen her make this soup thousands of times. A large bowl with a mixture of ground beef and pork sat alongside her, along with an egg, rice, and herbs for the meatballs.

She glanced up from chopping for a brief second before returning to her task. I moved toward her, kissing her on the cheek before settling my hip against the thick wooden edge of the butcherblock table.

"How long have you known?" I asked without preamble, watching carefully to see her initial reaction.

Her eyes met mine and held them for a long moment as she tried to decipher how much I knew. With a long sigh, she replied, "Sebastian. Finally. I told him he didn't need to wait until he turned twenty-five, but I soon figured out he was using that as an excuse."

I inclined my head in acknowledgment of her admission. "How long?"

"A few years before your father's death. My son was a good man, but he made some foolish choices in his lifetime. Things that weren't worthy of his wife," she added, pressing her lips together in a thin line. Although, Tata was her son, she and my mother had an especially close relationship. "Who goes and falls in love with a fickle and silly woman like that American when he has a fine wife at home?" she asked, shaking her head in dismay.

"He knew his life was in danger when he moved in on Bratva territory, and so he told me. I've been part of Sebastian's and Emma's lives since then. It was hard to accept his double life, full of lies and deceit, but I had no choice. I never forgave him for that, you know? That and keeping the children separated."

"Does Mama know?" he rasped out.

"I'm pretty sure she does. That other woman wasn't subtle with her stupid notion that they could be one happy family and share the same man. She doesn't know Romanian women, the witch. I stayed out of it and focused on the children. But your mama dropped a hint here or there. She has a good idea," she clarified.

"I'm in shock, *Bunică*," I admitted. There were many things I anticipated in my life, but stumbling upon an extra sibling or two wasn't one of them.

"I bet you are," she said, a resigned shake of the head. Grabbing a skinned potato, she hacked at it with her chopping knife. "You worshiped the ground your father walked on, even when he didn't deserve it. You sacrificed Nina to marry Nelu's daughter so you could honor your oath to your father. But neither of those men deserve your sacrifice. Your father made little effort when it came to keeping it in his pants. And you gave in too easily to Nelu. I've known that man my entire life, his father before that, and his grandfather from when I was a girl. The Popescus are a dishonorable family, every last one of them."

"Cristo may be horrible, but Stegan beat him to a pulp. Regardless of his lack of personal qualities, he will be a prince, first and foremost. That needed to be made right," I defended. A pit in my stomach yawned open. Christ, *Bunică* knew about Nina and didn't condone my decision. That hit me hard in the solar plexus. I straightened my spine, more determined than ever to exploit my father's transgression for my own use. Soon every Lupu would know that Tata had had a second family, another set of full-grown children.

I had to talk to Mama and see where she was with this. Although, I knew she'd ultimately accept my decision, if only for the business angle of bringing Sebastian on board, it was my duty as the eldest to make this okay for her. Besides gaining two siblings, the upside to dredging up this soap opera was that it freed me to do what I wanted. Bowing out of my engagement would pale in comparison to this scandal.

I'd thought this through for a long time and decided I'd free Cătălina from marrying a man who cared nothing for her. My heart was with Nina, not that it'd change my situation beyond that. My stomach twisted in revolt, but I pushed through the agony because I realized I'd done the right thing to push Nina away. Right for her, at least. She deserved more from life than to be trapped with a *mafie* king like me. The notion left me hemorrhaging in my gut, but I was determined to do what was best for her, dammit. She was a bright ray of sunshine, and my darkness, the darkness of my world, would only dim her light. I'd never forgive myself for that.

I grasped something important from my father's

betrayal. I didn't need to be perfect for my clan, like my father had been. But I did need to be perfect for my mate, the one l loved above all else, the way my father hadn't. Nina was all I wanted, more than ever now that we were apart. I didn't know how I was going to make it without her, but I was damn well going to try. For her sake, not mine.

"There were other ways instead of agreeing to his extreme demands," she countered.

Focusing back on my grandmother, I was curious about something. "How did you find out about me and Nina anyway?"

"Pfft, I'm not blind. And that girl is good for you, even if she isn't Romanian *mafie*. I'm the first to respect tradition, but that doesn't mean following it blindly. It's clear as day you were meant for each other."

"Says the woman who had an affair," I retorted. It was a well-known story that *Bunică* and my grandfather had fallen in love and had had an affair before finally leaving their respective spouses.

"An affair with the man I fell in love with, who happened not to be my husband at the time," she returned with a wink. "But we fixed the situation. We both divorced our spouses and remarried. Neither of us had children, so the casualties were manageable. Sometimes allowances have to be made for true love. I would've wronged my husband by staying married to him when I'd fallen in love with another man. Think of the girl," she said with a little shrug.

Turning on the stove, she poured olive oil into a large pot and threw some vegetables in, sautéing them. Once she was satisfied, she added tomato paste and water.

"What I'm saying is that you can fix this now that you realize that your *tata* wasn't as holy as you made him out to be. He made bad mistakes, and while I agree that it's worthwhile to work with Nelu, you gave up too much. Don't do something you'll regret only to prove to yourself that you followed in your father's footsteps. I'm glad Sebastian finally came around and showed you what's what."

My jaw tightened. "It's not that simple. The woman you call 'the girl' knows this is not and will never be about love. I can't simply break off my engagement with Nelu, and honestly, Nina is better off without me," I finished, the bitter bile of my words coating my tongue.

Seriously though, it was pure selfishness on my part to try to keep Nina. She deserved a normal life, not with someone like me. My life was intertwined with violence. There were days when I came home with blood on my hands. Literally, caked with dried blood that I scrubbed off in the sink using a little brush. I fiddled with my cuff links, turning the square of gold to align with the seam of my jacket. What kind of life was that to offer her? I wasn't going to hide it from my spouse so it was better to marry someone who knew how dark my soul was. How tainted it was from the get-go.

I tried to focus on what a good thing I was doing but I was fucking miserable. Yes, I had my family and the businesses, but I was tired. Even before Nina and I got together, life had lost its flare. Now I knew what was missing. Nina. She gave my life new meaning. My drive had returned because I wanted to provide for her and, eventually, our children. I wanted to protect her. I wanted to love her, leaving no doubt that I owned her heart and she owned mine.

I'd found my calling when we came together. When her security and happiness was my priority. I was built to protect her, and not doing that shriveled my soul. Which was why I still had one of my guys trailing her, letting me know her every move.

Picking out a dollop of the ground meat and molding it into a meatball in the palm of her hand, my grandmother broke into my brooding with a question. "What's happening with Tasa?"

Good question. That was another fucking mess I couldn't seem to fix. I'd sent out several soldiers, along with Tasa's former bodyguard, Nikki, to search for her.

"Nikki's disappeared. He was somewhere Upstate. Told me he was in Albany already, even though the GPS I stashed in his phone last sighted him in a town called Poughkeepsie. Apparently, she passed through there. My contact last heard from him a few days ago, but since then, nothing. I have the Costa Nostra watching every city up north. I also have people combing through Montreal, but no one's seen her."

"She'll go to that workshop," *Bunică* said. "Even though I'd rather you left her alone."

I gritted my teeth. "You know I can't do that. It's not even about Tata's oath to keep her safe. It's about what could happen to her if the wrong person gets a hold of her. You may have confidence in her ability to elude them, but I don't. The marriage to Cristo is off, regardless. Nina changed my mind about what to do with Tasa once I found her. I'll let her go, I promise, but it's imperative that I know she's safe," I said in a decisive tone. "That's my final word on the matter. You can fight me all you want, but I will get what I want." After a beat, I threw in, "I always do."

"Following the logic of that statement, if you wanted Nina, then you'd figure out a way to get her back. You're choosing not to do anything," she concluded.

Between gnashing teeth, I gritted out, "It's the best thing for her."

Bunică slammed the metallic bowl down on the table and exclaimed, "It's not! Why don't you ask her what she wants before you decide for her? Has Tasa's running away not taught you anything about making decisions for others? When are you going to learn?"

She glared at me before returning to forming her meatballs.

A flare of anger burned in my chest. I loved my grandmother, really I did, but she was a continual thorn in my side. The real saint of the family must've been my grandfather for putting up with her for so many years.

I narrowed my eyes at her and ground out, "I'm doing what's best."

Dropping the meatballs, one by one, in the large pot of simmering soup, she muttered more to herself than to me, "No, I guess you haven't learned that lesson yet."

Fuck.

I came here to talk about Sebastian and ended up getting lectured about my love life by an eighty-year-old woman whose head barely reached my shoulder.

"Where's Mama?" I asked, bracing myself for what was coming. No son should be put in the position I was about to find myself in, introducing the subject of her beloved husband's *other* family. That was going to be one hell of a conversation.

25

I felt a pair of eyes on me. I'd sensed it since I started my run. After my conversation with Yo-Yo, I'd decided to get my butt in gear by going for a run first thing in the morning. It made waking up alone in my pink bed marginally better. Having something to do the instant I woke up didn't give me the chance to dwell on the fact that I was alone, without Alex's arms wrapped around me or his scent enveloping me. Nope, instead, I jumped out of bed the instant my eyes opened, splashed water on my face, tugged on some clothes, and stumbled down the stairs. Once I was out the door, cold air smacked me, joggling my brain awake.

As usual, I jogged in the direction of the park along the East River. It was still semidark outside, but there were always people on the street, so I felt safe enough.

That was until the hairs on the back of my neck pricked up.

Turning my head, I caught sight of a man in a black car, but I shook off the feeling as I started down my block, passing the red-brick, post-war apartment buildings and rows of single-family townhouses. As I turned the corner onto Skillman Avenue, I saw a flash of the same car. Normally, I didn't notice one particular vehicle, out of the hundreds that passed me by, so it was strange that I'd notice it again. Perhaps I was paranoid since I was coming up to the underpass I had to go through to get to the park. Shaking off my nervousness, I reasoned that I'd be fine. The tunnel was short and there was now enough daylight.

I made it through the underpass without a glitch and continued to the park, along the river. But as I retraced my steps to go home, I spotted the same man that had been in the car earlier. He was pacing on the street by the park entrance. Close enough to him, I finally recognized him as one of Alex's soldiers. A flurry of emotions clogged my throat as I gave him a glare on my way by.

His head snapped up when I passed, and he briskly walked after me, no longer bothering to hide the fact that he was following me. *What the hell, Alex?*

The relief I felt that it was only Alex watching me quickly morphed into indignation. I had specifically told him I didn't want any more guards. Who the hell did he think he was, keeping tabs on me? I didn't care if he thought it was for my own safety. I was no longer his responsibility. He'd done it behind my back, which infuriated me even more. The bossy bastard couldn't stay in his lane. It was one thing to have me trailed when I belonged to him, when I was in potential danger because I was with him. But if he broke it off with me, then he had to do it completely. Not this pick-and-choose nonsense.

As my feet pounded the sidewalk, my fury doubled and tripled. Alex's man followed me in his car at a consistent distance until I got home. Fury radiating off me, I turned and gave him the middle finger before stomping up the stairs. Yes, I got that it was immature, but I didn't care.

In my bedroom, I stripped off my clothes and jumped into the shower. Twisting the knob until waves of cold water dumped over my head, I hoped it would cool me off. No such luck. I dressed and grabbed breakfast, eyeing the clock until I knew Alex would be at his office at the café. I'd have to miss my morning class but I didn't care because my temper had been triggered and I was in rare form to confront him.

When the clock ticked past nine o'clock, I stalked over to the café. Swinging the door open, the little bell attached to the top of the door chimed lightly. A gust of warm air and the familiar *plink, plink* of porcelain clinking on porcelain filtered through the fog of my anger.

The café had a long bar on the left, with a large shiny espresso machine and a glass display for pastries and cakes. The back wall was exposed brick, and the copper-tin ceiling, along with the black-and-white-checkered floor, gave the café the feel of a bygone era. The fragrance of coffee hit my senses as I stepped inside, reminding me of the many times I'd stopped by when Tasa was working. I was assaulted by another wave of longing for my friend. I felt her absence more than ever, standing in the center of the café as a few of the old men, playing backgammon with their cups of Turkish coffee and shots of *țuică*, halted their game to look at me. There were always a few bottles tucked away behind the coffee bar for the old men who asked for the Romanian brandy.

Scouring the café, I searched for someone to lead me to his office. Instead, I found the man himself, seated near the back.

Alex rose from his seat, his hair tousled as if he'd been raking his fingers through it in frustration. His eyes looked... stark. Hungry. Greedy. They ate me up as if I would vanish at any moment. After I was done with him, I'd make him wish I'd vanish.

A sharp stab of pain hit me in the chest, but I pushed past it. I was here on a mission, and I wasn't leaving until it was done. Until we were done. All ties severed. It was the only way I could survive. The only way forward.

Stalking over to him, I gritted out between clenched teeth, "Alex, do you have a moment?"

His eyes scanned over my face, which I knew was screwed tight with anger. "What's wrong? What's happened?" he insisted, his tone edged with worry.

I let out an exasperated sigh. I didn't want his concern. It would only erode my aggravation, and I had every right to be irate about his heavy-handedness. I *needed* my anger. It came over me so rarely and dissipated so quickly that I had to take advantage of it while it lasted. I was already risking so much by being in his presence, and I was in no mood to weaken.

"Could we speak in private? I don't want to have this discussion in public," I replied, my eyes drifting to Stegan, who was sitting at his table, and then back to him. His laptop and paperwork were spread out across two tables pulled close together. My brows stitched together. Why was he working here when he had a quiet, comfortable office upstairs? It was on the tip of my tongue to ask, but I bit down on my tongue.

His mouth turned down on the sides, his eyes narrowing as he tried to figure out what had pushed me to cross the invisible boundary line of the café and seek him out.

"Of course," he answered, gesturing to the stairway that led up to his office. Skirting the table, he gave Stegan a nod to stay and followed me as I stalked toward the stairs. Ascending the dark, narrow stairway, I felt the heat of his big body behind me. My mouth went dry, but I clenched my jaws to tamp down my nerves.

He unlocked the door to his office and pushed it open for me, one hand on the handle. As I passed, my shoulder brushed against his. That one little touch jolted me. Just as I feared, my fury began leaking away, replaced by a longing that struck me as sharp as a whip. *This* was why I moved out of his apartment. *This* was why I refused to see him. *This* was why I averted my eyes whenever I passed the Dacia Café. The man made me weak.

A different wave of longing, coming in right behind the one I had for Tasa, swept over me and left me gutted. I'd made a grave mistake coming, I realized. I'd greatly overestimated the strength I could draw on from my anger. Since it was so uncommon, I had little experience with it. I thought I could stroll into his place, hurt him with my words, and get out unscathed. Now that my fury leached out of me, it laid bare my desperate yearning for him.

But I couldn't turn around and walk out. Besides my pride, he wouldn't let me go until he found out why I'd come.

Turning around to face him, I stood there and took him in for a moment. Besides his messy hair, there was a new hollowness to his cheekbones, as if he'd lost weight. Dark circles swam under his eyes. He wasn't sleeping, either. *Good*, I thought with a viciousness that surprised me.

My gaze roved over his torso. He was still fit. His biceps bulged under the wool sleeves of his jacket. I'd forgotten how big he was, how broad his shoulders were. *Damn.* I bit down on the inside of my cheek as a familiar flare of arousal shot through me.

"How are you doing?" he inquired, his voice deep, gravelly, and dripping with sin.

"Good," I answered automatically. I cleared my throat and averted my eyes. It hurt to look at him for too long.

"You have to call off your dogs, Alex," I launched in without preamble. "I told you I didn't want anyone watching me. We're not together anymore. There's no reason for it."

He took a step closer. "Is that really why you came?"

"Yes," I hissed. "Goddamn you, yes that's why I came!" I twisted away and stomped to the far corner of the office. The more distance between us, the better. His beguiling spicy, woody scent was already driving me crazy. "I can't believe you went behind my back after I clearly told you I didn't want them around. I didn't think I needed to extract an oath from you."

Soft steps crossed the thick Persian carpet, and his heat was at my back once more. Goose bumps coasted over my skin. I broke out into a light sweat. The hair on the back of my arms rose in awareness as his hands fell on my shoulders.

"I can't," he replied simply. Too simple for my liking. As if he'd already fought himself over it and long given up the fight. "You should've thought of that before you handed that untouched pussy over to me. With the blood bond, I couldn't let you go even if I wanted to. I will *always* protect you."

Oh. God. Images of the time he took my virginity in the employee bathroom bombarded me. Of the time he'd made me that omelet the morning after. Of the times I woke up in his bed with him behind me, curled over me as if he could protect me from the harshness of the world. My shoulders slumped forward.

Licking my lips, I admitted, "He scared me. He followed me when I went running this morning, and I was really scared, until I recognized him."

His fingers unconsciously squeezed my shoulders.

"I'm sorry about that. I never meant for you to find out, and I certainly never meant to frighten you." His fingers lifted swaths of my hair and gently slid them off my shoulder. "But I can barely sleep as it is. If I don't at least know you're safe, I won't get the little that I do manage."

Swinging my head over my shoulder, I persisted, "That's not good enough, Alex. You can't have me watched. It-it's a boundary issue. I won't have it. I *can't*." Already, I was barely holding on by a thread. I was inches away from surrendering.

He took a step closer. Close enough that I could feel his hot breath drifting over the bare skin of my neck. "Do you miss me, firefly?" he asked, as soft as a whisper. It was a whisper, but it sounded loud in the stillness of his office.

Firefly.

I squeezed my eyes shut. I ached to hear that endearment said in his husky voice. *No, please don't call me that. I won't survive.*

His front pressed against my back, molding against me like he did when we'd slept side by side in his large bed. My walls were crashing around me, leaving only puffs of dust in their wake.

"It doesn't matter whether I do or not," I said, my voice scraping out of a throat so tight that it was painful to speak.

"It matters to me," he murmured in the shell of my ear. "I miss you so much, firefly. I can't sleep. I can't eat. I can hardly breathe."

A harsh breath stuttered out of me. My hands began to tremble at my sides.

"I fucking need you, Nina. You shouldn't have come here," he muttered, gliding his lips up the side of my neck. "Did you really think I could keep my hands off you?"

"Yes," I replied, gasping as he fluttered his tongue against my pulse. "You're the strongest person I know."

"Not this strong. Not when it comes to you," he replied, his hands tugging off my coat.

"What are you doing?" I cried out as my coat tumbled to the ground.

"I need to taste you, baby girl."

The rasping sounds of the fine wool of his jacket coming off his shoulders and falling to join my coat triggered something in me.

An instant later, it was a mad fury between us.

We ripped at each other's clothes, our sole purpose to be skin to skin.

Our mouths smashed together, teeth clanging as we moaned and devoured each other.

I dropped to my hands and knees on the thick carpet. Behind me, his belt clanged as he unbuckled it. I closed my eyes in anticipation as I heard the slide of his zipper. My head swerved around, over my shoulder to watch. He tore at his tie and whipped it off. His shirt hung to the sides; several buttons had popped off.

His hand slid up and down his shaft, pre-come beading on the indentation of his slit.

"You don't know how many times I've fucked my cock raw since you left," he said darkly. "Thinking I'd never get a chance to sink into your cunt again. Fucking hell."

Sinking to his knees behind me, his gaze zipped from my eyes to my pussy and back, as if he couldn't tear himself away from one or the other. His crown swiped against my slickness, and my eyes rolled back in my head.

"You want this, baby? Tell me you want it," he pleaded, his voice smoky dark.

"Yes, pleeease," I begged. I was dripping wet, craving

him. My interior muscles clenched and released as arousal exploded in my veins, and I started whimpering. If he didn't take me soon, I'd tackle him to the ground and impale myself on his cock. That's how bad I needed relief after weeks apart. I hadn't been able to get off that entire time, as if my body had gone on strike. Deprived of Alex, it withheld satisfaction.

Seizing my mouth in another filthy kiss, he shoved deep, taking me in one stroke.

"Hah, hah," I panted out. It'd been weeks, and he'd just speared me with his huge cock.

"*Tiiight*," he ground out, holding still for me to adjust.

The instant I stopped my wiggling, he took over, fucking me with a touch of wildness I'd never experienced from him before. He was always dominant, but also always in control.

Not so much now.

"God, I missed this," I admitted when he hammered into one spot that had my body shuddering.

He gave a harsh laugh. "You've missed this? Christ, I can't live without this again. I *won't*."

His hand went to my nape, holding me down as he took me with long, deep thrusts. With each downturn, he bottomed out, his balls slapping against my pussy. My thighs quivered, turning to jelly, but I forced myself to spread them wider. Arching my back further, I gave him more access, and still I felt the stretch each time he pushed back in. The way he fucked me was a claiming. A marking of whom I belonged to.

Clenching down on his cock, I could hear the squelching of my pussy each time he withdrew. One hand came around my front and toyed with my clit. The other hand wrapped around the base of my throat, cutting off more and more air so that when he finally let go, I drew in a deep breath at the same time as my climax crashed over me. I let out a strangled cry-scream as I toppled down and mashed my cheek against the rug.

Not breaking his gait, his hips snapped against my buttocks as he rode me. Hearing him, feeling him straining behind me, punctuated by delicious greedy grunts as his cock grew thicker built me back up again. Croaking out my name, his pace became disjointed. I felt the moment he broke behind me, jacking into me with wild thrusts. My gaze swung around to witness his unraveling, and it was glorious. His eyes glazed over into blindness, his jaw slackened, and his body stiffened as he took pleasure in my body. When he came, I crested again.

I heaved in great gusts of air while Alex ground his cock deeper, as if to prove a point. Then he pulled my limp body up to his chest, his arms wrapped around my middle, and held me tight while his cock continued to pulse and soften inside me. My head lolled back on his chest while tingles skated over my skin as I came down.

Nuzzling my cheek, he swore, "I'm not letting you go. I could've fought it longer if you hadn't walked into my café again. Never again, Nina."

Yanked out of my blissful state, my eyes slammed to his. *What the hell is he talking about?*

26

I was fucked the moment Nina walked into the café, her deep brown eyes flashing at me in anger. The air in the place shifted at her arrival. My men went on the alert, but the only thing on my mind was to bend her over the table and fuck her in front of them. Show them who she belonged to. Yes, I was an animal. I got that. Even now, I wanted to come all over again, but this time, I wanted to leave streaks of come on her delectable peach-shaped ass. Mark her and lather her in my scent until she smelled more like me than her beguiling fragrance.

My heart stuttered as she crossed the threshold, my eyes glued to her. And once I caught her gaze, I latched on. Like a taut rope, I pulled her toward me, one step at a time with excruciating slowness, while greedily drinking her in.

I heard the wobble in her voice when she asked to speak to me. My heart clogged my throat, thinking something had happened to her. If I thought that was bad, once we were alone, everything got exponentially worse. I couldn't keep my hands off her. The first chance I got, I attacked her mouth, hungry and consuming. Instinct took over and I lost it. Nothing mattered but claiming her.

The moment I finished fucking her, I knew I was never letting her go. My one chance at staying away, at doing what was best for her, had gone to hell. Dragging her into my embrace, I laid us down on the rug. Cradling her head in the crook of my arm, I stared deep into those big, beautiful, wide-set eyes I'd missed more than anything.

"Talk, firefly," I ordered gruffly. My chest was tight, and I had trouble pulling in the necessary amount of air as I waited for her reaction.

"I was with you because I didn't want to regret anything. But when 'maybe' turned to 'no,' I had to leave. It wasn't because of pride, although maybe it should've been. It was survival. Simply because I happened to walk into the café, you've decided we're back together again?" A puff of surprise left her lips. "That's not how it works, Alex. I'm not a volleyball you can punch back and forth over a net."

Dragging her closer, I took her mouth. Ravenous, I gorged on her lips, pressing my advantage and forcing her submission. Finally, when she went limp in my arms, although it'd never be enough, I was able to pull back and break our kiss.

"I want to be with you. I've always wanted that, but I was trying to do right by you. I'm plotting a way to break my engagement, but even though every day without you is hell, I figured you were better off without me."

She curled into me. I released a little breath of relief that she didn't pull away.

Her forehead was set in a little frown as she turned to face me and said, "I don't understand."

I swiped a hand over my face. "Baby, I'm a fucking criminal. I may be a high-end criminal, but a criminal all the same. I hope to be a free man soon, but I'll never be free of my clan and what I do for them. So I convinced myself you were better off without me. Look, you don't even want my guards on you—"

"That's because we're no longer together," she cut in, her tone exasperated. "It's about maintaining boundaries. About staying sane after we broke up. I don't have an issue with you protecting me if I'm yours."

"I was only making sure you were safe," I argued.

"No, you weren't. Once you dumped me and had a fancy new fiancée, I wasn't worth anything to your enemies. I'm not like Tasa, who has worth on her own. My worth was only linked to being with you. If people thought you didn't care about me anymore, then they couldn't hurt you by harming me. You had me followed for you," she accused, poking her forefinger into my chest.

"Yes, dammit," I growled, my patience snapping. "I was going fucking insane. I couldn't stand not knowing what you were doing, who you were seeing," I seethed. Okay, so apparently, I had a jealous streak. It's not like I didn't know I was a fucking savage when it came to her. Just the way I fucked her showed I barely had any self-control when it came to her.

"Exactly," she drawled with a smug smile, crossing her arms over her chest in a way that was distracting as hell. "Finally, we're getting somewhere. As for deciding whether we should be together or not, that wasn't your decision to make alone, buddy."

"*Bunică* said something to that effect," I muttered.

"What?" she asked cheekily, cupping her ear. "I didn't hear that. Can you repeat it louder this time?"

"I said, *Bunică* said something like that," I returned.

"Oh, you mean the old, wise woman who's your grand-mother? Haven't you already gotten yourself in trouble for making decisions on behalf of Tasa? When are you going to learn?" she pondered with a shake of her head.

"Okay, you've made your point." Did she and *Bunică* share a brain? I gave her my signature smirk, relieved that instead of smacking me like I deserved, she was teasing me. God, I fucking loved her. "I'm a work in progress, alright."

Her eyes turned serious, her lips pulling down at the corners. "So you would've kept us apart if I hadn't stopped by?" A little shudder shook through her shoulders, and I pulled her into my embrace.

I shook my head vehemently. "Oh, babe, I doubt I could've lasted much longer. It was a continual fight, and I could feel myself slipping by the day. I'm a selfish bastard at heart, but I want you to at least give me credit for attempting to do what's best for you."

"*Humph.* I would if you weren't so misguided," she huffed, cuddling into me. She was so open and giving, inno-cently nestling into my arms. Did she realize what a gift she gave me? She'd effectively forgiven me. I didn't deserve it, but that didn't mean that I wasn't going to take it as a win and run with it.

After a few moments of silence, she inquired softly, "You told your grandmother about us?"

"She guessed. She's too clever by half and then she cursed me for being a fool. Told me I was trying to follow in my father's footsteps, who it turns out was a hot fucking mess. I have two half siblings from his secret family, for Christ's sake," I confided in her.

Her eyes widened, lifting her head off my biceps, which she was using as a pillow. "What?"

"Yeah, turns out my perfect father had a very dirty

secret. A second family. I have another brother, Sebastian, and a little sister, God help me, named Emma."

"You're not going to push her into marriage are you?" she asked, concern lining her face.

"God no, I should think I've at least learned one lesson there. My new brother may come into the fold, but I'm keeping the girl far, far away from this world. Even if she is some sort of computer whiz that could be of great use to us, I don't care. I still haven't found Tasa, for fuck's sake. Let me find my sister before I try screwing up another girl's life."

Her hand lay on top of mine, her worried eyes on me. "How are you feeling about this?"

I let out a breath. It was so damn good to talk to her like this. It felt right, lying beside her, with her curled up against me. Constantly feeling shackled by responsibilities, the only time I let my guard down was around Nina. She didn't expect or ask anything of me. Her primary concern was to be by my side, to help me. With her, I could just...relax.

"It was a shock, for sure, but Sebastian looks so much like me there's no doubt we're related. Then *Bunică* confirmed it. She's known them since they were children. I was worried about my mother, but she's too understanding for her own good. Much like you." My arms tucked her svelte body closer into my chest. "More than anything, it was liberating. I was trying to emulate something that didn't exist. He was a fraud. I mean, not that I would've wanted my parents to divorce, but what kind of man has *two* families? Lying to one and torturing the other with the knowledge that they came in second best."

"I can hardly believe it..."

"Oh, believe it. He might not have been a sadist like Nelu, but he definitely fell off his pedestal. Nicu is crushed. Luca is gleeful. Me? I'm resigned, but I also get to welcome a new brother into the family. And now I'm freed to do what's best for me, the family be damned. *Bunică* was right that I was a fool to give you up," I finished.

Her large chocolate eyes gazed at me. "But what about Nelu? Nothing's changed. You can't hand Stegan over to him."

"No, I'm digging into his business. I'll eventually discover something to hang over his head in exchange for releasing me," I said confidently, because for once, I had hope. No, hope was a dangerous thing to have. I had more than hope, I had conviction. She was never going to get out of my grasp again. "The man's dirty, through and through. Nicu agreed to take my place so the contract between the families will remain intact as long as Nelu accepts that I won't become his son-in-law." Foisting the youngest son on his was an insult but, after what I had planned for him, he'd be grateful for whatever he could get. Shame burned in my belly that I panicked and allowed my world to tear us apart. Even if I'd agreed at that moment, I should've kept fighting for us. Eyes boring into hers, I snarled, "Honestly, I don't know what the fuck I was thinking."

Being Nina, she tried to comfort me. "You were doing what you thought was best. I always knew that. It was never a question of you not loving me."

"Damn straight, it wasn't. I blame myself, though," I said harshly. "I could've lost you forever. If you weren't the angel you are, willing to love me despite my idiocy, I could've lost you from sheer stupidity alone." Just the thought of it made me want to claim her again, to prove that she was real. It dawned on me that this is how it would be: I'd always want more. If nothing else, these last few weeks showed that she was as essential as breathing.

I was reveling in digging up dirt on Nelu, and I hoped to

be free of him soon. Thank fuck, the fates had smiled down on me. I didn't care what she'd come here to do. Reprimand me, curse me out in front of my soldiers. What I knew was that the moment I set eyes on her again, it was game over.

"The guard stays," I declared. "And you're moving back in with me."

A flush spread over her cheeks, and she slid her nose along my throat, cooing. "I love when you're bossy."

"Then you're in for a treat. I plan to boss you all night long."

I couldn't wait until we were in my bed again. Tonight, I reminded myself. As soon as tonight, I'd have her where I wanted her. I could finally breathe fully again. My hand glided up her spine and grabbed hold of her tresses. Steadying her, I swooped in for a languid kiss.

Canting her head to the side, she asked, "Are you sure I should move in so soon. Is that a good idea when you don't have the situation with Nelu resolved?"

"Nothing will keep me away from you, Nina. That's fucking over with. I already told you, the instant you walked through that door, it was over. I'm not keeping us separated for Nelu's benefit. Fuck him. You're going to pack up and move back in with me tonight," I ordered hoarsely. "We're not sleeping another night apart."

Her lips parted, and she bit down on the plump bottom one, hiding a tremble. Fuck, I was making her cry.

"That I ever made you doubt how much I care for you is a goddamn travesty," I said, my voice guttural. I'd already put her through so much. I'd spend the rest of my days proving to her how precious she was.

Sniffing back her tears, she buried her face in the crook of my neck.

"And the jade choker goes back on, first thing," I warned her gruffly, holding her by the nape. At least, until I got a ring on her finger.

27

I walked out of the steam room of the Russian-Turkish bath into the gentle heat of a blue-and-green-tiled room, where my meeting with Nelu was to take place. He was already seated on a stone bench, his large, bloated belly protruding over the knot of his bath-wrap, waiting for me. We'd chosen a neutral location in Brighton Beach, at a bath house not affiliated with any mafia family. The trickling sounds of a small fountain in the center, flanked by palm trees on either side, gave off a false sense of peace. Several small windows punctuated the top of the wall, the frosted glass letting in uniform, pale squares of light over the tiles and stone slabs jutting out of the walls of the circular room.

Seeing his smug expression, I wanted to slam my fist into his face, but I gave him my signature smirk instead. Sauntering toward him, I took a seat on the bench adjacent to him. Dropping my head back against the tiled wall, I lowered my eyelids and breathed in the humid, perfumed air.

"What did you want to talk about that needed this?" he asked, his hand waving to encompass the room.

"My youngest brother, Nicu, will take my place and marry Cătălina," I stated calmly.

Nelu's already flushed skin turned a mottled red. "What?" he rasped out, disbelief streaking through the one-word question. "What is the meaning of this? We had a deal. You have to pay for Cristo, and that was the payment. You. *Not* your brother."

"That payment was made in good faith, something you know nothing about," I replied calmly, my eyes slitted toward him.

"*Pula mea...* What the fuck are you talking about, you backstabbing asshole? *Du-te dracului!* Go to hell!" he hissed, rising to his feet.

I was on him in a second, clasping his shoulder and pressing him down until he buckled under the force of my grip.

"You thought you could trick me? I would've fucking honored my promise if it weren't based on treachery," I sneered. "I found out every sick detail, you bastard."

Fear sparked in his eyes for an instant before he smothered it. His jaw ticking, he said, "I have no idea what you're talking about."

"Oh no? You lie like a dog," I shot back, shaking my head. "Cristo set it up. Beating Una might have been real, but the miscarriage sure as hell wasn't. The blood? Nice touch, Nelu. Did you come up with that fucked up little detail yourself or was it Cristo?" My lips turned upward into a dark smile, all teeth and no sympathy. "No, that was all you. Cristo isn't that smart."

"How did you find out?" he rasped out.

"Like I'd tell you," I scoffed, my hand moving to his throat and squeezing.

Una, that was how. Stegan had saved her from Cristo, and she was under our protection. Once I had Luca break into the hospital database and check through her medical records, we found the doctor's notes. There was no miscarriage. The blood was fake. Then it all came together. Her other injuries were real, but not that one. I had Stegan confront Una, and she crumbled instantly. She already felt guilty but was too scared to confess on her own, fearful that we would toss her away like Nelu did. Part of me wanted to punish her but forgiving her was the better choice. Now, she was indebted to us. She'd told Stegan that Nelu threatened to kill her mother if she didn't do what he said. The girl was only trying to survive a monster, and I couldn't penalize her for that.

He watched me carefully as my fingers pressed deeper into the sides of his throat. I wouldn't kill him, but while we were alone in this room, I'd give him a little taste of my fury.

"I always knew you were a dirty rat, but now I'll be on the lookout for every fucking move you make. You're lucky my brother's a good soldier and willing to come forward and seal this deal, because if he wasn't"—I tipped my face down to him, pressing deeper until I knew he was struggling to breathe—"this would deteriorate into war."

I spoke the truth. Nicu had saved the day because I sure as fuck wasn't going to sacrifice myself. Knowing I'd been played, I would've had to step down, in any case. Luca was no more willing than before. He didn't give a damn if there was a war or not. With the bloodlust running through his veins, hell, he'd welcome it.

That left the youngest.

Nicu wasn't one to back down from a fight either, but

finding out about Tata had put him in a dark place. Realizing he was the only one left to fulfill our disgraced father's wishes, he'd taken up the mantle. Poor girl. I almost felt sorry for Cătălina. Almost...if I didn't know who I was saving her from. Hell, she was better off with coldhearted Nicu than with brutes like her father and brother. Those men had no soul, and would've sold her off to the highest bidder anyway. I was doing her a fucking favor.

My fingers tightened as I stared down at the fucker. His hands grasped my own, trying to pry my fingers off as they cut off the breathing of this bloated pig.

"Our contract stands, but the first three months are free, and I swear to fucking God, Nelu, if you cross me again, I will end you," I snarled in his face before releasing him.

Clutching his throat, he drew in gasping breaths. His narrowed eyes turned to me, but he said nothing. Smart man. Caught red-handed, he had no standing to speak. My main concern was that I couldn't afford a war right now. Not with Tasa still somewhere out there. Not when I was starting a new chapter with Nina. I wanted these next few months to be peaceful so we could begin to build our new life together. Once we had our honeymoon, and I had Tasa back home safely, then I'd consider it. But Nelu was no fool. Besides getting off easy, he wanted his daughter in our family. It was a feather in his cap that he wouldn't get from any other family.

Spitting at his feet, my lips peel back in a snarl before I pivoted on my heel and stalked out. Nicu and Stegan were milling outside the door, ears cocked for any sounds of danger. I gave them a nod and threw Cristo a scowl as I strode past him to change. I was more than done with this place and ready to get back to the woman currently warming my bed. She'd better be where I'd left her when I headed out for this meeting, or there'd be hell to pay.

When I came out of the locker room, Cristo was waiting, legs apart and arms crossed over his chest. He wrenched my arm as I passed him.

I stared down at his hard grip on my arm.

"Get your hands off me," I warned. A fight had been brewing between us for years, but we'd kept it civil. Till now.

Touching me without permission was spoiling for a fight. Bring it.

Bunching my shoulders together, I ripped his hand off me. I was a fencer. Fencers and fighters shared the same footwork, and mine was legendary.

"What did you do to my father back there? There are red finger marks on his throat. And then taking Una from me—"

Feet apart, knees bent, I barked out a sharp laugh. "You beat her half to death, you dumb fuck."

That got him.

He came swinging. I pulled back in the nick of time. He stumbled forward, and I plowed a fist into his face, catching him in the jaw. His head jerked back. *Crack.* It smacked against the wall, leaving an imprint.

Stegan stepped forward, but I waved him back. This was long overdue and I was more than ready to take him on.

Bouncing on the balls of my feet, I waited. Cristo massaged his flexing jaw as he shoved off the wall and righted himself.

Shoulders hunched forward, he barreled toward me. I sidestepped him, and he ran passed me and crashed into a vase on a pedestal. Shards of porcelain flew everywhere. The sound reverberated throughout the room as he slammed into the wall. Twisting around, he hurled toward me with a roar.

I blocked his uplifted hand and threw a series of punches—*one-two, one-two, one-two*—into his flank.

"You think I'm a pussy 'cause I don't street fight anymore," I grunted out. Hands flying up, his body jerked back with each round. "Think again." I gave him a little jab with my right fist just to mess with him.

Pulling his fist back, this time he swung and connected with my cheekbone. There was a burst of pain. *Fuck!* With a growl, I shoved my shoulder into his chest, driving him back until his back smashed against the wall. Plaster fell in chunks around the outline of his body.

Hand wrapped around his throat, I pinned him in place. His fingers grasped my forearm, fighting my grip. Leveraging my weight, I pushed forward and smacked him into the wall again. His nails tore my skin bloody, but I held tight. Strengthening my hold, I squelched his breathing. Hissing like a pissed-off animal, spittle flew from his mouth.

Teeth bared; I shoved my face into his. "Don't fucking touch me again."

Thrusting him hard one more time, I unclenched my fingers and stepped back.

Legs buckling, he slid to the ground, gasping for air at my feet. With a death stare on him, I casually adjusted my tie, flicked nonexistent dirt off the lapels of my jacket. "In case you're wondering, it's your temper that makes you such a bad fighter." He glared up at me, chest heaving as he regained his breath.

I spat at his feet, as I had done to his father. With a jerk of my head to Stegan and Nicu, I marched out. I'd gotten what I wanted. Now, it was time to return to my woman.

❋❋❋

ON THE RIDE HOME, I ordered Stegan to have Una move in with him so he could keep an eye on her for the time being. I wouldn't put it past Nelu or Cristo to kill her for her betrayal. They'd lost face, and that wasn't going to go down well for her. The way I'd humiliated them would be seared into their brains for a long time to come.

I was walking out of the elevator onto my floor when Tatum poked his head out of his apartment.

"How'd it go?" he asked, eyeing the blossoming bruise around my eye.

"As well as could be expected. I made my position clear. He didn't exactly have the clout to do much except to agree to my terms. Three months of free supply is going to hit him where it hurts. You know how stingy he is. Haggling is his damn religion. Everything okay?" I asked with a nod to my front door. It had been five days since Nina came back, and I'd basically forced her to spend every minute of it with me.

"Yeah. Not a sound. You must have worn her out," he replied with a smirk.

That got a chuckle out of me. "The walls are thick. You wouldn't be able to tell if she was out of bed."

He shrugged. "If you say so. Listen, I think I've got a trace on Tasa. Nothing conclusive yet, but a contact thinks she's been spotted in Montreal."

I raised an eyebrow. "It's still weeks before the workshop is supposed to start."

"Like I said, nothing conclusive. I wanted to give you a heads-up so you can be ready to leave the second we get a lock on her location," he said.

My eyelids dropped closed. Thank fuck. While this might be a false lead and too soon to guarantee relief, I felt it in my gut that we were getting close. Other than learning about Tata's betrayal of our family, things had been going my way lately.

"Call the airport and make sure the plane is ready. The moment you get a confirmation, you let me know."

"You want me to come with?"

I clapped his shoulder, squeezing to communicate my appreciation of his support. "This is between Tasa and I. We need to settle our differences on our own."

"She may not want to come back," he warned me.

I blew out a breath. This was something I had already thought of. When my sister first left, I was ready to drag her back at all costs and lock her up until I married her off to someone who could keep her safe. After Nina helped me realize Tasa hadn't left like a spoiled toddler having a fit, I decided I wouldn't force her to return, despite my deep desire to have her directly under my protection. I'd still do everything in my power to convince her to come back. This was her home. This was where her family was. But as long as I could assure her safety, I'd indulge her in her wanderlust. For a while. At this point, I had nothing more to lose. I'd already lost her, and that was on me and my arrogance.

"I'm going to meet her where she is and try my best to salvage our relationship," I revealed. "As long as she's safe, I can be flexible."

His lips twitched. "You can? Since when?"

"Ha, ha, you're a funny guy. Real funny," I retorted. "Now let me get back to my woman."

Unlocking the door, I dismissed Tatum and stepped into the apartment. It was quiet. I'd made my meeting with Nelu early to get it out of the way so I could have the day free to be with Nina. Shrugging off my jacket, I made my way through the apartment until I reached the bedroom. Perhaps I should've gotten an ice pack for my eye and cheek, but I decided it would be a good reminder to my soldiers that, despite my penchant for Ermenegildo Zegna suits, I was still a fighter.

Nina was so attuned to me that she sensed my presence and stirred in the semidarkness of the room. Our bed looked like a nest as she rose to her elbow, eye-fucking me as I strode toward her. It was a silent offer to join her so who was I to say no? Her skin was warm and fragrant as I dropped kisses down the side of her throat before taking a moment to draw in her scent.

"How did it go?" she asked in a husky voice that made me groan.

"It's done," I replied simply. I didn't want to waste precious time talking about Nelu when she was easily within reach. Stripping out of my clothes, I threw the covers back and slipped in beside her. My arms opened, and she instantly came to me, laying her cheek against my chest. I'd never take a moment like this for granted for as long as I was alive. "He had no choice after I told him," I added. "He'll play by my rules. For now, at least."

She squinted her eyes, processing my bruise. "Was it that simple because your eye is swollen?" Her fingertips gingerly traced the area.

"Yes, well, I did threaten his life." One of my eyebrows curved up. "Did I forget to mention that?"

She didn't flinch away from me. She wasn't even shocked. Not by my bruise or by my threat. Her throaty laugh vibrated through my chest cavity. The sound made its way down my body, settled in my cock and hardened it. No surprise there. Fuck, this woman was made for me.

"Your skin is damp," she noticed.

"We met at a Turkish bath," I explained.

"Huh. I've never been. I've been to a Korean bath before, but not Turkish."

"I'm sure they're similar. We own a bathhouse in Queens, although we met the Popescus on neutral territory in a bath in Brooklyn," I told her, stroking down her back and sliding my hand beneath her thin silk tank top. She only slept naked when I was in bed with her. Otherwise, I noticed she'd slip something on.

The days since we'd come back together had been incredible. Even better than before, because now I knew what I'd been missing. She tilted her hips toward my pelvis, and my cock was ready to play. The sweet scent of her pussy wafted up to me as she shifted under the covers, suddenly antsy. My hand cupped her tight ass, bringing her flush against me. I craved the sense of connection and rightness she brought me.

Hiking her up until her lips were within reach, I whispered over her mouth, "I love you."

I felt her little intake of breath against my skin before I swept in and devoured her. Even after everything we'd been through, it was the first time I said it out loud. I pulled the top off her, wiggled her panties down her long legs and slipped my thigh between them, groaning at the touch of her wet slit.

Nina's head dropped back, and she let out a low moan, "Now you tell me? Not over a nice dinner when I'm not desperate to have you inside me and can focus on what you said."

"It's better this way," I promised, sliding her on top of me. Lifting her to her knees, I placed my cock at her slippery entrance. Gritting my teeth to hold on, I brought her down with excruciating slowness. Her hands slapped on my chest, her blunt fingernails digging into my skin. She scraped them down my chest, the little tease, as she shimmied her way down the length of my cock.

Eyes hooded with desire, she said, "I'm in love with you, Alex. I have been for years."

"That was puppy love, baby. This is real," I elucidated. "To take me back after what I did..." I shook my head, still a bit incredulous at my luck. "That's true fucking love."

I watched as her tits bounced as she rocked herself on my cock with a swerve of her hips that had me baring my teeth. Fuck, her pussy was a gold mine. Whenever I hit it, I hit gold. The jade wolf of her choker bounded off the base of her throat, reminding me of my claim on her.

"And you're getting the tat," I pronounced.

"Ahhh," she gasped out, her pace stuttering in her surprise. "Really?"

Did she not believe me when I'd just declared my love to her?

"Christ, Nina. Of course," I said. "As soon as possible."

A wide grin spread over her face, lighting her melted-chocolate eyes. Pure joy radiated from every inch of her.

I thrust my nose into her neck and growled, "Firefly, I fucking love you. I *love* you, baby. I'll never deserve you." My heart broke in two that she didn't own it, didn't take it for granted that I was fixated on her, didn't *assume* I'd do everything in my power to fulfill her every wish. I was going to dedicate my life to showing her how obsessed I was with her. Every. Single. Day.

Starting now.

As I thrust up into her, I told her all the things I loved about her. With every caress, I praised her, calling her my good girl. The curve of her hip, the bow of her back, the arch of her neck when she came. The way her pussy tightened and milked me like it was its only job on earth. And when I raced after my own climax, I shouted her name until my throat was hoarse, because this woman deserved everything from me.

She was my everything.

EPILOGUE

I was beside Alex in the car, trying to give him a stern stare-down but I wasn't having much success. Sitting in the middle of traffic on the FDR Drive, I'd spent the past quarter hour pressing him to tell me where we were going for dinner. The man wouldn't break.

"Come on, Alex, just tell me already," I persisted. I wasn't a fan of surprises. Besides, I was both giddy and famished. I'd finished the last session for my Lupu tat, inked by a famous Danish tattoo artist who'd closed his shop to work on me. The colors were gorgeous, and I loved, loved, loved it. A sense of wholeness had settled on me as he worked away. Meanwhile, Alex fretted beside me like I was having life-saving surgery instead of getting ink on my skin, the baby. His pacing was distracting me, so I could only imagine what it was doing to poor Henning. Finally, I put my foot down and gave him an ultimatum to either settle down or leave the room.

I'd already sent Tasa a pic, who texted back with a series of smiley and celebratory emojis. I planned to check on her later. Tasa was up in Montreal, but going through a difficult time, and I was worried for her. At least Alex and Tasa had finally found common ground. Once Alex's contact had gotten a location on Tasa in Montreal, he flew up to see her.

Apparently, their discussion had lasted through the night. Tasa had divulged that she was pregnant. The baby daddy was a former Bratva prince whose name was Whistle. Apparently, he was a biker in a city an hour north of New York City. She'd left him and was on her own, working in Montreal while waiting for Mrs. Pierrette's workshop to begin.

Alex was livid, but he'd rallied to support her. I'd had to stop him from intervening more than once, after he tried to bully Whistle into going after Tasa and force her to return with him. Luckily, Whistle wasn't an idiot and refused to get pushed around by Alex. I already liked him for standing his ground. He knew his woman and that was a sign that he was stable. Tasa needed someone strong and steady by her side.

For now, her plan was to attend the dance workshop while she worked through her feelings for Whistle. I tried to talk her into following her heart. That was the one thing I'd done right with Alex, so it was the only advice I could confidently give her. If she followed her heart, I told her, the rest would work itself out. Of course, I didn't have the intense craving for independence that she had, but it was also obvious she was in love with him.

As for Tasa and me? At first, I was worried about how she would react about Alex and me. Like with my mother, my first tendency was to hide. But Tasa was my best friend, and she loved me. She was thrilled for us, although, to Alex's great frustration, she routinely checked in with me to make certain this is what I *really* wanted. He genuinely seemed worried that she would change my mind. As if!

Once the tat was completed, my skin was red, itchy, and

burned. Sensing my discomfort, Alex declared that he was taking me somewhere special for dinner. But he refused to tell me more. *Grrr, stubborn man.*

We took the downtown exit and wound around Chinatown until we pulled up to a restaurant. From the roast ducks hanging in the window, I guessed we were at a restaurant from northern China.

"Is this a hot-pot place?" I asked, peeking through the window at the awning. "I've had hot pot a few times, buuuttt my mother's from the south," I reminded him with a wry smile.

"I'm aware," he replied in an offended tone. "Seriously, Nina, do you really think I don't know that? That I don't know the most basic aspects of who you are."

"Sorry," I mumbled, because yes, that was exactly what I'd assumed.

"I thought we could learn about this cuisine together. Share the experience. Create a new set of memories that are only ours."

My heart melted right then and there.

Passing the unpretentious storefront, we stepped into the foyer and I blinked a few times. While the front was like any typical Chinese takeout restaurant, the interior was...*whoa.*

Elaborate. Luxurious. The floor beneath my feet was made of thick floorboards of dark wood, something like mahogany. The back wall was deep-red velvet. The color scheme was accentuated by the semicircular, red velvet seats situated around tables with impeccable settings that looked like artwork in themselves. Small red lanterns were scattered throughout the space, punctuated by calligraphy-inspired chandeliers hanging from the ceiling at regular intervals. The focal point was a pond in the center with what I assumed were koi fish, and squinting, I saw lily pads with...flowers? How did they even manage that in such dim lighting.

"This is quite something," I breathed out, my eyes pinging all over the place as the hostess led us to our table.

"Wait until you try the food. And they have champagne," he added.

My forehead wrinkled. "Champagne with Chinese food?"

"Apparently, they have a sommelier who works with the chef to pair the dishes with different wines and champagne," he explained with a shrug.

We took our seats and perused the drinks menu, or rather Alex did, as I took in the sumptuous surroundings. "I have to say, I'm surprised by the interior when they have Peking ducks hanging from the windows in the front like any ordinary Chinese place."

"Yes," he mused. "When the son took over his father's more modest restaurant, he kept the front to remind him of his roots. It's become something of a gimmick, now. Kind of like underground speakeasies and jazz clubs that can only be found by a bare light bulb in a dark alley."

"Huh," I replied.

After ordering a bottle, Alex inspected me closely. "How are you feeling, firefly? I hate the idea of you in pain, and I know it burns like a bitch after a session like the one you had today. At least he got it done in only two sessions. I think I'd lose my mind if I had to go back there and watch him touch you again."

I rolled my eyes. "He was working. It's not like he was groping me or something. Henning was a complete professional."

"Pfft," he scoffed. "God only knows what would've happened if I hadn't been there."

I grinned. Poor Alex was delusional. He was convinced that I was irresistible to every man and in imminent danger to getting taken from him. And I was the meanie who let him run wild with that thought. If he wanted to get possessive and growly with me, I was all in for shamelessly promoting that sort of behavior, because it meant he'd inevitably get dominant in bed later.

Pitching my voice low, I mischievously licked me lips and said, "Are you going to teach me who's the boss when we get home?"

His green eyes glittered. "Baby girl, you don't want to poke the bear after the afternoon I had to endure."

"Mm-hmm."

Leaning over, he warned, "If I didn't know for a fact that you're hungry, we'd be leaving right this instant. But don't worry. When we get home, I'll find something useful to occupy that bratty mouth of yours."

"Promises, promises," I trilled. It still felt unreal...this bliss between us. Alex had cut down on his hours, delegating more responsibility to Luca and Nicu because he said that after what we'd been through, we deserved a moment to bask in each other.

He crossed his arms over his chest. Gulping, I gazed at the sleeves stretching over the width of his biceps as Alex reprimanded me with his eyes. Ha, like that would do anything. Ever since he'd casually brought up the subject of marriage after telling me it was time for my tat, I'd been insatiable.

"Behave," he demanded, his voice deep and commanding.

"Okay, okay," I huffed. I'd kept him in bed half the day as

it was. He put his hand out, and I grabbed it, our fingers tangling. The waiter came and opened the champagne with a little pop and poured us each a glass.

I took a sip and felt something in my glass as I tipped it to my lips. Glancing down, I caught a glitter of something at the bottom of my flute. My eyebrows drew together as I examined it carefully, tipping my flute this way and that but the lighting was too low for me to tell what it was.

"Um, there's something at the bottom of my drink," I said.

"Drink up to see what it is," Alex said casually.

My gaze shot to his face. He returned my gaze with a hooded one of his own. *Okay, what's going on?*

"Go on," he prodded me.

Unable to resist, I angled my glass up and let the liquid slide down my throat. Just as cold metal hit my lip, I pulled away and stared at a wet ring caught by the lip of the glass. It had a huge diamond surrounded by little pearls. Gingerly taking it up, I raised it to eye level, my gaze darting from the ring to Alex and back to the ring. This went on for a long moment before I cleared my throat and asked, "W-what is this?"

"I should think it's obvious, no?" he said simply, with a shrug of his shoulders as if he hadn't had something to do with a huge-ass diamond ring being dropped in my glass of champagne.

"A ring?"

"For you," he said hoarsely, his eyes flickering away from mine.

Oh. My. God. It dawned on me that he was nervous. Alex Lupu, the *Lupul*, was nervous. It was the first time I'd ever seen him like this.

"Nina..." he said in a hoarse voice, paused and restarted,

"Nina, I fucking love you, and it's growing by the day. Since you've been mine, my jealousy is off the charts, and I imagine it will only get worse until I get you in front of a priest and put a wedding ring on your finger. Hell, who am I kidding. Not until I make you fat with a baby in your belly."

I gasped, but he went on, "I never wanted to be a better man until I was with you. You make me want to be better. For you. For us. For the family I pray you want to have with me. Please, firefly, be mine."

Tears rolled down my cheeks by the time he finished. All I could do was nod because, otherwise, I was going to ball. My heart was pounding out of my rib cage with emotion. Joy and gratitude and such an outpouring of love for this man. Plucking the ring from my fingers, he got out of his seat.

My hand went to my mouth, and I shook my head, aghast as he took a knee in front of me. Lifting my shaking hand, he pressed a kiss on each knuckle before sliding the ring onto my finger.

"Oh, God, Alex. You don't know... I've never let myself dream of this happening."

He frowned. "Why not? I've been dropping hints constantly."

"Yes, but I didn't want to get my hopes up. I figured the tat was such a huge step..."

"Fuck the tat. The tat is nothing compared to what I'm going to do to brand your ass for doubting me." He rose to his feet. Bending over, he seared me with a blistering kiss that left me breathless before returning to his seat.

Taking my hand, he murmured, "I fucking love you, Nina. I'd kill for you, and I'd die for you, do you understand?"

"Yeah," I replied, nodding like a loon. "I can't remember a time when I didn't love you."

"I will do everything in my power to be worthy of you, baby. I will take care of you. Never ever doubt that you deserve everything from me. You're my reason for breathing. For living. Without you, I'm nothing.

"And once we're married, I want you off birth control. You know my mother's expectations for grandchildren," he said nonchalantly with a cheeky wink. "I always try to keep my mother happy."

I let out a gasp. *What?*

"We'll move into a bigger place if that's what you want. With enough room for Yo-Yo to come and go as he needs, whenever he wants a break from your mother."

This man. This man was everything to me. He paid attention and gave me everything I'd ever wanted.

In the middle of the restaurant, I stood up and moved toward him. He pushed his seat back, and I sat on his lap, linking my hands behind his nape. Twirling the soft ends of his hair in my fingers, I breathed in the familiar scent of sandalwood from his cologne, which I now knew was Serge Lutens.

"You've given me everything, Alex. Everything."

We'd fought the odds, odds that almost tore us apart permanently, and I swore I would hold on tight to our love. I was his, and he was mine, and nothing would come between us again. With the tat rubbing against the bandage and the delicious weight of the ring around my finger, I felt it in my bones. We were bound for life.

BONUS EPILOGUE

CAT

I had to escape the suffocating pressure of being dragged around by my mother, who prodded me to smile wider and laugh quieter in order to seem more ladylike. Pfft, as if any of that would help my case. It didn't matter what I said or how I acted. The man, or rather stranger, who was my fiancé, was as stuck as me with our engagement.

My mother relished every moment of the charade, especially since the Lupu clan was paying for the entire engagement party weekend. Considering our financial problems, I tried talking her out of a big wedding, but she said it was a matter of Popescu pride. I didn't see what pride had to do with it. If we couldn't afford it, we couldn't afford it. My father was already in debt, and the idea of adding to it to pay for my wedding seemed insane. While my mother was ecstatic, I was trying to manage Cristo, who slunk in the background, growling and snapping at anyone who passed by.

My mother got embroiled in a deep conversation with another *mafie* matriarch, and seeing my chance, I held my breath and inched away slowly until I melted into the crowd. When I was far enough away, engulfed in the large, bustling reception room, I scooped up a champagne flute from a passing waiter, took a deep swallow, and slipped out the nearest open French doors onto a patio.

Guzzling down half the glass, I felt the bubbly blend with the acid roiling in my stomach. Not the best combination but screw it. I followed the wraparound patio around the corner of the house and pressed my spine against the rounded, ancient-looking stones protruding from the wall. The back of my head thumped lightly on the wall as I closed my eyes and expelled a long sigh.

"Needed an escape, huh?"

A gasp slipped past my lips as my eyes popped open wide. My head spun in the direction of the intruder. My gaze landed on a man, half a dozen feet away from me. Leaning a shoulder against the stone wall, a cigarette dangled from his full, sculpted lips. I gaped at his face. God, what a face. His expression confirmed that he was a devil. Wasn't every man here? But damn if his features didn't give him the look of an angel.

How unfair.

A spring breeze blew blond curls off a face that might as well have been carved out of marble. All the angles were hard, from his strong, wide forehead to his high cheekbones to the jut of his jawbone. But his eyes were what paralyzed me, rooting me to my spot. Bright silver and hard, but with a faint trace of mischief in them. Staring at him was an experience in and of itself. An unusual mixture of the desire to scream and laugh hysterically warred inside me.

"Uhhh..." I trailed off. Caught off guard by his cruel beauty, my brain hiccupped. "I-I didn't see you there."

A feral smirk curled the edges of his lips upward as his eyes slowly made their way down my body. Heat singed every inch he touched with his eyes. It took every ounce of pride I had not to fidget under his blatant perusal. Sheesh, at least he found me attractive, which was more than I could say for my fiancé. The thought burned a hole in my gut. Normally, I didn't seek the approval of others, but it was a doozy to experience Nicu's eyes gloss over me like I didn't even exist.

Nothing like that could be said of this man.

"Hmm, apparently not. Who are you running from, beautiful? Or were you also escaping the general bullshit of this absurd party?" he asked, his voice doused in mockery.

I cleared my throat.

"General bullshit," I croaked out.

He nodded knowingly, as if we shared a mutual secret. As if we were co-conspirators of some kind. Good God, I wish I could conspire with him. Preferably between the sheets. I didn't really mean that, of course. It was my unbridled libido talking. But that's what happened when a woman of eighteen, who had never been touched, was faced with such raw, sensual beauty.

Between the arrogance that oozed from him and the fact that I didn't recognize him, he was most definitely a Lupu. Lupu men were dangerous, and this one had to be the most perilous of them all. There was a wild, rough energy that rolled off him in waves, even though he hadn't moved a muscle. He reminded me of a caged feline.

Powerful. Untamed. Unsafe.

The smartest move I could make was to leave his presence, but then my eyes dipped to the cigarette in his hand.

I stammered out, "D-do you have another one of those?"

Alcohol. Nicotine. Anything to help me get through this ludicrous farce of an engagement party. If it wasn't for the fact that it was my duty, that I wanted to make my family proud, and that my mother was having the time of her life, I'd never have put up with this ridiculous situation.

His eyes slid over my face critically. "Are you even legal?" he asked, tipping his chin toward the glass that I gripped. His lips turned up into a half smile and a deadly dimple popped out on his left cheek.

"Yes and no," I teased.

His eyebrows drew down. "What the hell does that mean?" he ground out.

Jeez, no patience, this one.

"I'm eighteen," I clarified.

He nodded sagely. Instead of giving me a cigarette of my own, he passed me his own, butt facing me. I glanced down, searching for the imprint of those full lips on the filter. Finding nothing, I snatched it and took a drag. The burn exploded in my lungs, giving me a little head rush, but I savored it.

"You're not going to tell on me, are you?" I threw him one of my toss-away flirty smiles.

His eyes turned hard. Clearly, it didn't melt him. He snorted. "No. I'm the last one to tattle."

I didn't know exactly what he meant by that, but as long as I had a moment to regroup before I returned to my mother, I was good.

"You must be a Popescu," he said neutrally.

"Obviously," I said before taking another drag. "And you must be a Lupu."

He gave a bark of disbelief at the snark in my tone.

"A little attitude. I like it."

Those last three words coming out of his mouth did something to my tummy. It was like a swarm of butterflies had suddenly found refuge in there. Damn, with that edginess and rough tone, he was too sexy by half.

A few curls of sandy blond hair flopped over his fore-head, and I itched to reach out and sweep them out of the way. I always had a thing for blonds, a rare unicorn among dark-haired, olive-skinned Romanians, like Nicu.

"A little," I agreed, giving him a real grin this time, with a shrug of one bare shoulder. My dress was pretty revealing, with a plunging neckline from my spaghetti straps. I cupped my elbows to warm myself in the still-cool weather of the late spring day. While not far north of the city, being away from the incubation of the concrete jungle dropped the temperature by a few degrees.

Searching for something else to say, I observed, "It's pretty here. Different from the usual *mafie* parties, always on some fancy rooftop or, even worse, a blinged-out reception hall." My gaze absorbed the garden, with its swaths of tulips in brilliant colors. There was a marble fountain of a woman, water pouring out of the urn she was holding.

"You're the pretty one," he commented, his voice drip-ping with dark promises. His gaze coasted over me, and there was a snap, crackle, and pop on every inch of skin he pored over. *Holy hell.* Suddenly, I was burning up.

"Ahh...a player. I should've known," I replied with a sardonic shake of my head.

"How would you know?" he scoffed. "You're barely an adult."

Delectable heat turned to hot shame. Okay, that was uncalled for. Grinding my teeth together, I took a turn at patently looking *him* over. Two could play this game, and oh, was I going to take advantage of my one and only chance to look. Tease him with my overtly sexual gaze. It might be my engagement party, but screw that, this man was taunting me. Besides, I was no delusional miss who thought my engagement and marriage had anything to do with love. I was a pawn, and my marriage was a contract. Nothing more. Nothing less. So, while I had a teensy bit of freedom, I'd snatch it up.

And he was nothing like the immature teenage boys from school that left me unimpressed and uninspired. This Lupu was a full-grown male. Biting into my bottom lip, I took in his broad shoulders and defined chest, obvious beneath his jacket and tie, down to his tapered waist and fitted slacks. This one was a lady-killer. He exuded a combination of sensuality and dominance that would bring women to their knees.

"For a little girl, you have a dangerous way of looking at a man. Could get you in trouble," he murmured low, the gray in his eyes turning darker and more turbulent as he moved closer. Close enough for me to catch the musky scent of him, with a hint of bergamot.

That and the way he called me "little girl" shot lust down my middle and settled in between my thighs. I may have felt something when I'd kissed Simu, but what this man made me feel was in a whole other category of heat.

It could go no further than this moment, but I enjoyed the flirting, even with the edginess he threw into the mix. I chuckled, dismissing his comment. "I seriously doubt that."

My fiancé had barely looked my way since I arrived, over an hour and a half ago. And I was watching his behavior closely. I got nothing. *Nada. Nichts.* You couldn't feign that level of disinterest. Again, I knew this wasn't love. *But couldn't lust at least make an appearance?* Boys at school hit on me. Simu liked me. Hell, he could've at least glanced my way. I wasn't ugly. In fact, people had commented on my looks in the past. I'd been called pretty.

But clearly not by my fiancé. Maybe he had a side girl,

like Cristo had. Or maybe he was at the bottom of the totem pole and didn't have the clout to reject me.

This one, on the other hand...I checked him out beneath my lashes and caught him staring at me again. This one was...something else. He took out another cigarette from a gold cigarette holder and lit it with a Zippo that he'd extracted from his jacket pocket. There was interest in his eyes. Deep interest. And I loved being the center of his attention. I felt like a butterfly coming out of a chrysalis and stretching its wings for the first time.

His hand moved, picked a strand of hair that had flown across my face, and rubbed it between his fingers. My tummy swooped. The gesture felt proprietary. The cigarette I was holding had burnt down to the butt. Mesmerized by him, I dropped it to the ground. He crushed it beneath his heel.

"It's quiet here. So different from the city," I said, to cut through the heavy tension between us. I'd never felt this with a man before.

"It's my hideaway," he divulged, continuing to caress my hair.

"I love flowers," I confided on a gentle sigh. His hand paused on my hair for a moment. There was an emotion in his eyes that I couldn't interpret, him being a stranger and all. If I wasn't mistaken, there was warmth in his gaze, along with a glint of pride.

Breaking our connection, he looked across the explosion of blooming flowers. Why would a man like him want to hide out? Men who looked like him were meant to rule in nightclubs, getting to choose the pick of the litter of women that inevitably flocked them. And yet, at the same time, I completely related. Boarding school was a hideout for me. It offered me an escape from the parts of my family and the *mafie* world that I hated, necessary evil that they were. I just assumed that only women, who were locked away most of their lives, were desperate to break away.

Before I could ponder this enigma or the man behind it any further, I caught a flash of red.

My cousin, Dina, turned the corner and I pulled away from him. He held on for an instant before letting go just as Dina noticed me. Letting out a huff, she gave him a brief nod of respect before chastising me, "Your mother's been looking for you everywhere. God, you can be such a pain sometimes."

"I haven't been gone for more than ten minutes. I needed a break."

Her eyes softened as she came to me and pulled me into a hug. "I know, I know. The whole situation is maddening, but this is our lot in life. We have to make do, sweetie," she said as she wrapped her fingers around my upper arm and dragged me off the wall like I was a child. Ugh. My head snapped to him when I heard a low growl, but I must have imagined it because his face was a mask of nonchalance.

"Come on, things could be worse," she muttered.

His eyes were narrowed on Dina's hold around my arm, and my heart soared. As we passed him, he brought his hand up and broke her contact on me. She drew back, rattled, but he ignored her, his eyes on me now.

"Could they?" I replied as I nodded a thanks to him before following her. Glancing over my shoulder, I gave the sexy Lupu a little wink and downed the rest of my champagne before Dina poked me in the side to get moving. Would I ever see this sexy stranger again?

God, I hoped so.

Thank you for reading THE CHOSEN HEIR! I hope you loved meeting Alex and Nina. The next book in the Lupu Chronicles dark mafia series is The Recluse Heir.

I am Luca, the black sheep of the Romanian mafie Lupu clan.

Cat, the woman I want as mine, happens to be my brother's fiancée.

I will do anything to make her mine. Consequences bedamned.

GET THE RECLUSE HEIR ON AMAZON, APPLE, KOBO, NOOK & GOOGLEPLAY >>

Want a taste now?

Virginity is power, dragă mea. *One of our great powers as women. Do not be careless with it.*

My mother's words rang in my head while I sat through the droning lecture in my senior history class, causing heat to crawl up my nape. The sounds of clacking on keyboards and riffling through books sifted through the classroom. I tore a few sheets of paper from my notebook and used them to fan myself.

"Ms. Popescu?"

My head snapped up; my gaze fixed on my history teacher, who'd approached my desk without me noticing. His frowning visage pinned me to the back of my seat.

Clearing my throat, I stammered, "Y-yes, Mr. Holland."

"And exactly how did the Reagan administration's massive military spending program, the largest in US history, impact the Soviet economy, pray tell, Ms. Popescu?"

Shoot. This is what happened when my mind wandered. What was once a rare occurrence happened much too often lately. Of course, it would come as no surprise to anyone who knew what my life was really like.

Although I'd worked my butt off to graduate at the top of my class in this exclusive boarding school, none of it mattered because I wasn't going on to college like every other kid in my school.

No, instead, I was getting married to a man I barely knew.

Nicu. The youngest, and most vicious, son of the Lupu clan. Ugh.

My mother already sent me a pic of my engagement ring, along with posting it on her social media. Yes, so help me God, my mother was on Insta.

The ring was truly atrocious. Huge. Sparkly. *Tacky.* My family had a rep for not being classy. *His* family was known for their refinement, so there could only be one reason for picking the ring he did. To taunt me. To show the world that the Lupu clan was powerful and rich *and* to flaunt the fact that they now owned me. Me and my virginity. We were nothing more than expensive possessions, like that horrid ring.

"I'm waiting, Ms. Popesc*u*," Mr. Holland said, dragging out the *ou* sound of my last name as if it were an ugly thing. The classroom was so quiet that I could hear the branches of the tree outside scratching against the windowpane as it swayed in the wind.

"I'm sorry, Mr. Holland. I got distracted and didn't..."

My eyes darted to my side. My best friend, Jewel, shot her hand up. Yet again, trying to save me, but Mr. Holland wasn't having any of it.

"Ms. Popescu, Reagan's massive spending program was one of the pivotal factors that led to the final downfall of the Soviet Union. *That* is the answer, and it behooves you to pay closer attention in this class if you wish to continue your sparkling educational career. More importantly, to become an educated citizen of the world, because that is the real goal behind an education at Roman Academy."

"Yes, Mr. Holland. I'll try to do better," I muttered, heat creeping up my neck and flushing my face.

"I should hope you do more than *try*, Ms. Popescu," he replied tersely.

"Yes, sir," I whispered, slouching down in my seat, eyes glued to my desk.

He was right, of course. Mr. Holland wasn't being rude on purpose. He believed in the worthiness of history and the importance of a stellar education. Normally, I agreed with him. Being called out in front of the class was so humiliating precisely because I was one of his favorites. I was a model student. A teacher's pet. It came from my heart, not from the pressure to please my parents, like so many students here. My parents couldn't care less. My father hadn't even completed high school. He was running the streets of Bucharest by the time he was in his teens, hustling to feed his mother and siblings, selling drugs or anything he could get his hands on. These were the suppertime stories I grew up listening to, not about fraternity hazing rituals at an Ivy League college.

I did well academically because being the best was the only kind of positive feedback I got, and negative attention wasn't an option for a *mafie* girl like me. While some of my classmates rebelled, I came from a world where you didn't bring unwanted notice to you or your family. Yet, despite my love for school, the impending doom of my wedding had blunted my drive to learn.

Bending my head down and pretending to focus on whatever was on the screen of my laptop, I let out a weary sigh. The only silver lining of going back to New York City after I graduated was that Jewel had gotten accepted to Barnard College, the women's college, so she'd be in the city as well.

It would be painful to watch her go off to classes while I rotted away in a lonely apartment with my new husband, but, at least, we'd be in the same city. Besides living vicariously through her, I harbored a secret hope that once I settled into the marriage with Nicu, I could convince him to let me take a couple of classes with Jewel.

My eyes darted briefly to Jewel. She caught my look, her expression softening with pity. The Popescu pride should have burned at the sympathy on her face, but it didn't even penetrate the cloud of sadness enveloping me. She knew how determined I had once been to be the perfect student and how now I was...lost. What was the point of it all now that I wouldn't join the rest of my graduating class off to college next year? Of course, I always knew I was destined to marry a *mafie* made man, but I hadn't expected to be thrust into an engagement quite this soon.

Despite the guilt of being away from my family, I should be grateful for this opportunity, this slice of heaven that I was afforded. No other *mafie* girl got a chance like this. They stayed at home, to ensure they were virgins when they got engaged after graduation. It took witnessing my father, the head of my clan no less, killing a man in front of me at the ripe old age of twelve for that to happen.

A shudder racked through me as the memory flittered into my mind. I'd been on my way to the kitchen in the middle of the night to grab a glass of water when I'd heard strange sounds and bumps beneath me. Half asleep and confused, I'd crept down the steps to the basement.

Glancing around a corner, I had arrived just in time for

the main attraction. Frozen in place, I'd watched as he choked the life out of a man, his face in a twisted grimace of pleasure and pain.

Hearing my sharp inhalation, his head had whipped toward me. With a curse, he'd snapped at me sharply to *go back upstairs.* My heart stuttered at the murder in his eyes.

Taking advantage of my father's distraction, the man tore out of his grip and lunged toward me. I shrieked as I dodged his clawing fingers. In a flash, my father tackled him to the ground. Knee on his victim's chest, my father choked him. Gasping and gurgling, his eyes bulged open, and his face turned an unnatural shade of red.

Tearing my gaze away, I spun around and bolted up the stairs. Diving under the covers, I huddled in my bed in a fetal position. Much later, he came to my room and apologized. "None of that was meant for your eyes, and I promise it won't happen again," he said in the same heavy accent that was usually a source of comfort to me.

I'd been too freaked out to say much of anything, but I couldn't help the full-body shudder that racked my body. My tongue lay thick in my mouth, unable to move. *No biggie, Dad. I now know, without a shadow of a doubt, that you're a cold-blooded killer.* Of course, I had known what my father and brother did for a living but had been spared the violent reality up to that point. I had worshipped my dad. Scratch that; I had worshipped them both. Still did.

That night, I hadn't slept. The following night, I'd fallen into an exhausted stupor, but with it came the nightmares.

Nightmares where I shrieked so loudly that I'd wake up the entire house. My mother was upset, my father worried. It had caused a rift with my mother; she blamed me for allowing this to happen. Only months of endless nightmares and my father's persuasion convinced her to forgive me. Soon after, my father decided that a change of scenery was the best solution, and I had been sent to boarding school.

It was only supposed to be for a year, but then I met Jewel, a New Yorker like me, and one year turned into two. Now six years later, I was in the last semester of my senior year.

The bell rang.

"That's all for today," Mr. Holland said with a dismissive wave of his hand. The class broke into movement as students slapped their notebooks or laptops shut and gathered their stuff. In the midst of all the noise, I slowly turned to Jewel.

"It's okay, Cat. It's okay," she said in a soothing tone, patting my forearm in reassurance.

I was the good girl. The good student. Sure, I had a mouth on me, but I strove to be number one in everything I did. Who knew where it came from, this overachieving gene? Cristo certainly hadn't inherited it. Whereas his entire life revolved around our *mafie* family, I didn't want to limit myself to being a wife and mother. I may have known better than to yearn for a career, but I dreamed of continuing my education. At the very least, I wanted to make it through college.

"Come on," she coaxed, as she helped me collect my things. "You'll be late for your next class."

My shoulders drooped. "What does it matter, Jewel? Seriously, with my current GPA, I could flunk out of every one of my classes and still graduate. It's not like it matters what my GPA is anyway. I'm not moving on up," I replied as I dragged myself to my feet.

"Hush now, stop that. It matters a whole lot because you're one of the smartest people here, and you busted your butt to become valedictorian. Don't let what's going to happen in the future get to you," she said guardedly, not wanting to mention my engagement out loud. "Don't let anyone undermine the work you've put in these past four years, Cat. You can still graduate valedictorian. You know you'll regret it if you don't."

With a pained groan, I meekly followed her out into the hallway. She was right. I may not be able to get the image of that engagement ring out of my head, but I had long ago set a goal for myself to be the best. To graduate and give that stupid speech that only valedictorians give. No one besides Jewel and my guidance counselor knew I wasn't going on to college. My best friend told everyone that we were going to attend Barnard College together.

The valedictorian graduation speech was my last hurrah before I went under lockdown as a trophy wife-slash-arm candy-slash-breeding heifer. I had no choice in my future. There was no way I'd disappoint my mother, bring shame down on the family name, and turn my back on my community. Not only would it be a tragedy to give up after working so hard but focusing on academics had saved me once before. I had to believe that it would do the trick again.

God, please let me be right.

I appreciate your help in spreading the word, including telling a friend. Reviews help readers find books! Please leave a review on your favorite book site.

Sign up to my newsletter to find out when I have new books!

MORE BY MONIQUE MOREAU

The Lupu Chronicles

The Recluse Heir (Luca's story)
The Savage Heir (Nicu's story)
The Perfect Heir (Tatum's story)
The Bastard Heir (Sebastian's story)
The Princess Heir (Emma's story)

Fans of sizzling hot alpha bikers and the sassy, strong women who tame them will love Monique Moreau's steamy MC series.

The Demon Squad MC Series
Kingdom's Reign
Cutter's Claim
Loki's Luck
Stanton's Sins
Puck's Property
Whistle's War
Her Hidden Valentine, A Squad Novella

ACKNOWLEDGMENTS

Thank you to my family for your support and patience each time I say, "Hold that thought!" while I pound out one more sentence. Thank you Alison Aimes for your encouragement, for being a fantastic and supportive beta reader, a mentor, and an all-around incredible person. Thank you Joy Daniels for brainstorming with me. A shout out to Monica Bogza of the Trusted Accomplice for editing and Lisa for spectacular proof-reading. To my special readers in my FB Reader Group, Possessive Alpha Reads, thanks for picking up an Advanced Reader Copy and getting excited about this book. To all the bloggers and booklovers who help spread the word and finally, but not least, to every single one of you who've picked up this book and given it a chance. Thank you!

Join Monique's Mailing list to receive goodies and release information
I have a Facebook group just for readers
Like my Facebook Page
Follow me on TikTok @moniquemoreauthor
Follow me on Instagram
Follow me on BookBub
Learn all about my books: moniquemoreau.com